NAKED LIES *the* TRUTH

MICHAEL L. NICHOLAS

Archway Publishing books may be ordered through booksellers or by contacting:

Archway Publishing
1663 Liberty Drive
Bloomington, IN 47403
www.archwaypublishing.com
844-669-3957

ISBN: 978-1-6657-0342-0 (sc)
ISBN: 978-1-6657-0341-3 (hc)
ISBN: 978-1-6657-0317-8 (e)

Library of Congress Control Number: 2021903445

Print information available on the last page.

Archway Publishing rev. date: 4/6/2021

Acknowledgment

To my friend Damir and first reader: Thank you for urging me to write this novel. And thank you for your encouragement as it progressed and your wise counsel when I strayed. This novel wouldn't exist without your consistent support during the writing process. Gratitude!

1

The Bean Field

Los Angeles, 1929. A real place full of imaginary people. In ten years, the population had doubled to over a million. It was a city where newcomers could invent their own stories. That's why they came—that and the weather.

The year is remembered now in black and white but was lived in a hazy pink and golden light when the scent of orange groves still perfumed the air with the promise of paradise. Paradise if you were white that is. Because how you looked in this town was all that mattered. And Officer Mathieu looked white.

The young officer stepped onto the porch and undid his holster snap. He looked around before knocking; he was cautious. Domestic disturbance calls in this part of town were dangerous, especially at night. It was the last house on a dead-end street next to a bean field. There were streets like this all over Los Angeles. Tentative forays into the vast agricultural lands that still dotted the landscape.

Officer Mathieu knocked. There was no answer. Keeping his hand on his sidearm, he tried the doorknob. It was unlocked. Entering, he announced himself, "Police! Is anyone here?"

And then he saw her.

A naked young woman lying on the floor shot twice just below the rib cage.

Had she been black, no one would have ever heard of the case. But she was white, so they would. And she was beautiful. Perhaps the most beautiful woman Mathieu had ever seen—movie-star beautiful. There was an expression of surprise frozen on her face. Her lush blonde hair seemed to flow even in death. Her silken skin still had a golden hue to it. Mathieu bent down and touched her wrist. It was warm, but there was no pulse.

Standing up, Mathieu drew his handgun. He listened for any sounds. The house was quiet. He yelled again, "Police!"

He scanned the rest of the room before heading toward the hallway. With his back to the wall, he inched down the narrow corridor. He came to a kitchen on his left. A half-filled coffee cup with lipstick on the rim sat on the table. Further down the hall was the bathroom. A nightdress hung over the open door; a wet towel lay on the floor. At the end of the hallway was the bedroom.

Cautiously, Mathieu entered the room, pointing his handgun with his outstretched arm. Startled by a movement out of the corner of his eye, he swung quickly to his left and yelled, "Police!" Only to be confronted with his own tall, lean image reflected back at him in the full-length mirror. He sighed in relief, laughed at himself, and holstered the gun.

Her perfume hung in the air. The bed had been slept in. The contents of a purse were scattered across the crumpled sheets. A small suitcase lay open on the floor, bras and panties tossed about next to it.

He picked through the items on the bed, hoping to find an ID. He spotted a business card. He read the name "Irene Simpson," then the title "Personal Secretary to …"

Shocked by her employer's name, Mathieu froze. He stared at it in disbelief. If this got out, there would be a scandal that would rock the city.

Backtracking through the house, Mathieu went outside. There was a late model black Cadillac Cabriolet Town car parked at the curb in front. He searched the glove compartment until he found the registration, the name matched the victim's business card.

Mathieu walked to his Henderson police motorcycle and radioed in his report. He didn't mention who the victim's employer was over the radio. Better to do that in person when the detectives arrived. Then he reentered the house to secure the scene and wait for the shit storm that was sure to come.

2

Bull

Back inside the house, Mathieu searched the bedroom again. He found the victim's driver's license and a set of keys lying on the bed next to her purse. Using his handkerchief, he picked up the keyring and went to the front door. He tried a key that looked like it might fit the lock. It did. Next, he went outside to check if a car key on the ring was for the Cadillac parked in front. It was.

Mathieu was puzzled. Irene Simpson had presumably driven herself to the house and let herself in. What was the personal secretary to one of the most powerful men in Los Angeles doing here? Mathieu returned the keyring to where he'd found it, then searched the main room.

The room was simply furnished but neat and clean. In one corner, Mathieu found a well-worn saxophone case. He opened it; it was empty. On the mantel, he noticed a photograph of someone he recognized. A handsome young Black man was standing next to Duke Ellington. The photo was signed, "Great jamming with you, Paul—The Duke." Mathieu turned it over. An inscription on the back read, "Duke Ellington and Paul Thornton at the Dunbar Hotel Feb 2, 1929—the best day of my life."

While he stared at the photo, Mathieu heard a car drive up and stop in front of the house. He walked to the window and parted the curtains. It was a late model Buick Phaeton with a police light mounted on its ragtop and a siren on the front grill. Mathieu laughed to himself, no Model A Fords for the detectives. Then he saw who stepped out of the passenger side, and it made sense.

It was the Chief Detective Inspector himself, William "Bull" Braden. Mathieu wondered why they'd sent Bull. Maybe it was because it was the murder of a beautiful white woman in a black neighborhood. Braden loved sensational cases. Bull and the driver got something out of the trunk and then walked toward the house.

Mathieu watched Bull approach. He had a head shaped like a square block. It was difficult to tell where his jaw ended and his neck started. His ruddy complexion forewarned of a temper just below the surface. Yet he was impeccably dressed, his hair neatly combed and pomaded. He looked more like a banker than a cop. Behind him was a tall man carrying a camera. Bull marched toward the house as if he was going to bust the door down. Mathieu opened it to save him the trouble.

Bull entered and stopped in his tracks when he saw the blonde woman lying on the floor. "Mother of God! What do we have here?"

He was still looking at her when the tall man entered, almost scraping his bald head on the doorframe. He whistled when he saw the dead woman, "Look at the tits on that broad!"

Bull turned on him and said, "Shut the fuck up, Leonard … show some respect for the dead."

Chastised, the tall man said, "Sorry, Chief."

Turning to Mathieu, Bull asked, "Did you find the body, officer?"

"Yes, sir."

"Was there anyone else here?"

"No, sir."

Bull stared at Mathieu, appraising him. He was a good-looking young man with intelligent, watchful eyes.

"What's the victim's name?"

"Irene Simpson, twenty-nine years old … a resident of Los Angeles."

"Whose car is it outside?"

"The victim's."

Bull nodded. "It's an expensive car. I wonder what she was doing here?" he said almost to himself. "Whose house is it?"

"A musician, Paul Thornton."

"Negro?"

"Yes, sir. There's a picture of him on the mantle with Duke Ellington."

"How do you know it's him?"

"There's an inscription on the back of the photo," Mathieu said. "And I've heard him play at the Dunbar. He plays the saxophone."

"You a Negro lover, son?" Bull asked.

"I'm a jazz lover, sir," Mathieu responded.

Bull let the answer go. The kid had spunk. He didn't back down from him. Most patrolmen did. But this one didn't seem to be intimidated. Maybe he was too young to be.

Bull turned to Leonard. "Let's get the pictures over with."

"Okay, Chief."

Leonard told Mathieu to move out of the shot. Bull posed for a couple of photos looking down at the dead woman's body. Then Leonard took closeups of her face and chest wound. After that, he started moving down her body, clicking the shutter as he went.

"That's enough, Leonard," Bull said. "She wasn't shot in the crotch."

Turning red, Leonard stood up and backed away.

Still looking at the body, Leonard said, "What do you think, Chief? Looks to me like the Negro kidnapped, raped, and killed her."

Bull didn't respond.

Leonard noticed a look of disdain on Mathieu's face. "Do you have something to say, patrolman?"

With a hint of irony, Mathieu said, "Well, I was just wondering if he kidnapped her before or after he gave her the keys to his house."

Caught off guard, Leonard didn't know what to say.

Bull seemed to delight in Leonard's discomfort. "What do you mean, young man?"

"She has a key to the house on her keychain in the bedroom, sir. And her suitcase is there also, and her dresses are hanging in the closet."

Pointing at the hallway, Bull said, "Lead the way, son ... show me what you found."

As if they were making the Stations of the Cross on Good Friday, Mathieu lead Bull down the hallway, pointing out what he'd found in each room. Leonard brought up the rear, taking photos. When they got to the bedroom, Mathieu pointed out the victim's clothes in the closet, her suitcase on the floor, and the contents of her purse on the bed.

Mathieu said, "It looks like whoever killed her did a hasty search of her purse and suitcase afterward. It wasn't a robbery; there's money in her purse, almost three hundred dollars."

Bull nodded quietly, taking it all in.

"And there's something else, sir," Mathieu said.

He handed Bull Irene's business card.

Bull looked at it in shock. "Sweet Jesus, we're screwed."

"What is it, Chief?" Leonard asked.

"The victim is Harry Chandler's personal secretary."

"Harry Chandler, the publisher of the Los Angeles Times?"

"The one and only," Bull said. "Leonard, go out to the car and radio in for the crime scene team. We've got to do this one strictly by the book. And don't mention Chandler's name."

"Yes, sir," Leonard said, as he turned and ran in haste down the hallway.

After Leonard left, it was just Bull and Mathieu in the small room. Mathieu could see Bull mulling over the situation in his head.

Bull sat down on the bed and put his head in his hands. To no one, in particular, he said, "What a fucking mess. How the fuck am I going to tell Harry Chandler that his personal secretary was found totally naked and murdered in a Negro's house?"

Mathieu hesitated before he spoke. "I could tell him, sir."

Bull looked at him, confused. "What are you talking about, kid?"

"I know him, sir."

"You know Harry 'fucking' Chandler, the most powerful man in Los Angeles?"

"Yes, sir," Mathieu said.

"How?"

"He's my godfather."

At that moment, it was hard to tell who looked more surprised, Bull, or the dead woman in the front room.

3

Harry

After the forensic team finished their work at the house, Mathieu followed Bull and Leonard back to police headquarters. Mathieu waited until eight in the morning then phoned the LA Times. He got a hold of Francine, Chandler's appointment secretary, who knew him.

She had been one of Mathieu's babysitters when he was a little boy. She was in her mid-forties, a spinster, and still very fond of him. She set up an appointment for him with Chandler for seven o'clock that evening.

At dusk, Bull and Mathieu stood at the corner of First and Broadway. They gazed up at the domed cupola of the LA Times headquarters across the street. The lights had just come on. Mathieu glanced over at Bull. He looked as nervous as Mathieu felt, which was somewhat reassuring. Dodging a Red Car trolley, they crossed the street, entered the building and took the elevator up to the third floor, which emptied into Chandler's anteroom.

The room was filled with that day's array of "supplicants," as the staff called them. Like a feudal lord, Chandler met with his supplicants each evening after the paper went to press. Some had business deals to discuss. Others were looking for a handout, which surprisingly, he often accommodated.

Mathieu spotted Francine and walked over to her desk. She made a quick call to see if Chandler was free, then escorted Mathieu and Bull into his office.

While intimidating, the wood-paneled office was not ostentatious, like the man himself, who still walked to work each morning. Chandler was sitting at his desk in the far corner of the room, engrossed in reviewing a document. When he finished with it and spotted Mathieu, a grin spread across his face, and he stood up.

Chandler was an imposing presence, over six feet tall with a broad frame. His gray hair was neatly combed with his signature right-hand part. He was wearing his usual dark pinstripe suit, the chain of a pocket-watch visible across his vest. He strode over to Mathieu and grabbed him by both shoulders.

"Theo, how you've grown, you're almost as tall as I am," Chandler said. "I can't remember the last time I saw you."

"Three years ago, on my eighteenth birthday, sir."

"Ah, yes, now I remember at your father's restaurant."

"Speaking of your father, he tells me he hasn't seen you in a while."

"I've been busy with police work," Mathieu lied.

Chandler grinned. "You look great in that uniform, Theo. Luckily for you, you take after your mother. You're as handsome as she is beautiful."

It was an old family mantra that his father often repeated until everyone believed it, but it wasn't true. Mathieu had no idea who his real mother was. Only his parents and the woman who gave birth to him did. But Mathieu was determined to find out. That's why he had joined the police force, much to the displeasure of his father.

Always the businessman, Chandler added, "You know Theo, your father and I are going to make a ton of money on that new

Hollywoodland development. Have you been up there yet? It looks like a French mountain village as the roads wind up into the hills. The lots and houses are selling like hotcakes."

"No, sir, I haven't had a chance yet, but I've seen the sign," Mathieu said, distracted.

Noticing the discomfort on Mathieu's face, Chandler asked, "What brings you here today, Theo? What can I do for you, son?"

Mathieu looked down at the floor. "Something rather serious has happened, sir."

"What is it?"

"It concerns your personal secretary Irene Simpson," Mathieu said tentatively.

"What happened? Irene didn't come to work today. Has she been in an accident?"

"I'm afraid it's more serious than that, sir," Mathieu said. "Miss Simpson has been murdered."

Chandler turned ashen; all the joy drained from his body. He staggered a little, then caught himself. He suddenly looked older than his sixty-four years. Without saying a word, he went over to the seating area near his desk and sat down.

Mathieu moved closer to him but remained standing.

"Where did it happen?" Chandler asked, his voice breaking as he spoke. He cleared his throat, trying to cover his distress.

"In a house at the edge of a bean field below the hill where the Inglewood Oil fields are located," Mathieu said.

He'd decided beforehand to spare Chandler the details of how they had found her naked body.

"That's a Negro area, isn't it?"

"Yes, sir."

"What was she doing there?"

"We're not sure, sir ... but she had a key to the house."

"Are you sure it's Irene?"

"We found her business card, and the car parked outside had her name on the registration."

Chandler seemed in a daze. "I didn't even know she drove."

"Do you have a picture of her, sir?"

Chandler pointed absently over his shoulder toward a framed photograph on the wall. Mathieu walked over to take a look. It was a Christmas party photo. Chandler was in the center with his staff gathered around him. Irene was at the end of the second row. She was demurely dressed, a blank cautious smile on her face. It was almost as if she was trying to make herself invisible. But she couldn't hide her beauty. Mathieu's eye was drawn to her immediately.

Mathieu came back around in front of Chandler and said, "I'm sorry, sir, but it's her."

Chandler seemed lost and adrift. He was a man used to being in control. He started asking all the questions everyone does when confronted with violent death.

"How was she killed?"

"Gunshot, sir."

Chandler winced. "Did she suffer?"

"No, sir, she died instantly."

"Who found her body?"

"I did."

Chandler nodded silently as if that somehow made it better.

"What was she doing there?" he repeated almost to himself.

"We were hoping you or someone on your staff might know."

Chandler shook his head. "I don't know anything about Irene's personal life. But you're free to ask the staff."

"Thank you, sir."

Regaining some control, he looked at Mathieu and said, "Just don't say anything about how she died or where. Just say it was an accident. The details can't get out."

"I understand, sir."

"Whose house is it?"

"A Negro jazz musician, sir."

"Is he in custody?"

"The house was empty except for Irene. We've put out an APB for him."

"Did he kill her?"

"We don't that yet, sir, but we'll find him and question him."

All this time, Bull had been standing quietly near the door, a silent witness to the proceedings. He was more than willing to play second fiddle on this visit. He was grateful to Mathieu for delivering the bad news. And Mathieu's handling of the situation impressed him.

For the first time, Chandler looked over and noticed Bull.

Mathieu introduced him, "Sir, this is Chief Detective Inspector William Braden. He's in charge of the investigation."

Chandler stared at Bull without speaking. A look of recognition came over his face as he stood and approached him.

Looking down at him, he said, "You're Bull Braden, right?"

"Yes, sir."

A smile broke out on Chandler's face. "I remember you. Years ago, you were on the front lines doing some union-busting, knocking a few heads after those commie bastards bombed our old building. That was a long time ago. You were a patrolman then."

"Yes, sir."

Chandler reached out his hand. "It's an honor to meet you, Bull."

Bull relaxed for the first time since entering the office as he shook Chandler's hand.

Chandler seemed reinvigorated. He started walking around the room, deep in thought, slowly regaining his strength and composure. Bull and Mathieu watched him silently, observing his changing mood.

Chandler turned and looked at Bull. "You know this can't get out. It would cause a scandal. I'm holding you personally responsible for keeping a lid on this, Bull. Is that clear?"

"Yes, sir."

"This is personal, Bull. I want the guilty party found and punished. Don't let me down on this."

"No, sir, I won't."

With nothing left to say, Chandler said, "I'll let you get to it then."

Realizing they had been dismissed, Bull and Mathieu turned to leave.

Chandler stopped them. "Bull, I want to be kept personally informed. As a favor to me, I'd like you to put Officer Mathieu on your team."

Bull looked surprised but didn't resist. "Yes, sir ... consider it done."

And then they left.

Outside on the street, Bull looked at Mathieu as if he was going to reprimand him, then said, "Nice job in there, kid."

"Thank you, sir."

4

Paul

Paul Thornton never had a chance. When he arrived home a few days after Irene's murder, the cops watching his house beat him within an inch of his life before he could say a word. The beating was more about finding a naked white woman in his home than about her being dead.

When Thornton regained consciousness in the hospital three days later, the police confronted him with the murder charges. Thornton asked the officer guarding him to look in his wallet. Inside there was a receipt for a hotel room in San Francisco the day of the murder, and a Greyhound bus ticket back to Los Angeles the following day. Thornton had been in San Francisco playing a gig at the Astoria Hotel on Market Street. After the police checked his alibi with the hotel and Greyhound, they dropped all the charges against him.

Fortunately for Thornton, the cops hadn't broken his fingers or knocked out any teeth. He was grateful for that, at least. But there was no apology forthcoming. They trumped up a charge about him resisting arrest as their excuse for the beating. They warned Thornton to keep his mouth shut, or next time they'd break his fingers and knock out all of his teeth. The impeccable logic of their threat won the day. Thornton declined to file a complaint.

Thinking he was free of the police, Thornton was understandably wary when Mathieu showed up in uniform at the hospital a week later. By that time, Thornton was able to sit up in bed and eat solid food. The wounds to his face had healed, but the bruises were still visible. His chest and stomach no longer throbbed from the beating he had taken. He was scheduled to be released in a few days.

Now that the swelling on Thornton's face had gone down, Mathieu could see he was a handsome man. He had regular features and smooth chocolate-brown skin as if he was from Jamaica or somewhere in the West Indies.

Mathieu smiled at Thornton, trying to put him at ease. "I'm not here to cause you any trouble, Paul. I just have a few questions about Irene."

Thornton looked at him with suspicious eyes, wondering if it was some kind of trap.

"Sorry, those guys beat you up. Are you in a lot of pain still?"

Thornton shrugged, resigned to what had happened.

"Are you going to be able to play again?" Mathieu asked.

Thornton nodded, yes.

"I saw you at the Dunbar a few times … you play a wicked sax."

Thornton seemed surprised that this white cop went to a black club.

"I play a little jazz piano," Mathieu offered as an explanation. "Nothing like you, of course, I'm just an amateur, but I get lost in it."

Thornton was curious now but didn't say anything.

Mathieu tried a different approach. "I could use your help, Paul," he said. "If we're going to find Irene's killer, we need to understand who she was. So far, she's a mystery."

Thornton retained his stony look despite Mathieu's appeal.

"Look, man, I don't know anyone who knew Irene like you did. I'm sure you cared about her. I know you didn't kill her. Help me."

Not taking his eyes off Mathieu, Thornton tested him. "Name the most common jazz chord progression."

Without hesitation, Mathieu replied, "two-five-one."

"How do you find the seventh degree of a major seventh chord?"

"Half step below the root," Mathieu said.

Thornton laughed. "You do know a little about jazz. What do you want to know about Irene?"

"Where did you meet her?"

"At the Dunbar ... the night I jammed with Duke Ellington."

Mathieu nodded but kept quiet, hoping Thornton would keep talking.

"She came up to me after the set and put her arm through mine. She said, 'I could lick you like a chocolate ice cream cone.'"

"She was that bold?" Mathieu asked, surprised.

Thornton smiled at the memory. "She was fearless."

"What did you say?"

Thornton shrugged. "I have no idea. I was speechless. Did you ever see her?"

"I was the one who found her body."

Thornton's face saddened. "Man, what a waste."

Trying to bring Thornton back to happier memories, Mathieu asked, "What happened next?"

"The Duke invited all of us upstairs to the band's suite. There were bottles of champagne and beautiful women everywhere. We drank and sang. Irene never left my side. At some point, she whispered in my ear, 'Take me home.' I told her I didn't have a car.

She said that wasn't a problem because she did. Then she drove us back to my house."

"What happened there?"

"She asked me to play for her," Paul said, reliving the moment. "So, I did, and she started dancing around the room while I played. And ever so slowly, she started taking off her clothes. Man, it was hard to keep playing. But every time I stopped, she stopped. She would stand still and smile a wicked smile at me. So, I started playing again, and she started dancing again and taking her clothes off until she was totally naked. We did that for hours. It was the most erotic thing I've ever experienced in my life."

"What happened after that?"

"She put her clothes back on, kissed me on the cheek, and left."

"You didn't make love?" Mathieu asked.

Paul looked sheepish. "I hate to admit it, man, but I never touched her ... ever."

"Never?" Mathieu asked, finding it hard to believe.

Paul shook his head. "Never. You saw her man what I was supposed to do when she came over, tell her to go home?"

Mathieu shrugged.

"Anyway, that's how it started. But it was always on her terms. I could never set anything up. She controlled everything that happened. She'd come when she wanted to, show up unexpectedly at all hours of the night, ready to dance naked while I played the sax. So, I gave her a key. What could I do? It was like magic when she was around. Time stopped. But afterward, when she'd gone home, the house felt empty. It was like coming down from the worst drug high ever. I didn't know where she lived or where she worked. I didn't know her phone number. Sometimes she'd be gone for weeks then suddenly show up at two in the morning.

And it would start all over again. Totally crazy but absolutely addictive."

"Where did she get the money for that expensive car?"

Thornton shrugged. "I have no idea, man, never asked didn't care ... as long as she kept showing up."

"Did she talk about her family, her dreams, anything personal?"

"No. I tried asking a few times, but I could tell it bothered her, so I stopped."

"Nobody I've talked to so far seems to know much about her," Mathieu said.

"That sounds like Irene ... a total mystery," Thornton said.

Both men were silent for a few moments. Thornton spotted Mathieu's name tag on his uniform. "You related to the Mathieu that owns that restaurant over in Frenchtown?"

"Yes, he's my father."

"I played there once with my trio at a private party ... nice place."

"I know that's when I first heard you play."

Thornton looked confused.

"I was a just teenager then, working in the kitchen. Later, when I was old enough, I went to the Dunbar to hear your quartet."

"You a Negro lover, Mathieu?"

"I'm a jazz lover."

"Safer choice," Thornton said, laughing. "What's your first name?"

"Theo."

"Nice to meet you, Theo ... you're not too bad for a cop."

Mathieu returned the compliment. "You're not too bad either, Paul ... for a murder suspect."

They both laughed.

Before leaving, Mathieu told Thornton what little he knew about Irene's life. He didn't mention Chandler's name but said she had worked for a prominent land developer. Thornton was surprised by the revelation. Both men were learning things about Irene they didn't know before. Mathieu gave Thornton his phone number in case he thought of anything else.

As Mathieu was leaving, Thornton said, "When I get out of here, I'll call you. We can jam a little at the house."

"Can you handle an amateur?"

"Don't worry, man," Thornton said. "I can make anyone sound good." Then he laughed until his side started to hurt.

Mathieu said his goodbyes and left. Irene was a little less of a mystery now but still an enigma.

5

Francine

Bull didn't know what to do with Mathieu. He was a smart young officer, and he had handled himself well with Chandler, but he couldn't put him to work with his other detectives.

They were a close-knit group who would never accept an outsider in their midst, especially a lowly motorcycle patrolman. But Bull was stuck with him, and he wasn't prepared to defy Chandler's request. So, he decided to give Mathieu assignments he could do on his own. That's why he had sent him to interview Thornton.

Bull was impressed that Mathieu had been able to get Thornton to talk after the beating he'd taken. He was also surprised by what Mathieu had learned. Irene wasn't the prim secretary that Chandler thought she was. But he could never tell Chandler that; he'd go ballistic with rage. The next assignment Bull gave Mathieu was to interview Chandler's staff.

Mathieu began with Francine because he knew her the best. He called and invited her to tea at the Biltmore Hotel one evening after work. The sun had just set as they started walking south on Broadway toward the hotel. The spring air was balmy with a hint of a cool breeze. At Pershing Square, they cut across the park to the hotel entrance on Olive Street.

Entering the Moorish-style lobby, they both gazed up at the beautiful vaulted ceiling, painted in golds and browns. A curved archway to their left led them to a small bistro that faced Olive Street. There they found a cozy table near the window that gave them a view of the park. When the waitress came, Mathieu order tea for both of them.

Even with Prohibition, had they wanted to have alcohol, they could have gone to the Gold Room. There hidden behind an ornate mirror, was a secret passageway where drinks were discreetly delivered. But the bistro was more intimate. And Mathieu would have had to change out of his uniform if they went to the Gold Room so as not to scare the other patrons.

Francine seemed happy to be in Mathieu's presence. He'd always been one of her favorites. And for a spinster like herself, she briefly fantasized that she was on a date with a handsome young policeman in uniform. She primped her hair a little and caught herself self-consciously looking around to see if anyone was looking at them.

Mathieu put her at ease when the waitress returned with their tea by toasting her. "Thank you for coming, Francine. I appreciate that you could make a little time for me."

"It's my pleasure, Theo, it's not often I get invited to the Biltmore … it's so beautiful here," she said. "Like a fairy tale."

"Yes, it is," he said.

They took their first sip of tea while looking out the window at the lights starting to come on in the park across the street.

Francine made it easy for Mathieu by starting. "You mentioned on the phone you had some questions about Irene?"

Appreciative of the segue, Mathieu said, "Yes, I do. It's kind of a delicate situation, Francine. And I hope you can understand that I can't go into any details. But there are a few open questions about the circumstances surrounding Irene's death."

Francine looked slightly shocked by the revelation.

"It's nothing for you to worry about, Francine," he said, trying to reassure her. "And I'd appreciate it if you didn't repeat our conversation to anyone. But I need to find out a little more about Irene's personal life."

"I didn't know her that well," Francine began. "Irene kept to herself. She didn't socialize with the rest of the staff except at Christmas parties and such. But she was very polite and professional. Always willing to do more than her share of the work. She never put on any airs. That's pretty rare for a woman as beautiful as she was."

Mathieu was grateful to Francine for bringing up the subject of Irene's beauty. He hadn't known how to broach it.

"Did any of the male staff try to flirt with her?"

"Only if they were new," Francine said. "The regular male staff knew that any overtures of that type would be met by a cold blank stare from Irene. She didn't tolerate it. Even the reporters, who are a randy bunch, knew better than to try to come onto her. Besides, she was Chandler's personal secretary. No one was stupid enough to risk being fired for flirting with her regardless of how beautiful she was."

"Did any of the 'supplicants' ever try to flirt with her?"

"Oh, Lord, no! They're all so grateful to meet with Chandler; they'd never do such a thing. They're always on their best behavior. For them meeting Chandler is like an audience with the Pope."

Mathieu nodded. "What about Mr. Chandler's business associates?"

Francine took a sip of tea. "Now that's a different story," she said with a wry smile.

Mathieu was surprised by Francine's worldliness. He'd often thought she was a bit of a prude. He was glad he was wrong.

"How so?" Mathieu asked.

"Most successful businessmen think they're gods, don't they," she said with a touch of bitterness. "They think they can have anything they want just because they're rich."

Mathieu was silent, encouraging her to continue.

"More than once, I saw some fat cat standing in front of her desk flirting with her. The real creeps would lean over her desk and try to look down her blouse. Some even tried slipping notes across her desk before going in to see Harry."

"How did she respond?"

"She'd smile politely and nod. Then when they went in to see Chandler, she'd tear up the notes and throw them in the trash."

"Was anyone particularly aggressive?"

"I'd rather not say, Theo, I don't want to get anyone in trouble."

Mathieu nodded, then asked. "Would it be possible to see Mr. Chandler's appointment log for the last month?"

Francine smiled at Mathieu's negotiating skills. He'd given her a way out by finding a different way to get what he wanted.

"Of course," she said. "I don't see any harm in that."

Changing subjects, Mathieu asked, "Do you know if she had any boyfriends?"

"None ever came around. No flowers ever arrived at the office for her. If she did, she never mentioned them to me."

"What about her family?"

"There was a rumor she grew up in an orphanage. But I don't know if it's true."

"Which one?"

"According to the rumor, it was St. Anne's."

"The one in Westlake?"

"Yes."

"I thought that's a hospital for unwed mothers, not an orphanage."

"It is, but according to the rumor, they made an exception for Irene, and she grew up there."

"Irene's driver's license listed the LA Times as her address. Do you where she lived?" Mathieu asked.

"Nearby at the Figueroa Hotel. She rented a small room there. It's owned by the YWCA and caters only to single professional women." Francine added, "No men are allowed on the premises."

Mathieu was silent, wondering why a beautiful woman like Irene had lived such a strange cloistered life.

Francine broke the silence by asking, "What about you, Theo, any girlfriends?"

Mathieu smiled, embarrassed by the question. "None at the moment. I'm too busy with police work."

"You don't live at home anymore?"

"No, I moved out a couple of years ago," he said.

"Your father brags about you whenever he comes to the office to see Chandler."

"That's funny," Mathieu said almost to himself. "I can't remember him ever praising me in person."

"You're pretty hard on your father, Theo … he means well."

"Does he? I'm not so sure."

Francine tried to lighten the mood by changing the subject. "I hear one of Chandler's nieces has a crush on you."

"Which one?"

"Bridgette … the curvy redhead."

Mathieu laughed. "You mean the socialite?"

"Yes, that's the one."

Mathieu leaned across the table with his best smile and said, "Can you see me at a society ball, Francine?"

"No, Theo, I can't," she answered with a laugh. "Not in a thousand years."

Toasting her, Mathieu said, "You always knew me the best, Francine."

6

St. Anne's

The next day Mathieu rode his motorcycle west on Temple Street to the Westlake area. He turned onto Occidental and went two short blocks to St. Anne's. There he stopped and looked at the handsome Spanish revival building and its beautiful vine that enveloped an entire corner of the two-story structure.

A sign over the porticoed entranceway stated its mission: "St. Anne's Maternity Hospital." Started in 1908 as a twelve-bed maternity ward for unwed mothers, St. Anne's had more than doubled its capacity since then.

Mathieu walked up the porch steps and knocked on the front door. He took off his police cap while he waited. After a short delay, a young female docent came to greet him. He told her he'd like to see the Mother Superior.

The docent invited him in and escorted him down an immaculately clean hallway that smelled slightly of disinfectant. The building was quiet except for the occasional muffled cry of an infant. Nuns walked silently by him, some cradling newborns in their arms, others carrying supplies. The docent knocked on the Mother Superior's door, and when they both heard a cheerful "Come in!" they entered.

Behind a sturdy wooden desk, bearing her nameplate, sat

Sister Mary Catherine. She stood up and walked to the center of the room to greet Mathieu. In her mid-fifties, she was as substantial as her desk, stout and hardy, almost peasant-like.

The nun extended her soft hand in greeting. "How can I help you, Officer?" she asked, as the docent quietly left the office and closed the door behind her.

"My name is Officer Mathieu, Sister. I'm with the LAPD. I'm investigating the suspicious death of a young woman who may have lived here years ago."

"What was her name?"

"Irene Simpson," Mathieu said.

A look of sadness came over Sister Mary Catherine's face as if the sky had just darkened. She made the sign of the cross and said to herself, "God Bless Irene's soul."

She motioned toward a small sitting area near her desk, "Perhaps we can sit, Officer. Your news weighs heavily on my heart."

They sat down. Mathieu gave her a few minutes to adjust to the news and compose herself.

"I take it you knew Irene, Sister?"

"Yes, I knew her very well," she said. "Irene came here when she was five years old. We normally don't take children that weren't born here for adoption, but she was a special case. Her mother pleaded with us to take her. It was the only way she could protect Irene from being abused by her husband."

"What kind of abuse?"

"Sexual abuse … daily sexual abuse," the nun answered in a matter of fact tone.

Mathieu was surprised by her directness. She saw the reaction on his face.

"Like the police, we see the real world here. Nothing shocks us. By the time I arrived here two years later and took my vows, Irene was almost seven."

She added almost apologetically, "I realized my true vocation rather late in life."

"Why was she never adopted? She must have been a beautiful child."

"She was," Sister Mary Catherine said. "But she was terrified of men."

"She would scream and throw a tantrum when couples came to adopt her. So, we let her stay on and help out in the wards. She was a shy, sweet child. I guess I was the closest to her. She would grab my waist for protection anytime a man came near her. Trying to get her tiny arms around my big waist," she said, smiling at the memory.

Sister Mary Catherine's smile faded. "But all that changed when she turned seventeen."

"Why?"

"The obvious, she started to blossom."

Mathieu nodded.

"She was stunning. She started to notice how men looked at her. She realized the power she had over them. The tables had turned. Now she was in control; they were putty in her hands. She hardened and left soon after with hardly a word. I never saw her again or heard from her. Then about two years ago, she started making sizeable donations. The first one included a note."

Sister Mary Catherine rose and went to her desk and quickly found the note in her top drawer. She handed it to Mathieu.

It read. "Dear Sister Mary Catherine, I'm sorry. All my love Irene."

"What was she sorry for?"

"I guess for leaving so suddenly, for never letting me know

how she was. I confess I probably got too close to her. She felt like my daughter. She was such a sweet girl. I grieved when she left."

Sister Mary Catherine sniffed and dabbed the tears around her eyes. "I'm an old softy," she said, laughing at herself. "Irene's note didn't provide any way to contact her. That was all I knew about her until today."

"I'm sorry to be the bearer of such bad news, Sister."

She shrugged. "It's not your fault, young man. You've been very kind."

After a moment, she asked, "What did she do for a living?"

"Irene was the personal secretary to Harry Chandler, the publisher of the LA Times."

The sister's face brightened. "Oh my, she did very well for herself, didn't she?"

"Yes, she did, Sister. Do you mind me asking how much she donated?"

"A thousand dollars each time," she said. "Mr. Chandler must pay very well."

Mathieu knew he didn't pay that well; a thousand dollars was more than her yearly salary.

"You're probably wondering why I didn't ask how she died."

"No, Sister, I understand. A lot of people prefer not to know." And Mathieu was grateful she hadn't asked. It would have been painful to tell her the truth.

Composing herself, she asked. "When is the funeral?"

"I don't know yet, Sister … the coroner hasn't released her body."

"Will you let me know?"

"Yes, of course."

"We'll have a mass said for her tomorrow."

Mathieu nodded.

"If you think of anything else, here is my card," he said, handing it to her. She studied the card.

As Mathieu stood to leave, she asked, "Does your father own Mathieu's restaurant in Frenchtown?"

"Yes, he does, Sister. Why do you ask?"

"He's a long-time donor to St. Anne's."

"I didn't know that," Mathieu said, surprised.

"Oh yes, he's been very generous over the years."

Trying to be casual, Mathieu asked, "How long has he been a donor?"

Sister Mary Catherine thought about it for a moment. "Oh, it must be almost eighteen years ago in 1911. I'd just been put in charge of the St. Anne's a few years earlier."

Mathieu tried not to visibly react, but his mind was in turmoil, 1911 was three years after he was born.

"Yes, every year on April 7, your father sends us a check. We always give the sisters extra ice cream at dinner that night," she said, smiling.

"Thank you for help, Sister," Mathieu said, distracted. "I may be back another time to ask a few more questions."

"Anytime, young man. You're always welcome here at St. Anne's."

Mathieu turned and walked away, deeply troubled.

April 7 was his birthday.

7

The Mourners

After the coroner released Irene's body, Chandler's staff made the funeral arrangements. Chandler was so devastated by Irene's death that he paid for her burial out of his own pocket.

Francine let Mathieu know the date and time of the services. In turn, Mathieu called Sister Mary Catherine as he had promised. It was to be a private memorial service; only a select few were invited. There was no notice published in the paper.

Mathieu wanted to see who came to Irene's funeral, and for a good reason. In more cases than the public realized, the killer would often show up. Sometimes to grieve, other times as a kind of taunt to the victim.

He decided to forego the church service and focus on the cemetery. He thought only those closest to Irene would be at the burial site. And it would be much easier to observe their reactions out in the open than in a church. Irene was to be buried at the Hollywood Cemetery, a tranquil oasis in the middle of Hollywood bordered by Paramount Studios to the south.

He got there well before the funeral procession arrived. He wore civilian clothes and stood near a cluster of fir trees, close to the memorial obelisk for Harrison Gray Otis, the LA Times founder. Irene's gravesite was about twenty yards away in an open grassy meadow.

Looking toward Santa Monica Boulevard, Mathieu saw the hearse bearing Irene's body, followed by several expensive vehicles, turn into the cemetery. The funeral procession drove down the entranceway, then turned left onto a small lane that led to the burial site. The hearse came to a stop near Harrison Gray's obelisk; the other vehicles stopped in a line behind it.

Chandler, his wife, and one of his daughters got out of the first car. Francine and several other staff members got out of the second. After that, it was hard to keep track of who got out of which vehicle. Mathieu saw Sister Mary Catherine walking toward the gravesite with two other nuns. Behind them, he spotted a famous character actor but couldn't remember his name. The actor was walking with three men who looked like business associates of Chandler.

Francine had lent Mathieu a Leica 35mm camera from the newsroom. It was a marvel, light, compact, and beautifully made. Fitting snugly in the palm of his hand, it was a testament to fine German engineering.

From the safety of the tree line, Mathieu raised the viewfinder to his eye and began pressing the shutter release. He would find out the mourner's names from Francine after the film was developed. In truth, he wasn't sure what he was looking for or if the surveillance would bear any fruit. But he dutifully took photos of everyone who walked toward the gravesite.

He turned his attention back to the hearse. He was curious who the pallbearers would be. Eight men stood behind the vehicle as the coffin was rolled onto a foldable gurney. The men were an odd mixture of shapes and sizes. There were four slightly built men and four burly ones. The latter looked like laborers, but all of them wore their best suits. Though for the burlier ones, their suit jacket cuffs barely made it down to their thick wrists.

Mathieu recognized a few of the thinner men. One was a noted society columnist, another a movie critic, and a third was a staff member he'd seen in Chandler's anteroom. He assumed all the pallbearers worked at the Times. The burlier ones probably worked in the print factory. He had to admire Chandler; the LA Times took care of its own.

The coffin was brought to the gravesite and placed on a rigging above it. Chandler stepped forward, his wife at his side to steady him. He started in a halting voice, then slowly gained strength so that Mathieu could hear him clearly from where he stood.

"I want to thank all of you for coming today. We are gathered here to honor the memory of our coworker and friend Irene Simpson who was tragically killed in a car accident."

It was a lie, of course, but Chandler's force of character made it sound like the truth. And for his staff who worshipped him and his business associates who depended on him, whatever Chandler said was the truth—even when it wasn't.

Mathieu tuned out the rest of Chandler's speech. Regardless of whatever else he said, it was clear his intent was not the truth but a coverup, a coverup that suited his interests, and the LA Times.

When Chandler finished, the minister led the group in the Lord's Prayer. Then one by one, the mourners came forward to pay their last respects. Each was given a flower to place on the casket. Sister Mary Catherine lingered at the coffin, obviously distraught, until one of the other nuns helped her walk away. The ceremony now over, the mourners gathered in small groups to talk. Some came up to Chandler to shake his hand and thank him for his speech. The rest began to disperse, walking alone or in groups back to the waiting cars.

Mathieu was about to leave when he noticed someone out of

the corner of his eye, a lone man standing away from the others. He must have arrived late; Mathieu hadn't seen him earlier.

Mathieu turned to observe the man. He was in his early fifties, tall and lean with elegant posture. He was impeccably dressed, his full head of thick gray hair neatly combed. With his hands clasped in front of him, the man bowed his head in respect, a somber look on his handsome face. The man's presence troubled Mathieu, but he didn't take his photo. He didn't need to. He knew who he was.

It was his father, Pierre Mathieu.

8

The Blowups

Mathieu didn't confront his father at the cemetery. He wasn't ready to. He wasn't sure what his father knew and what he didn't at this point. But Mathieu did know that his father could evade anything. He'd confront him when he was better prepared.

He took the film to the police photo lab the next day. He asked the technicians to make enlargements of all the faces in the crowd. A few hours later, they were ready. He was surprised how crisp and clear the images were when he saw them. He had feared they would be out of focus or too indistinct, but they were like standing right next to the people.

Then Mathieu called Francine and asked for her help identifying the faces in the crowd. They met again at the Biltmore after work. They sat at the same table as last time. Francine looked around at the other patrons with a mischievous look on her face.

"What is it?" Mathieu asked.

"If we keep meeting here like this, people will think we're having an affair," she said.

"I think we should encourage that, Francine," Mathieu said, teasing her.

She blushed at his joke.

Mathieu handed her the photos of the pallbearers. "I know a few of these men, but not all of them," he said.

Pointing to a burly man with a flat-top haircut and broad shoulders, he asked, "Who's that?"

Francine studied the photo and said, "Oh, that's Frank Steward. He's the shop foreman in the printing factory on the ground floor."

"Did he know Irene?"

"No, the men who work on the printing press rarely come up to Mr. Chandler's office. But Chandler goes down there occasionally to check on things. Irene went with him a few times when there was an emergency."

"What kind of an emergency?"

"If a story has to be pulled or changed at the last-minute, Chandler goes downstairs and personally tells the shop foreman. Then it's all hands on deck. All the pages that have been printed have to be destroyed while the workers reset the presses. Irene often pitched in and helped with burning the pages. I'm told she was quite the sight, pushing a cart of papers to the incinerator in her high heels while the boys were busy changing the typesetting machines. I know Frank was impressed with how she helped out. He told me so a couple of times. All the men on the printing room floor were."

Mathieu nodded, encouraging Francine to continue.

"Frank asked if he and some of his men could come to the funeral and pay their respects to Irene," she said. "Chandler agreed and suggested they be pallbearers."

Mathieu took notes in a small notepad as Francine spoke. He pointed to the three other sturdy-looking men in the photo. "And these men are in his crew?"

"Yes, I don't know their names, but they all work downstairs on the press."

Pointing to another photo of the pallbearers, Mathieu said, "And he's a columnist, correct?"

"Yes, that's Darrell Franklin," Francine said. "He writes the society column."

"Did he know Irene?"

"Not really, but she would often compliment him on his column when he came up to see Chandler." Francine laughed. "Irene was curious about the rich and famous. Like all of us, I suppose that fantasize about their lives."

"And him?" Mathieu asked, pointing to a man with a rakish mustache and bleached hair.

"That's Steven Silverman, our movie critic."

"What was Irene's relationship with him?"

"Same as with the society columnist. Irene would compliment him on his column and ask about things he couldn't print. Irene was prim and proper, but she had a wide range of interests."

Mathieu thought Irene's interest in high society and movie stars seemed pretty typical for a young woman. He picked out another photo and pointed to a young man he'd seen in Chandler's anteroom. "Who is this young man? He works in Chandler's offices, doesn't he?"

"Yes, that's Bobby Stevenson."

"What does he do?"

"He's a story runner. He takes instructions from Mr. Chandler down to the newsroom."

"He looks pretty young."

"He's barely nineteen, I think."

"How did he treat Irene?"

"He had such a huge crush on her. He could barely speak to her," Francine laughed.

"He's not the stalker type, is he?" Mathieu asked.

"Oh, no, Bobby's harmless. It was kind of sweet to watch him try to hide his infatuation with her. Sometimes it was painful, though, as he would stammer trying to speak to her."

Mathieu handed Francine another photo and pointed to a bald man with a familiar face. "Who is that? He looks like an actor I've seen in the movies."

"Yes, that's Samuel Johnston. He's a famous character actor. He's been in a ton of movies. He's one of the lucky ones that made the transition from silent films to talkies." Anticipating his next question, Francine said, "He's a good friend of Mr. Chandler, who's a big fan of his."

In the next photo, there were several men who looked like business associates of Chandler. One of them had a mustache and wore wire-rim classes. He was thin, almost scarecrow thin. With his severe scowl, he looked like a fundamentalist preacher.

Pointing to him in the photo, Mathieu asked, "Who's that?"

"That's Thaddeus Harrison," Francine said immediately. "He's one of the richest men in Los Angeles, with a grand mansion in Pasadena. He and Chandler go way back. They've been in almost every big land development deal together. He's also co-chairman of the Eugenics Society that Mr. Chandler belongs to."

Mathieu didn't know anything about them. "What do they do?"

Francine seemed reluctant to answer. "Well, they believe in improving the genetic quality of the human population through selective breeding."

Mathieu shook his head in disgust. "You mean to preserve the white race at the expense of other races, don't you? Chandler believes in that crap?"

"I knew you would disapprove, Theo. But yes, Mr. Chandler does believe in it." Quick to defend her boss Francine added. "Despite some of his beliefs, Mr. Chandler does a lot of good for Los Angeles. He helped start Caltech, and he's nurtured the aircraft industry in LA. He's pretty progressive on a lot of issues."

Mathieu didn't respond to her comment. "What was Harrison's relationship with Irene?"

"He didn't have one as far as I know. I never even saw him talk to her."

"Why did he come to the funeral then?"

"I think out of respect for Mr. Chandler. As I said, they're pretty close business partners."

"Who's this man standing next to Harrison?" Mathieu asked.

"That's Jeremy Eckert. He's a wealthy financial advisor. Some of the richest men in California are his clients, including the Governor and the Secretary of State."

"Did you ever see him talking to Irene?"

"Once or twice in the office," Francine said reluctantly. "He has a bit of a reputation as a lady's man."

"What have you heard about him?"

"Not too much, just that he likes his women kind of young."

"Do you know anything else about him?"

"He has a private retreat in Ojai where the Sundowners Club meets."

"What's that?"

"A men's only social club. He's the president."

"Who are the club members?"

Francine shrugged. "The same as his clients, I presume," she said. "Rich and powerful men."

"Is Chandler a member?"

"Oh no, Mr. Chandler is a stay-at-home family man. He doesn't indulge in frivolous things like that."

Francine identified the other businessmen standing next to Eckert. Then they studied the rest of the photos together. Mathieu took detailed notes on who was in each photograph, what they did, and their relationship with Irene. When they finished, Mathieu thanked Francine for all her help. He handed the camera back to her.

She stopped him. "Why don't you keep it for a little while. It might come in handy."

"Are you sure it's okay?"

She nodded that it was.

"Thanks, I will."

Francine's face turned serious. "Irene didn't die the way Chandler said she did at the funeral, did she? You wouldn't be doing all this for a car accident. How did she really die?"

Mathieu looked away to avoid Francine's gaze. He'd been wondering since their first meeting when she would ask that question.

"No, she didn't die in a car accident. But I think it's best for you that you don't know how she died. I can only tell you that everything you've told me has been helpful. I do appreciate it." He added, "And I'll keep it just between us."

"I understand, Theo," she said. "Thanks for being honest with me."

Francine brought up another subject Mathieu had been avoiding, "I saw your father at the gravesite."

"So, did I," Mathieu said. "What was his relationship with Irene?"

"I don't think he had one, Theo, at least not the kind your thinking. He took her to lunch a few times. Irene told me he was giving her investment advice."

Mathieu nodded, not totally convinced.

"But I think the main thing your father did for Irene was he made her laugh."

"What do you mean?"

"Your father can be very charming, Theo."

"So, I've been told."

"You're more like your father than you want to admit. I know he always says you look like your mother, but it's not true. Except for your darker features, you look just like him."

Mathieu ignored her comment and changed the subject. "What did my father do to make her laugh?"

"I think it was his easy manner with her. Your father is smart and quick. He's good at seeing the absurdity of things. And he can laugh at himself. Irene responded to all of that. She had a kind of a mask, always kept her emotions under tight check. But when your father came into the office, he was able to break through it. He gently tugged at that mask in a non-threatening way and got her to laugh at herself, a real laugh, not a fake one. I think she needed that. It was the only time I ever saw her really let go."

Mathieu stared at his hands on the table. When he heard other people describe his father, he almost sounded like someone Mathieu would like to know. So unlike the father, he did know.

9

The Hotel Figueroa

Mathieu met with Bull the next day. He showed him the photos of the mourners and went over his notes on who had attended. Bull was impressed. He thought Mathieu would make a good detective someday. For a young patrolman, his judgment and attention to detail were exceptional.

"I'd like to take a look at Irene's apartment," Mathieu said after discussing the photos.

Bull shrugged. "My boys have already been over it with a fine-tooth comb. I don't think you'll find anything there. But if you want to go ahead."

He reached into his desk drawer and found the evidence bag for Irene's apartment. He handed it to Mathieu. "The search warrant is on the front. The key is inside," he said.

Bull was still convinced the culprit was black. His detectives had brought in five more suspects for "questioning" who lived near the bean field house. All were black. But so far, their strong-arm tactics hadn't yielded any results. If Mathieu wanted to focus on the victim, that was okay with Bull if it kept him out of the way.

Mathieu rode south on Figueroa Street. As he crossed West Ninth, he caught sight of the Hotel Figueroa. The handsome fourteen-story brick building had three towers, one behind the other. The separate towers allowed all five hundred rooms to have exterior windows.

He parked in front of the hotel, its entrance faced in stone with arches several stories high, framing the windows of a street-level café. Canopy-shaded doorways flanked the café on each side. Mathieu entered through the one on the left with the number Nine Three Nine above its doorframe.

The Spanish Colonial-style interior was stunning. It was three stories high, with sturdy rectangular columns supporting a beamed ceiling. Off to the left was a fireplace, with the YWCA's triangle symbol etched into the mantelpiece. There were seating areas on both sides of the lobby, lit from above by wagon wheel-shaped chandeliers. Past the lobby, Mathieu could see the arched corridors that led to the towers.

Mathieu approached the woman at the reception desk. Her nametag read 'Mildred". She was short with long black curly hair that fell to her shoulders and an unsmiling face.

"How can I help you, Officer?" she asked in a tone implying she had little desire to do so.

Mildred had regular but plain features that a smile would have enhanced. But given the tone of her greeting, Mathieu had little expectation he would see one during his visit.

"My name is Officer Mathieu. I'm here to examine Irene Simpson's room," he said, holding up the evidence bag with the search warrant attached.

Mildred frowned and said, "It's already been searched."

"I'm aware of that ... I'm here to search it again," Mathieu said, not giving any ground. "It's an ongoing investigation."

"When are the police going to release Miss Simpson's room so we can rent it?"

"When the investigation is complete," he said.

Defeated, Mildred gave an indifferent shrug.

"Is the rent past due on her room?" Mathieu asked.

"No, Miss Simpson paid a year in advance. We give special rates to permanent residents."

Mathieu nodded but wondered how even with a special rate, Irene could've afforded to pay a year in advance on her salary.

"Did she have any close friends here at the hotel?"

In answer to his question, Mildred said, "The hotel was a safe haven for Miss Simpson. Free from the unwanted advances of men."

"Did Miss Simpson express that opinion to you?"

"No, but she implied it. With her beauty, it must have been tedious for her to have to constantly rebuff the crude propositions of men."

Mathieu thought Mildred's opinion of men was far harsher and less Christian than Sister Mary Catherine's.

"Did Miss Simpson have any visitors?"

"Men aren't allowed here."

"I understand that. I meant female visitors."

"Are you implying Miss Simpson was a lesbian because she chose to live here?"

"I'm not implying anything. I'm asking a question."

"No," Mildred conceded. "Miss Simpson didn't have any female visitors."

"Did she take part in the social life of the hotel? I understand there are active political discussions here every week in the salon."

Mildred narrowed her eyes at Mathieu. He expected to receive a Socialist harangue in response to his question.

Instead, Mildred said, "Miss Simpson traveled a lot for her work. She wasn't here that often."

Mathieu smiled to himself. Irene was a chimera; no one knew

anything about her. The farthest Irene traveled for work was nine blocks to the LA Times headquarters.

"Can you tell me where her room is?"

"Third-floor second door to the left of the elevator," she replied in a mechanical tone.

"Thank you, Mildred," he said, hoping the use of her first name would break the ice. It didn't. Her face retained its stony glare. Mathieu nodded his thanks, then turned and walked to the elevators.

Mathieu got off on the third floor. The attractive arched hallway here was identical to those on the ground floor. Following Mildred's directions, he found Irene's room, removed the crime scene tape, inserted the key, and opened the door. The room had a stale, musty smell as he entered.

Compared to the elegance of the lobby, the room was simple and basic. Three white ceiling beams ran the length of the narrow chamber. A wood-frame double bed was on the left, beyond it, a small desk beside a curtained window. On the other side of the window was a sitting chair and floor lamp. Across from the bed stood a sizeable dresser, next to it a small closet and a door leading to the private bathroom.

The bed was neatly made. There were no personal items or photographs on the desk or dresser. Mathieu opened the closet door to his right, and a whiff of Irene's perfume temporarily paralyzed him. The scent transported him back to the moment he had found her naked body lying dead on the floor.

Shaking himself free of the memory, he took a deep breath and examined the closet's contents. No causal clothes were hanging there, only Irene's business attire. Also absent was any evening wear. It seemed to be the closet of a no-nonsense businesswoman.

Next, he went to the dresser. He opened the top drawer and saw neatly folded but modest panties and bras; the middle drawer contained blouses, pajamas, and a nightdress. The bottom drawer had some extra blankets, presumably provided by the hotel for Los Angeles' rare chilly nights.

Mathieu bent down to feel around under the blankets; his hand hit something hard. He pulled the object out and set it down on the dresser. It was a finely crafted chess set about eighteen inches square and five inches tall. The top of the case was the chessboard with a pullout drawer underneath for the chess pieces. Mathieu had seen similar chess sets in Chinatown.

The chess set was the only personal item in the room. Its presence puzzled Mathieu. Supposedly Irene didn't have any friends in the hotel and didn't have visitors. Why would she have a chess set then? Did she play alone? The case seemed too big and bulky for her to take on her "travels." And why was it hidden? He took the case over to the desk and sat down to examine it.

The surface of the chessboard had the classic red and black squares. The sides of the case, in contrast, sported an ornate Chinese design in gold leaf. Mathieu tugged gently on the brass pull to open the drawer underneath. Inside, carved soapstone chess pieces lay on a green felt inlay. He removed the white and maroon painted figurines and placed them on the chessboard. Then he closed the drawer.

Mathieu looked at the figurines on the board then around the room. He tried to imagine Irene sitting here playing chess by herself, but he couldn't.

He opened the drawer again, this time pulling it all the way out of the case. There was something odd about it. The drawer was much deeper than where the inlay sat. He removed the felt covering. Underneath was a thin cedar board. He tapped on it; it made a hollow sound. He tried to remove it but couldn't.

He felt around the sides of the drawer. On one of the front corners, he felt a dowel. He pressed it; nothing happened. He moved his finger around until he found a similar dowel on the opposite front corner. He pressed it, but still, nothing happened. Then he pushed both of them at the same time, and the thin cedar board popped open. He lifted the hinged lid. What he saw astonished him.

There, lying on a second green felt inlay were over thirty keys. Each key had a tag with a cryptic set of letters neatly hand-printed on it. The majority of the keys looked like house or apartment keys. But some looked like lockbox keys, and at least four were obviously car keys.

Mathieu sat back in the chair and pondered what he'd found. Why had Irene hidden these keys so carefully? Had she been involved in something illegal? Is that why she was killed? He wasn't sure what to do next.

10

Mathieu's Dilemma

Mathieu realized he had a dilemma. If he told Bull about the keys, he would probably give the lead to his detectives to pursue, shutting Mathieu out. If Mathieu didn't tell him and Bull found out later, he might throw him off the case.

But Mathieu didn't want to be shut out. He wanted to pursue the lead himself, at least for a while. So, in the end, he decided to risk it. He wouldn't tell Bull about finding the chest set. He'd only mention the automobiles; if he could find them.

But first, he needed to photograph what he'd found. Luckily, he'd brought along the Leica. He opened the drapes to let in more light and took a shot of all the keys together. Next, he moved in closer, framing three or four at a time to capture the codes printed on each tag.

After that, he went into the bathroom and got a couple hand towels. Using them, he carefully turned over each tag to see if there was any writing on the back. There wasn't any. He set the chess case upside down on the desk and photographed the maker's mark on the bottom. He would try to find out who made it later on.

Then using the hand towels, he wiped clean everything he'd touched. He knew he might be destroying evidence. But he was pretty sure the only person who had ever handled the chess set was Irene. He put everything back in the case then returned it to where he'd found it in the dresser.

Before leaving, Mathieu took several photos of the room and the clothes in her closet. At the last minute, he decided to check her clothes' pockets but didn't find anything. He left, locked the door, replaced the crime scene tape, and took the lift down to the lobby.

Outside the hotel, Mathieu took a moment to make sure he hadn't forgotten anything. Then he went in search of garages in the area that provided long-term parking. He knew it was like looking for a needle in a haystack. But that was what police work was like sometimes.

He rode north on Figueroa then turned left on Eighth Street. Two blocks down, he pulled into a narrow parking lot between two brick buildings. The hand-lettered sign read "Emilio's Daily and Monthly Parking." The wiry young attendant looked at Mathieu with a mixture of suspicion and fear.

Mathieu had experienced this kind of reaction before when approaching civilians. Encounters with the police often brought out a guilty conscience in people. Trying to reassure him, Mathieu smiled and showed him a photo of Irene that he got from Francine.

"Does this young woman park her cars here on a long-term basis?" he asked.

The attendant looked at the picture but didn't react. Mathieu was about to ask again when the attendant asked, "What kind of cars?"

Mathieu shrugged. "I'm not sure, but at least one is a Cadillac Cabriolet Town car."

Impressed, the attendant raised his eyebrows and shook his head no.

Mathieu didn't expect him to say anything else, so he started to walk away.

The attendant stopped him and said, "We mostly get Model As here. But there's a covered parking garage on Olive just south of Eleventh that stores luxury cars."

Mathieu nodded his thanks and left.

A few minutes later, riding south on Olive, Mathieu spotted the garage on the east side of the street, a long one-story brick building. The first part of the building had a flat roof and industrial-style windows. The second half had a hangar shaped roof with two roll-up garage doors. The sign above the entrance read "Aldo's Luxury Car Storage and Repair."

Mathieu parked his Henderson Streamline on the street and entered the building. The garage was cavernous, almost as deep as it was long. Sunlight streamed in from the windows and skylights, providing an even illumination throughout. Generously spaced support-posts, painted red on the bottom, held up the roof beams. The spacing provided ample room to maneuver cars in and out of the parking bays. A sign hung from the center beam that read "Positively No Admittance in Rear."

To his right, Mathieu noticed several bays with chain hoists and dollies. At each one, a uniformed mechanic was at work on a vehicle. Off to the left, there were three long rows of parked automobiles. On the east side of the building, there was another large roll-up door. It was open, providing a welcome cross breeze on this warm day. Next to the door was a small office with glass windows. Mathieu approached the office and knocked on the doorframe.

Seated at a tiny desk was a large man with slicked-back black hair engrossed in some paperwork in front of him. The name tag on his starched uniform was "Aldo." The man looked up at the sound of the knock and seemed surprised to see a policeman. He took the cigarette out of his mouth and said in a friendly voice, "How can I help you, Officer?"

Mathieu reached across the desk to shake his hand and said, "My name is Officer Mathieu."

"Mine's Aldo. Is there a problem with one of our cars parked on the street, Officer? Sometimes there's an overflow, and we have to park them outside."

"No, not at all," Mathieu said, shaking his head. "I've come on a different matter."

He handed Aldo Irene's photograph and asked, "By chance, does this young woman store any vehicles here?"

Looking at the photo, Aldo said, "Of course that's Miss Simpson. We store several of her automobiles here." Then added. "Is there anything wrong? I haven't seen Miss Simpson in several weeks. She never brought back her Cadillac Cabriolet. Usually, she's not gone so long."

Without answering the question, Mathieu said, "Can you show me her vehicles, please?"

"Sure," Aldo said as he stood and negotiated his bulging belly around the desk, then grabbed a set of keys from a pegboard near the door. "This way, please," he said, leading Mathieu off to the right down the first aisle of cars.

They stopped at the end of the aisle. "This is where we park Miss Simpson's four cars," Aldo said. "As you can see, one of them is missing."

It was quite an eclectic collection. The most expensive vehicle was a 1928 Packard Custom Eight Roadster. It was black with a red pinstripe running along the side of the hood and doorframe. Attached to the chrome-trimmed radiator were chrome-encased headlights and fog lights. The vehicle sported immaculately clean whitewall tires with a spare tire mounted on the running board.

Pointing at the Packard, Aldo said, "That's Miss Simpson's favorite. She just got it last year."

Mathieu could see why. It was a beauty. Parked to the left of it was a sporty yellow Essex Boat Tail Roadster with a black convertible top.

"Miss Simpson likes to take that one to the beach on weekends," Aldo volunteered.

There was an empty spot next to the Essex, presumably where the Cadillac that Mathieu found in front of the bean field house was usually parked. Next to that against the wall was a highly polished Black Model A Ford.

"That was Miss Simpson's first car. I think she keeps it out of nostalgia and when she wants to be incognito. Nobody pays any attention to you if you drive a Model A," he said, laughing.

"How long have you been storing cars for Miss Simpson?"

Aldo let out a breath and looked at the floor. "Let me think … it must be at least five years now."

"How did she learn to drive?"

Aldo shrugged. "I don't know. She just showed up one day and said she wanted to store her car here. She said it was convenient to where she lived at the Hotel Figueroa. We don't usually store Fords, but I made an exception for her. Who could turn away a woman as beautiful as that?" he said with a smile.

"Later on, she brought the rest of them. At one time, she had five cars here. We also maintain all of them for her. If she wants to use one, she always calls in advance, and we get it out, gas it up, check the tires, and wash it for her. She's a great customer. And the guys in the shop always perk up when she comes in. She's a real classy lady and a very successful businesswoman."

Mathieu removed the Leica, hanging by its strap from his shoulder. He raised it to his eye and started taking photos of Irene's cars from different angles. Aldo realized this was something more than just a casual inquiry.

"Level with me, Officer, has something happened to Miss Simpson?" he asked.

Mathieu hesitated, reluctant to answer. But being the bearer of bad news came with the job. "I'm sorry to tell you that Miss Simpson has died. I can't share any details with you at the moment."

Aldo looked crestfallen as if there had been a death in the family. Staring at the floor, he made the sign of the cross. "Mio Dio ... how sad," he said. "When is her funeral?"

"A small private service was already held," Mathieu said, trying to cushion the blow.

Aldo nodded that he understood. "Do you know who's going to come and get her cars?"

"I'm sorry, I don't know when her estate will be settled," Mathieu said. "I'll let you know if I find out something."

"Thanks," Aldo said, adding. "She's paid up till the end of the year."

"How did Miss Simpson pay?" Mathieu asked.

"By check."

"Personal check?"

"No ... with her company's check."

"Do you remember the name?"

"Occidental Enterprises."

Mathieu smiled to himself. St. Anne's was on Occidental Street. Either Irene had a strange sense of humor or a deep sense of nostalgia.

11

Chinatown

More than anywhere else in Los Angeles, Chinatown was set apart by its distinctive mélange of scents. The heady mix of hot cooking oil, exotic spices, and burning incense characterized its uniqueness as much as the signs and paper lanterns hanging from the storefronts.

With the Southern Pacific railroad tracks running down its center, Alameda Street bisected Chinatown. To the west of it, Chinatown extended to Main Street. And to the east, it went for three blocks, where a spur of the main rail line and the LA River marked its eastern border. There were rumors that the area east of Alameda might be torn down for a new train station, but so far, these were only rumors.

Being next to Frenchtown, Chinatown was an area Mathieu knew well. He had played on its dusty streets as a kid. Most were paved now except for a few east of Alameda that were too narrow for cars. He remembered those cobbled lanes, flanked by two-story brick buildings with green balconies, as fun places for kids to play. Their nocks and crannies providing ample fuel for a child's imagination.

As a teen, Mathieu had taken Kung Fu lessons in Chinatown. And he'd probably eaten there more often than he had at his father's restaurant. Many of the older people had known him since he was a child, and even though he was a policeman now, they still welcomed him with a friendly smile or greeting. In turn, Mathieu knew enough Chinese to return their respect.

He parked his police motorcycle near the plaza, then walked down Marchessault and crossed Alameda. To the north, he could see a freight train slowly making its way down the center of the boulevard, flanked on both sides by vehicles. He had never gotten used to seeing huge locomotives and cars sharing the street. There had been horse-drawn carts on Alameda in his youth also, but now there were fewer of them. Those that remained were relegated to the side of the road so as not to impede traffic.

After crossing Alameda, he made a quick left and walked to Apablaza, where he turned right. When he was a kid, Apablaza was still a dirt road, but now it was paved. This was the area of Chinatown he loved the most with its warren of little cribs. In past times the cribs had housed prostitutes.

But now, a family or small business might be crammed into one of them. Most merchants in Chinatown still pursued the traditional trades, market owners, fishmongers, and the like. But the Chinese were also quick to adapt to new business opportunities. In the last few years, a film development shop had opened in an old crib off of Apablaza. It offered quality processing at prices far lower than you'd find downtown.

It was also the kind of place where you could develop photos of a certain type. Photographs that would be frowned upon in the more respectable parts of town. It was there where Mathieu was headed now. He couldn't risk developing the film he'd taken at Irene's apartment at the police lab. At least not until he'd decided what to tell Bull about the keys he'd found.

After a few blocks, Mathieu turned off Apablaza onto a narrow lane. Some children were playing in the pathway, watched over by an elderly man sitting in the shade. The buildings were closer together here, the smells more intense. Laundry hung from second-story clotheslines, and here and there, flowers grew in planters perched on the railings. At the end of the lane, a "Kodak Photo Supplies" sign hung in front of Hop Li's shop.

Mathieu entered the store. Hop Li was younger than he'd expected, a wiry man in his early twenties with nervous eyes and a cigarette hanging from his mouth. Mathieu gave him the roll of film. He asked him to make prints of all the negatives and to blow up those containing keys. If Hop Li wondered why a policeman was bringing a roll of film to his store, he didn't let it show. He told Mathieu it would take about an hour.

Mathieu left and made his way to a Chop Suey place on Marchessault, where he had eaten often as a kid. One of the old Aunties made a fuss over him, bringing him extra helpings to fatten him up.

When he returned to Hop Li's an hour later, the prints were ready. He took a quick look at them, paid, and started to leave. But then he remembered a question he wanted to ask. He showed Hop Li the photo of the maker's mark on the bottom of the chess set. "Do you know whose mark this is?"

Hop Li glanced at it and said, "Of course that's Mr. Wang's. He's two blocks over on Napier."

"Thanks … I have one more question," Mathieu said as he handed him Irene's photo. "Have you ever seen this young woman?"

Hop Li's face remained impassive, but his eyes darted quickly to the side as he replied, "No."

Mathieu knew he was lying but let it go. He handed him his card and said, "Here's my business card. If you should remember her later, call me."

Hop Li nodded, took the card, but remained silent.

When Mathieu returned to Alameda Street, he encountered his old Kung Fu instructor, Mr. Yang, on the sidewalk. He looked older and frailer than Mathieu remembered. Mathieu bowed to him in respect and said, "Sensei."

The teacher's wizened old face brightened wide enough so Mathieu could see a few of his teeth were missing. But also to see the affection he still had for Mathieu. They talked for a few minutes when a sudden instinct prompted Mathieu to ask him a question.

"Have you ever seen this woman, Sensei?" Mathieu asked as he showed him Irene's photo.

The old man stared at the photo for a long time. Mathieu wondered whether age had dulled his mind. Then he looked up at Mathieu with a mischievous smile and said, "Miss Simpson would be a formidable opponent even for you, Theo. She was one of my best students."

Mr. Yang explained that Irene had come to him several years earlier for training. She wanted to learn how to defend herself. Not shy as to the reason why the old man said it was because of her beauty. Irene had told him she wanted to know how to protect herself against the kind of men who didn't take no for an answer.

Mathieu nodded that he understood.

Before parting, Mathieu promised he would come and visit him soon. He left Chinatown perplexed. More and more, it seemed like Irene's life and his own were strangely intertwined.

12

The Vacant Lot

The next day, Mathieu showed Bull the photos he had taken of Irene's automobiles. Bull was intrigued, but his reaction was predictable.

Dismissing it, he said, "Maybe she was a call girl. She had the looks for it. But I don't see what that has to do with her death. I can't see any Negros being able to pay her enough money so she could afford those cars."

"Her money could have come from some other source," Mathieu said. "Maybe she got rich doing business deals behind Chandler's back. And one of his partners got wind of it and killed her."

"But why kill her in a Negro area?" Bull asked.

"Simple, so we'd suspect a Negro killed her."

Bull shook his head, "I doubt she was scamming Chandler. He's too smart for that. My gut says she was a high-priced hooker."

"Okay, let's supposed she was. Where's the most obvious place she could have met her rich clients?" Mathieu countered.

"In Chandler's office," Bull conceded with a shrug.

"Exactly! The richest men in Los Angeles are in and out of Chandler's office every day. Do you think they wouldn't have noticed Irene? That they wouldn't have desired her? Wanted to buy her, wanted to possess her? They're all used to getting whatever they want. They certainly could afford to give her expensive gifts like cars."

"Sure, they could," Bull said. "But Chandler's business partners are white, every last one of them. What's his slogan for Los Angeles 'Keep the White Spot White'. His lily-white partners sure as hell wouldn't follow Irene into a dangerous Negro area and kill her. They'd shit their pants before they got south of Jefferson Blvd. You're looking in the wrong place, Mathieu."

"But you don't mind if I keep looking, do you, Chief?" Mathieu asked innocently. "Just to keep me out of the way and keep Chandler happy."

Bull couldn't help but smile. He liked the kid; he understood how the game was played. "Sure … knock yourself out. Now get out of my office. I've got reports to sign."

"Thanks, Chief," Mathieu said. "By the way, can I keep Irene's apartment key? I may need to search it again."

Bull shrugged as if to say, why not.

Mathieu started to leave, but Bull stopped him.

"How did you know Irene had those other cars?" Bull asked as he leaned back in his chair and stared at him.

Mathieu had been expecting the question. "I didn't. But I figured she had to park that car we found somewhere. And the Hotel Figueroa doesn't have parking. So, I looked around the neighborhood and found the garage on Olive that had her other cars."

Bull wondered if Mathieu was telling him everything but let it pass by saying, "Get out of here, kid, before I change my mind."

Mathieu smiled and left. He went to the nearby Aztec coffee shop. The interior of the diner had the kind of muddled architecture you'd expect in Los Angeles. There were Aztec designs painted on hideous looking faux Moorish columns. Garish chandeliers hung over the counter, which would have been more appropriate in a bordello. But the coffee was good. And the spacious booths gave him enough privacy to look at the photos undisturbed.

He laid out the photos of the keys in front of him. Irene had devised a cryptic encoding that was hard to fathom. One of the tags read "CA – JF," another "CG – TH," a third one, "GA – SJ." The first two letters of each tag were unique. But the last two letters on some of the tags were identical. Mathieu wrote each code in his notebook. There were five tags each that ended in the letters "JF," "SJ," "TH," and "FF." And another two each, that ended in "KP," "AB," and "JE." Those tags alone accounted for twenty-six keys.

There were other tags with a different kind of encoding, such as "3096 Dur – PM." Mathieu noticed that those keys looked more like lockbox keys than house or apartment keys. He wrote their codes on a separate page in his notebook. The one constant was every tag ended with two-letters. Were they initials? Mathieu wasn't sure.

Mathieu was so engrossed in studying the photos he didn't notice the waitress standing next to him with a hot pot of coffee. "Want a refill, Hon?" she asked to get his attention.

"I'm sorry … yes, thank you," Mathieu said, looking up and smiling.

"No problem, Officer," she said, batting her eyes in a flirtatious way. "You want anything to eat, Hon?"

"Sure … how about a piece of your blueberry pie?"

"Coming up," she said as she turned and walked away, swaying her hips as she did.

While he waited for the pie, Mathieu had a sudden idea. He stood up and motioned to the waitress that he'd be right back. He went outside and got his "Thomas Guide Maps to Los Angeles" from his saddlebags.

Back in the diner, Mathieu examined each tag that started with a number and an abbreviation. He tried to find a matching street name in the Thomas Guide, beginning with those letters. To his surprise, he found a match for all of them. Excited now, Mathieu stood, left money for the bill and tip, and hurried outside.

One tag, in particular, intrigued Mathieu. The one for "3096 Dur," because it looked to be an address in Chandler's new Hollywoodland development. Deciding to check it out, he rode northwest to Hollywood. Once on Franklin Avenue, he took it to Beachwood Drive, where he turned right and headed up into the hills.

When he got to Belden Drive, he turned left and took it to Flagmoor, then Durand, where he wound up the narrow ridgeline road. Here and there were lone houses, but mostly the area was still empty lots. He rounded a sharp corner and got a great view of the Hollywoodland sign and downtown Los Angeles. He stopped in front of a vacant ridgeline lot with a For Sale sign on it.

The address on the sign was 3096 Durand Drive. The lot was small and would be challenging to build on because it was steep, but it had great views. The sign read, "For Sale - Hollywoodland Realty Office." Mathieu backtracked to Belden and Beachwood, then crossed the street to Westshire Drive, where the real estate office was located.

He parked in front of the blue-trimmed gingerbread house and went inside. The only person there was a finely coiffed blonde real estate agent with rigid posture and an equally stiff attitude. She looked at Mathieu as if he had made a mistake and was horribly out of place.

Trying to ignore her attitude, he said, "My name is Officer Mathieu. I wonder if you could tell me who owns the lot at 3096 Durand Drive?"

The agent had a pained look on her face at the question. "I'm afraid those lots are a little out of your price range, Officer," she said, not even trying to be pleasant.

Her smug attitude angered Mathieu. So, he did what he usually avoided doing. "I'm well aware of that, Miss, that's what my godfather told me."

Still dismissive, she asked, "And who may I ask is your godfather?"

"Harry Chandler," he said evenly.

Her face dropped, and her smug smile with it. She cleared her throat, trying to recover. "Well, now ... let me get that information for you right away, Officer," she said as she consulted a large binder on her desk.

"What was that address again?" she asked as she paged through the binder.

"3096 Durand Drive," Mathieu replied.

"That's curious," she said, finding the page for the property. She looked up at him and asked, "By any chance, are you Pierre Mathieu's son?"

"Yes, I am. Why?"

"The property you asked about used to be owned by your father?"

"Used to be ... who owns it now?"

"Occidental Holdings," she replied.

Mathieu was shocked but tried to hide it. "Do you have their phone number?"

"Yes, I do," she said, writing it on the back of her business card and handing it to him.

All smiles now, she said, "My name is Sharon Stevens ... don't hesitate to call if you have any further questions, Officer Mathieu."

He looked at Occidental's number on the back of the card, thanked her, and left.

Outside Mathieu was troubled. Why had his father transferred the lot to Irene? It was a question he would have to ask his father at some point, but for now, he had to track down Occidental Holdings.

13

The Office Manager

When Mathieu returned to police headquarters, he phoned Occidental Holdings. A young woman answered the phone on the second ring.

"Occidental Holdings, how may I help you?"

"I'm calling about a property you own," Mathieu replied.

"Which property is that?"

"A lot in Hollywoodland at 3096 Durand Drive."

"Just a moment, please, while I check our records," she said. "Yes, that is one of our properties. How may I help you with it?"

"Is it for sale?"

"Yes, sir, it is," she said. "May I ask your name, please."

"My name is Officer Mathieu. I'm with the LAPD. And what is your name, please?"

"My name is Rose Thompson. I'm the Office Manager," she replied, showing some concern in her voice. "Is there a problem, Officer?"

"Is your employer's name Irene Simpson?"

There was silence on the line while Rose decided how to respond. "Why are you asking?"

"This is an official police investigation, Miss Thompson."

"Yes, Irene Simpson is my employer," she said without offering any other information.

"When was the last time you spoke with Miss Simpson?"

There was another silence on the line while Rose tried to remember. "It was three weeks ago."

"Is it unusual to have such a long time between contacts?"

"No. Miss Simpson is a very busy woman, and she trusts me to handle her business affairs while she's away traveling."

"Where is your office located, Miss Thompson?"

"In the Bradbury Building ... third floor Suite 325," she answered.

"I'd like to come and visit you there now if that's okay with you."

Now concerned, Rose asked, "Has something happened? Has Miss Simpson been in an accident?"

"It's best if we discuss that in person. I'll see you in about fifteen minutes," Mathieu said, then hung up.

The Bradbury Building was close enough to walk to from police headquarters. Mathieu headed south on Broadway and, after crossing Third Street, paused in front of the Grand Central Market. He looked across the street at the Bradbury. It was his favorite building in downtown, but not because of its bland brick and sandstone exterior. He knew the real beauty lay inside.

Mathieu crossed the street, turned right, and walked to the arched entranceway. He paused in front of the doors with their dark-tinted glass inlays. Even here, one had no idea what delights awaited them inside. He opened the door and stepped in. It was as if he had entered a tunnel.

It took a moment for his eyes to adjust to the darkness of the foyer. As they did, he took in the honey-colored wood-paneling on the ceiling and the glazed brick walls. Ahead of him was a narrow corridor that led to the heart of the building, to the right of it, a staircase with intricate black metal railings. Instead of being claustrophobic, the corridor felt comforting, hinting at what was to come.

Passing through it, he came out into the light-filled central court. He stopped for a moment and gazed up at the skylights five stories above. It was like being in a secular cathedral.

Turning to his right, he boarded one of the "Bird-cage" elevators. The elevators were like a touch of Paris in LA with their black wrought-iron grillwork. He asked the lift operator to take him to the third floor and enjoyed the view unfold as they ascended. The elevator ride was a brief respite from what was to come. He wasn't looking forward to telling Miss Thompson about her employer's death.

When the elevator came to a stop on the third floor, he got off. He walked along the open-air passageway past closed office doors on his right, searching for Suite 325. As he walked, he occasionally glanced over the railing on his left to the lobby below.

At the end of the passageway, he spotted a door with "Occidental Enterprises" painted on its frosted glass inlay. He knocked and soon after was buzzed in. He entered the spacious office where a diffuse light from oak-framed windows filled the room. Metal file cabinets stood against the brick walls, and in the center of the room, there was a lone desk with several telephones.

It was there that Rose Thompson sat, eyeing Mathieu as he approached her. She was a woman in her early thirties, who some might judge as homely, except for her kind, attentive eyes.

Rose stood when Mathieu reached her desk and extended her hand in greeting. "Please have a seat, Officer," she said, pointing to a chair next to the desk. "I confess I'm somewhat anxious to know the reason for your visit."

Mathieu sat down, paused a moment, and said, "I apologize

for any anxiety I caused you on the phone, Miss Thompson. But I felt it was best to talk to you in person."

"I understand," she said, still on edge.

Looking at the floor, Mathieu said, "I'm sorry to inform you that your employer Irene Simpson is dead. I'm here because I'm investigating the circumstances of her death."

Rose stared at him with an open mouth but didn't say anything. She looked stunned and disoriented. Mathieu didn't know whether she was in shock.

"Can I get you some water or something?" he asked, unsure what to do.

Rose pointed vaguely at a water pitcher on top of one of the filing cabinets. Mathieu went over to the cabinet, found a glass, filled it, and brought it back to her. Rose took a sip from the glass, then took a deep breath to collect herself.

"I can't believe she's dead," Rose said. "Are you sure it's Miss Simpson?"

"Yes … I was the one who found Miss Simpson's body. She was properly identified afterward."

"How did she die?"

"I'm not at liberty to discuss that at the moment, but it's being treated as a suspicious death."

"When did this happen?" Rose asked, still trying to make sense of the incomprehensible.

"About two weeks ago," Mathieu replied.

"Why weren't we informed earlier?" she asked, now visibly upset.

"It wasn't until today that I learned of the existence of Occidental Holdings."

Rose nodded that she understood. "Miss Simpson was extremely private in her business affairs … I don't doubt it was difficult to track us down."

"You said 'us' how many people worked for Miss Simpson?"

"I'm sorry," she said. "That's just a habit of mine. Besides Miss Simpson and her lawyer, there's only me."

"I'm a little confused about the company name," Mathieu said. "The sign on the door says, 'Occidental Enterprises,' but you answered the phone saying, 'Occidental Holdings'."

"Occidental Enterprises is the umbrella name for the firm," Rose explained. "Under it are several different companies, including Occidental Holdings and Occidental Rentals. We have separate phone numbers for each."

"I see," Mathieu said. "Thanks for clearing that up."

"May I ask how you came to work for Miss Simpson?" Mathieu asked.

"I answered a help wanted ad in the Herald Examiner."

"When was this?"

"About five years ago."

"What did the ad say?"

"Independent Businesswoman seeks female Office Manager. Preference will be given to adoptees from St. Anne's."

Everything always came back to St. Anne's.

As the reality of Irene's death began to set in, Rose said, "I don't know what I'm going to do now."

She buried her face in her hands and started to cry. Mathieu gave her time to grieve. After a few minutes, Rose sat up straight and wipe her eyes with the back of her hands.

She looked at Mathieu and said, "I'm sorry, I just feel so lost. I don't know what to do next."

"Have you been getting paid regularly during the last few weeks?" Mathieu asked.

"Oh yes, Miss Simpson has that all set up with the bank. They pay me automatically every week by check. Miss Simpson was extremely efficient in her business affairs."

"Then, I would suggest you keep working as usual until Miss Simpson's estate is settled."

Mathieu's advice seemed to calm Rose. He took a few photos from a folder he'd brought with him and laid them on the desk.

"Do you recognize any of these keys?" he asked.

Rose studied the photos. "Yes, the keys with tags that have street addresses on them are lockbox keys," she said, pointing to the locked file cabinets against the wall. "Each one has all the legal documents for a particular land lot that Miss Simpson owns. Including the one on Durand you asked about on the phone."

Mathieu nodded. "And what about these other keys that look like house or apartment keys."

Rose looked at them carefully and shook her head. "No, I don't recognize them."

But then she quickly corrected herself. "Wait, I recognize these two keys."

"Which ones?" Mathieu asked.

"This one here that says "CA – SJ" is for an apartment Miss Simpson owns in the Carlton Arms in Hollywood. I don't know what SJ means, but CA stands for Carlton Arms. And the one that says "TT – SJ" is for her apartment in the Talmadge at Wilshire and Bernardo Boulevard."

"Why is it you recognize these two?"

"Because Miss Simpson recently started to rent them out, and I handled the leases," she answered. "We rent the apartments out under our Occidental Rentals name."

"What kind of apartments are they?" Mathieu asked.

"Oh, they're both quite luxurious," she said proudly.

"And you say she owns these apartments?" Mathieu asked, still confused.

"Technically, she holds long-term prepaid leases on them.

But it amounts to the same thing," Rose said, trying to clarify his confusion.

"For example, the lease on the Carlton Arms is prepaid for twenty years. With leases that long she had the freedom to either sub-lease or resell them at a profit. The demand for luxury apartments for the wealthy has skyrocketed in the past few years. Miss Simpson got into the market at a good time."

Now it was Mathieu's turn to be surprised at how profitable Irene's properties were. But how could she have afforded to prepay twenty-year leases on them? The only answer was she hadn't. Someone else had paid for them and given them to her. Someone rich. But who and why? He was quiet for a minute, trying to decide what to do next.

He looked at Rose and said, "Thank you for your help, Miss Thompson. I may need your assistance again in the next few days to figure out what these other keys are for."

"Certainly, Officer, I'd be glad to help," she said.

Rose was secretly grateful to be of some use. It would give her some focus and keep her from floundering in her own grief.

14

The Chauffeur

The chauffeur approached the ship's railing, leaned against it, and gazed out to sea. The water was calm. Light from a full moon danced off its surface. He took a long slow pull off his cigarette, drawing out the movement as he did. He knew his employer was watching him through the casino porthole, wondering if he would go through with it. The chauffeur made him wait. He was enjoying this.

He looked to his left to see if he was alone on deck, then reached into his finely tailored overcoat and pulled out a gun wrapped in a handkerchief. He tossed it over the railing and watched it sink immediately below the surface.

Looking back over his shoulder, the chauffeur smiled at his employer. The evidence was gone. Smiling back, his employer toasted him with his champagne, then returned to the party inside. They were three miles out to sea in Federal waters at least a thousand feet deep. They were effectively beyond the law out here for all but murder.

The night had started like most others when his employer called him into his richly furnished study after dinner. He informed him of the evening's plans, then handed him a heavy object wrapped in a handkerchief and secured with twine.

"I'd like you to keep this in your overcoat tonight, Albert, and dispose of it when we get out to sea on the S.S. Ritz."

"Understood, sir ... when would you like to leave?"

"The usual time around eight."

"And which vehicle?"

"The Bentley."

"As you wish, sir," Albert said and left to get ready.

Back in his quarters at the edge of the five-acre property, Albert put the package on his bed and untied it. Inside was a Colt 38 Special "snub-nosed" revolver, a favorite of detectives and bodyguards. He stared at it for a long time, thinking about how he could use it to his advantage. Having decided, he smiled to himself.

Careful not to touch it, he covered the revolver with his handkerchief, then hid it under a floorboard cache he used to store his private possessions. He substituted it with a German Luger he kept in the cache, wrapped that in the original handkerchief, and secured it with the twine. He replaced the floorboard, tapping it down with his foot. He had just bought an insurance policy for himself.

After dressing for the evening, Albert appraised himself in the room's full-length mirror. Satisfied with what he saw, he put on his overcoat and dropped the package into his inside pocket. Albert was ruggedly handsome, his face marred only by a bayonet scar obtained in the killing fields of Northern France during WWI. But Albert knew he was one of the lucky ones. He'd seen enough death during the war for a thousand lives.

Albert got the Bentley from the garage, brought it around to the front of the estate, and opened the rear door for his employer. Once his employer was seated, Albert came around to the driver's side, and they left. When they got downtown Albert turned right onto Pico, then drove west along its length to the Santa Monica Pier where they parked. They walked to the end of the pier, then down a ramp to a highly polished motorboat that ferried them three miles out to sea where the S.S. Ritz was anchored.

All the other gambling ships in the bay catered to the masses and were open twenty-four hours a day. But the Ritz was open only at night and only for the rich, famous, and elite. Their newspaper ads proclaimed, "High-class dining, dancing, dames, and games." Their motto was, "What happens at sea, stays at sea." Of course, everything was more expensive on the Ritz, the entrance fees, table stakes, booze, food, and the women. But it was worth it; it kept the riffraff away and made for a more exclusive experience.

The steel-hulled ship was long and narrow with a curved-roof-salon that ran the deck's length. The aft section had an area for dancing and parties. The longer middle section housed the casino, where tux wearing croupiers stood before every imaginable gaming table. The fore section of the salon was the dining area. To get from the dancing area to the dining area or vice versa, one walked through the casino. All roads led to Rome and the gaming tables.

Midship below deck, there were ten staterooms on each side of a polished teak corridor. The staterooms were available for "private entertainment." The engine room was in the stern, and the kitchen was beneath the dining area near the bow.

The Ritz had a crew of one hundred and fifty, including croupiers, waiters, waitresses, chefs, and a small orchestra. And like the other gambling ships in the bay, it employed gunmen and water cannons to repel any unwanted boardings by the authorities. Because of the gunmen's presence, many of the clientele, including Albert's boss, brought their chauffeurs along as bodyguards.

After throwing the gun overboard, Albert stayed at the railing for a while, thinking about the choice he'd made. The more he thought about it, the more he liked the feeling of having some potential leverage over his employer. He finished his cigarette, flicked it into the ocean, and went inside to the salon.

There were more celebrities onboard tonight than usual because of a premier party. Paramount Studios had rented the whole ship for the occasion. Albert spotted Charlie Chaplin in one corner of the room, chatting up three voluptuous blonds spilling out of their dresses as they gazed upon him with rapt attention. Albert made a private bet with himself, which blonde Chaplin would bed first. Of course, it probably didn't matter. He was sure to have them all before the night was over. Chaplin was an odd-looking guy in person. His head was so much bigger than the rest of his body that it was a mystery how his neck could hold it up.

In the center of the room, Albert saw Myrna Loy talking to some producers. He loved Myrna's exotic looks and femme fatale roles. Whenever he drove past Venice High, he tried to catch a glimpse of the Fountain of Education sculpture, which she'd posed for in high school. Standing here in the salon, she still had that same lithe teenage girl figure.

Despite his employer's wealth, he was a bit player in this crowd. Albert took secret pleasure watching Chaplin, and the others rebuff him as he strained a smile trying to fit in. He might have more money than them, but they were more glamourous and famous. And that's what counted in Hollywood.

In another corner of the room, Albert saw a tall, extremely handsome man with a cleft chin and British accent surrounded by several casting agents. He had them all laughing with his offbeat sense of humor and cockney slang. Albert had never seen the man before, but he had the easy charm and charisma of a star. He heard one of the casting agents call him Archie Leach.

They'd have to find a better name for him than that if he was to become a movie star.

Tired of watching the partygoers and gambling Albert made his way below deck. He walked along the corridor, past the private staterooms where all manner of debauchery was going on behind closed doors. A buxom brunette, totally naked, came out of one of them and puked on the floor right in front of him.

Trying to steady herself against the wall, she looked at Albert with a smile and said, "Excuse me, handsome." Then she turned and ran bare-assed down the corridor toward the ladies' room in the stern.

Albert casually stepped over her vomit and walked toward the kitchen in the bow. He spent the rest of the evening there smoking, talking to the crew, and eating while leaning against a galley wall.

When Albert headed back to the stern a few hours later, he spotted a platinum blonde exit a stateroom. She stopped to prim her hair and makeup in a small mirror, then stuffed some cash in her tiny purse and walked away. A minute later, his employer came out of the same room. Albert ducked into an exit aisle so he wouldn't be seen. He waited until he heard his employer's steps recede along the corridor and go up the stairs to the salon above. He laughed to himself. As usual, his boss hadn't gotten lucky and had to pay for it once again.

Back in the Bentley, after returning by motor launch to the Santa Monica Pier, Albert looked in the rearview mirror and asked, "Are we waiting for anyone, sir?"

"Not tonight, Albert … home, please."

"Yes, sir," Albert responded in a respectful tone but with a smirk on his face that couldn't be seen in the darkness.

15

The Reward

Mathieu hoped Chandler could shed some light on the properties Irene owned. Maybe there was some simple explanation for them. He called Francine and asked her to set up a private meeting on Thursday evening. He didn't let Bull know about the meeting. He didn't want him to blurt out his call-girl theory in front of Chandler.

By reputation, Chandler was a devoted family man. What might seem obvious to Bull that Irene had acquired her wealth through sexual favors would never occur to him. Mathieu needed Chandler to care about Irene for the investigation to go forward. Otherwise, it would be dropped, and her death would remain a mystery. More importantly, Bull's absence meant Mathieu could be more open with Chandler about what he had learned about Irene's properties.

Mathieu arrived at Chandler's office a little early. He waited in the anteroom while Chandler dealt with his supplicants, then Francine motioned for him to go in. As Mathieu entered, Chandler stood up and came around to the front of his desk. He took Mathieu's hand in both of his. Mathieu always felt somewhat intimidated in Chandler's presence. It brought up memories from his childhood when the kind but huge man loomed over him like a giant. But Chandler, unlike his father, was generous enough to recognize that he had grown up and was his own man now. He treated him like an equal.

Chandler motioned toward the seating area near his desk, and once they were seated, he said, "It's good to see you, Theo. I hope you brought me some good news about the investigation."

"I've made some progress, sir, but there's still a lot I don't understand. I was hoping you could help."

"If I can ... what is it you need?"

"I'd like to keep what I'm about to say between us for now, sir," Mathieu said. "I haven't told Bull yet."

"Of course," Chandler said with a smile, admiring that young Mathieu had a shrewd side to him.

"I've discovered that Irene owned quite a lot of property, including some apartments and several automobiles. Do you have any idea how she could have acquired them?"

Chandler looked a little dumbfounded. "Well, certainly not with what I paid her."

"Yes, that's what I thought also, but is it possible she inherited some money?"

"Well, as you've probably learned, she was brought up at St. Anne's."

"Yes, sir, I did find that out. But I was wondering if perhaps Irene's mother remarried and left her some money when she died. Or maybe some other relative like an aunt or an uncle did. Did she ever mention her relatives to you, sir?"

"No, not at all. Irene was very private. As far as I knew, she wasn't in touch with any of them. She had a pretty traumatic childhood."

"Yes, sir, that's what Sister Mary Catherine at St. Anne's told me."

They were each silent for a moment, both equally confused about how she had acquired her properties.

Chandler looked perplexed. He put his hand to his mouth and said, "I would hate to think Irene did something dishonest."

"Like what, sir?"

"For example, taking advantage of her position here," he said. "As my private secretary, she was aware of all my real estate dealings."

"It's possible, sir. But from what I've learned so far about Irene's character, she was fiercely loyal to those who were good to her. And that would include you."

Mathieu's instincts told him that Irene wouldn't have betrayed Chandler. But he chose not to bring up the subject of the lots she owned in Hollywoodland until he knew more. Especially since one of them came from his father. No sense in stoking Chandler's fears.

"You sound like her advocate, Theo."

"That's a policeman's job, sir … to be an advocate for the victim."

Chandler looked admiringly at Mathieu. "You love being a policeman, don't you?"

"Yes, sir, I do."

"It's sometimes hard for me to believe that you're your father's son."

"That's often difficult for me also, sir," Mathieu quipped, and they both shared a laugh.

Chandler changed the subject. "I still don't understand why she was in that Negro musician's house."

"She met him at the Dunbar where she heard him play with Duke Ellington," Mathieu said. "That's how they became friends."

"What was she doing at the Dunbar?"

Mathieu shrugged. "Apparently, she liked jazz. So do I. I've been to the Dunbar many times. And I've heard Thornton play. He's an excellent saxophone player."

Chandler didn't look pleased but let it go. There was no reason to upset himself and think poorly of both his godson and Irene because they liked jazz. But he still wasn't convinced that was the whole story.

"What aren't you telling me, Theo? I may be an old man, but I'm still a man. What was Irene's relationship with Thornton?" Chandler looked at Mathieu the way he must have looked at his adversaries in a business deal. He wasn't going to be fooled easily.

"According to Thornton, they were just friends. She'd drop by his house unannounced and ask him to play for her." Mathieu shrugged. "I mean, what man would have refused to play for a beautiful woman like Irene?"

"Then how did she get in the house if Thornton wasn't there?"

"He left a key outside for friends under the porch. Irene knew where it was and let herself in." Mathieu chose to lie instead of telling Chandler that Thornton had given her a key.

"Why did she go to his house if he was out of town?" Chandler pressed.

"Thornton told me he had no idea how to get a hold of Irene. He didn't know her phone number or where she lived or where she worked or anything. She would just show up unannounced," Mathieu said. "So, I guess when she got there, and Thornton wasn't home, she assumed he was playing a local gig and decided to wait for him. Unfortunately, when she went to the door, it was her killer, not Thornton."

"And you don't think some other Negro killed her? Like maybe one of Thornton's friends."

"No, sir, I don't," Mathieu said emphatically. "Bull's men have beaten up a half-dozen Negroes, and they still haven't found any leads."

Both men were silent. Mathieu watched Chandler think about the problem, perhaps in the same way he approached his business problems.

Chandler looked at Mathieu and said, "Maybe some reward money would help shake the tree, Theo. What do you think?"

"It might, sir ... with certain kinds of people," Mathieu replied.

"It would have to be handled discreetly, though," Chandler said. "I'm obviously not going to publish it in the LA Times."

"Understood, sir," Mathieu said. "It could be used to encourage people to talk who otherwise might be reluctant to."

"I'd like you to handle it, Theo," Chandler said, finally getting to the point. "Will you do that for me?"

Mathieu was uneasy about his request but agreed. "If you wish, sir. But what do I tell Bull?"

"Nothing for now," Chandler said. "When you leave, Francine will give you an envelope. There's some cash inside ... use it however you wish to get at the truth. And if you need more, tell me."

"Yes, sir ... I will."

Chandler sat back in his chair and rubbed his forehead. "This is a sad business, Theo," he said, sighing. "I've never been this close to violent death before. It's shaken me ... I feel out of my depth."

"That's understandable, sir," Mathieu said. "Especially since Irene was someone you knew and worked with. I've seen violent death before, but this is the first murder case I've ever investigated. I guess it's a policeman's curse, but it becomes quite personal. You start to identify with the victim ... the lines between you and them start to blur."

Neither knew what else to say about a death that had affected them both. To break the tension, they chatted for a few minutes

NAKED LIES THE TRUTH • 81

about trivial things. Then having said all they could, for now, they shook hands, and Mathieu left.

In the anteroom, Francine handed Mathieu a thick envelope. She had him sign for it. He did so mechanically without looking inside. Down in the lobby, he opened the envelope and counted the money. Inside was two thousand dollars in one-hundred-dollar bills. He was shocked by the amount.

He immediately walked to his bank a few blocks away at the corner of Fourth and Main. The handsome Classical Revival style building housed The Farmers and Merchants Bank. It was the first bank incorporated in Los Angeles and the only one his father would allow him to use. It was also the same bank Chandler used. The bank's policy of holding most of its capital in Treasury securities had enabled it to survive past economic downturns. And even though the economy was booming, his father had always advised him to be conservative with his savings.

Entering the lobby, Mathieu asked to access his safe deposit box. A bank clerk gave him a form to sign. After checking his signature, the clerk escorted Mathieu into a windowless backroom where steel cabinets filled with deposit boxes lined the walls.

They walked around the periphery of the room, looking for number twenty. Finding it, the clerk inserted his master key then asked for Mathieu for his. The clerk unlocked the door and removed the deposit box from the steel cabinet. He placed it on a waist-high counter, returned Mathieu's key, and left.

Mathieu took three hundred dollars from the envelope just in case he needed it to encourage a witness to come forward. He put the envelope with the rest of the money into the safe deposit box. Mathieu knew it would be foolish to carry that much cash around with him during the investigation. It was safer in the bank, and he could always access it quickly if he needed it.

As he began to close the deposit box, Mathieu spotted his

birth certificate on top of some Savings Bonds. He took it out and examined it. He had scrutinized it many times before searching for clues. But had always come to the same conclusion. It had been tampered with. The handwriting on the "Mother of Child" section was different than the handwriting on the rest of the form. As if it had been filled in later by someone else.

He started to put the certificate away when he spotted something barely legible under the physician's signature. Something that he'd never noticed before. He squinted at the scrawl to bring it into focus. In a tiny script, it read, "St. Anne's."

16

Not the Usual Suspects

Mathieu was beginning to understand the code Irene had used on her key tags. The last two letters were most likely the initials of who she got each the property from. If he could match initials to names, then he could create a list of suspects. But Mathieu needed help, so he called Francine again.

He read Francine the list of initials he'd recorded off the key tags, except for his father's. He asked her if she could match the initials to Chandler's close friends or business associates. Anyone that might have come in contact with Irene. Francine called back two days later with a preliminary list of names. They agreed to meet up again at the Biltmore Hotel after work.

Mathieu got there first and waited in front of the hotel. When Francine arrived a few minutes later, they entered the lobby through the revolving doors and turned left into the bistro grill. They found a table near the window and sat down. Soon after, a waitress approached and gave them their menus. With her narrow face and pinned up hair, the young waitress was prim and proper in her freshly starched uniform.

Mathieu glanced quickly at Francine then said to the waitress, "Two coffees to start with, please."

After the waitress left, Francine said, "Did you see the look she gave me?"

"What do you mean?"

"She waited on us the last time we were here," Francine said. "She looked at me like, 'What is this older woman doing robbing the cradle?'"

Mathieu laughed. He was glad Francine was enjoying the intrigue. "I wonder if she ever smiles?" he asked.

"It's unlikely," Francine said with her own warm smile.

A few minutes later, the waitress brought their coffee. When she left, they began discussing the list.

Francine said, "I've found names for some of the initials you gave me, but not all of them."

"That's fine ... what do you have so far?"

"Well, first of all, 'SJ' might be Samuel Johnston. He's that character actor you took a photo of at Irene's funeral. Do you remember him?"

Mathieu had brought along the photos from the gravesite and flipped through them until he found what he thought was the right photo. "You mean this stocky guy with the bald head."

"Yes, that's him. Johnston has made hundreds of films. And even though he's only a character actor, he's made a lot of money."

Looking at the list, Mathieu asked, "What about 'JF'?"

"'JF' could be Joseph Friedkin. He's a studio executive. He used to be married to Norma Russell, the actress. He's a Russian or Ukrainian Jew, I think."

"Was he at the funeral?"

"I don't think so, but he sent Mr. Chandler a condolence card. I brought along some press clippings of him," Francine said, laying them out on the table.

"That's him," she said, pointing to a dapperly dressed middle-aged man with a prominent nose and a receding hairline.

"How old is he?"

"About fifty."

"Did he remarry?"

"No."

"Is he still in the film business?"

"Oh, yes."

"Where does he live?"

"He has several homes in LA and another one out in Palm Springs."

Mathieu wrote some notes in his notepad, then asked, "Who's next?"

"Then there's 'FF,' which could be Fredrick Fallon. He's a rich oil tycoon who married an even wealthier heiress from Santa Barbara."

"Is he the same Fredrick Fallon who was involved in the Teapot Dome Scandal?"

"Yes, but I think he was acquitted of any wrongdoing."

"Probably because he had a good lawyer," Mathieu scoffed. "Wasn't he an associate of Edward Doheny?"

"Yes, and also of Edward's son Ned before his death."

"Didn't Ned commit suicide in the Greystone Mansion?"

"Yes, five months after he moved in," Francine said. "Wealth isn't a guarantee of happiness, is it?"

"No, it's often quite the opposite," Mathieu said.

"For 'KP,' I've got two possibilities, and one of them is kind of scary," Francine said.

"Why?"

"Because one of them could be Kent Parrot," she said.

"You mean the guy that pulls the strings behind the scenes in LA politics? The guy they call the 'shadow mayor' because he controls Mayor Cryer?"

"Yes."

Mathieu raised his eyebrows. Kent Parrot was a scary guy. He had been Cryer's campaign manager when Cryer ran for mayor on an anti-vice platform. Now people called Cryer "Parrot's Puppet." The rumors were that Parrot had strong ties to all of LA's major underworld figures. Mathieu had a hard time believing Irene would get involved with someone like Parrot. From what he knew about her, she liked to be in control. And there was no way she could control someone like Kent Parrot.

"Who else could 'KP' be?" Mathieu asked

Francine said, "Well, it could also be Professor Kevin Patterson."

"Who's he?"

"He's a Vice-Chancellor at USC and also heads the Architecture Department."

"Is he wealthy?" Mathieu asked, suspecting everyone on the list probably was.

"Oh yes, Vice-Chancellors are paid quite well. And Professor Patterson has also been an investor in some of Chandler's business deals."

Mathieu nodded. "Do you have a photo of him?"

"Yes," she said, handing him a news clipping from the LA Times, which included Patterson's formal portrait.

Mathieu studied Patterson's face. He looked to be in his late sixties and struck Mathieu as being both distinguished and troubled. In the photo, he wore wire-rim glasses and sported a gray Van Dyke beard that camouflaged a weak chin. But it was his eyes that Mathieu's gaze kept coming back to because they seemed to be in pain.

"Is he ill?" Mathieu asked.

"Not that I know of," Francine said. "But he is retiring next year after twenty-five years at USC."

Patterson seemed a more likely person for Irene to be involved with than Parrot. He looked weak, needy, troubled. Irene could control him. After taking a few more notes, Mathieu asked, "Who else do we have?"

"The only 'TH' I can think of is Thaddeus Harrison. He and Chandler go way back, to the syndicate they formed with Otis to buy forty-four thousand acres in the San Fernando Valley."

Mathieu shook his head in mock admiration at Otis and Chandler's scheme. In 1905 they convinced the voters to approve a bond issue to build an aqueduct that brought water from the Owens Valley to Los Angeles. The two hundred-mile-long aqueduct, designed by William Mulholland, was to terminate at a spot just north of the San Fernando Valley. Soon after the bond was approved, Chandler and Otis formed a syndicate that secretly bought up most of the land in the San Fernando Valley for next to nothing. By the time the water arrived, the land was worth many times over what they'd paid for it. The scheme was devious but brilliant, and it changed Los Angeles forever.

"Chandler, Otis, Harrison, and their partners made a king's ransom on that deal," Francine said.

"Is Harrison married?"

"No, he's a confirmed bachelor, I think."

"Where does he live?"

"He lives in Pasadena," Francine said. "You saw him at Irene's funeral, remember?"

"Is he that Eugenics Society guy?"

"Yes."

Mathieu picked through the pile of photos until he found one with Harrison in it.

Pointing to a thin man with a pinched face and sullen look, he asked, "Is that him?"

"Yes."

"I remember him now. He looks like a preacher. I can't see

Irene being involved with him. But I'll put him on the list. You never know."

"Any other names?" Mathieu asked.

"Not for now," Francine said. "But I'll keep looking."

Mathieu smiled at her. "Thank you, Francine, this has really been helpful."

"Where did you get the list of initials from?" she asked.

Mathieu hesitated before answering. He trusted Francine, but he didn't want the information about Irene's properties to get out yet. In the end, he decided to tell her part of the truth. "I found the initials in some of Irene's notes."

Francine looked troubled. "Do you think someone on the list killed her?"

Mathieu shrugged and said, "I don't know yet, Francine. Before I can determine that, I need to find out what kind of relationship these men had with Irene. Assuming they had any relationship with her at all."

"How will you do that?" she asked.

"I'll have to talk to all of them."

"Who will you start with?"

"The weakest one."

"Who's that?" Francine asked

"The actor, of course."

17

Inceville

Francine gave Mathieu the name and address of Samuel Johnston's agent in Hollywood. The agent's name was Sylvia Wosk. Initially, Mathieu was going to call her but decided instead to visit her office the next day.

The agent's office was in a bungalow near "Poverty Row" on Gower, where the three minor Hollywood studios were located. He arrived unannounced and knocked on the frosted glass door that read, "Sylvia Wosk Talent Agency."

He heard a muffled voice behind the door say, "Come in!"

Mathieu opened the door and entered. There was only one person in the room, a middle-aged woman with curly hair, tinted a shade of red not often found in nature, and a cigarette dangling from her mouth.

Without looking up, she said, "You're early, Hon. Did you bring your headshots?"

Mathieu didn't reply, so the woman lifted her head. "You didn't have to wear a costume, Hon. You could have come in your street clothes," she said.

"But you do look good in that uniform. You must be Bruce Steel." All this was spoken in a gravelly voice that some women get that smoke and drink too much.

"I'm sorry, Miss Wosk, there's been a mix-up. I am a police officer. My name is Officer Mathieu."

Sylvia seemed unfazed by this new information as she studied Mathieu's face. "That's a damn shame because the camera would love your face," she said. "Let me see it in profile."

Without thinking, Mathieu did as she requested and turned his head.

"You're in the wrong line of work, Hon. I could make you a star."

Mathieu reddened. "I'm here on a police matter, Miss Wosk."

"Is my car blocking the alley again?" she asked as she took a drag from her cigarette.

"No, mam, I'm here to talk to one of your clients."

"Who's that?"

"Samuel Johnston."

Looking concerned that one of her breadwinners might be threatened, she asked, "What did Samuel do now?"

"Nothing that I know of, Miss Wosk. I just need to speak with him."

"Have a seat, Hon," she said, relieved, as she pointed to a chair next to her desk piled high with scripts. "You can put that stuff on the floor."

"Samuel's basically a good boy … if he could only keep his dick in his pants. I keep telling him, 'Sam, you've got a reputation to protect. Your whole career is built on playing the good solid citizen, the family man, mayor, judge. You don't need bad publicity over some floozy'." She looked at Mathieu and sighed. "Being a man must be a terrible burden."

"Where's Mr. Johnston today?"

"He's out at Inceville filming a Western. He's playing the mayor … good part ten pages of dialog."

"I thought the sets at Inceville burned down," Mathieu said.

"They did. But when that Papist from Boston, Joe Kennedy, bought Inceville for FBO, he rebuilt the western town. Everybody still calls it Inceville even though it's officially now 'FBO Studios,'" she said with disdain.

"Where are you originally from, Miss Wosk?" Mathieu asked out of interest.

"The Bronx," she said, emphasizing her New York Jewish accent.

"I used to work at Astoria Studios … came out here for my health," she said as she took another long drag from her cigarette.

Watching Sylvia smoke was fascinating. She kept the cigarette in her mouth as long as possible, like a life support system. Until just at the last moment when the ash had grown to a length that defied gravity, she'd flick it into the ashtray, take another pull, and put it back between her lips.

"Would it be okay to visit him on the set?"

"Sure, there's a lot of time to chat between takes. It takes forever to set up some of those shots. Do you know how to get there?"

"I think so," Mathieu said.

"It's out in the Palisades. Take Sunset till just before it ends at the ocean, then take the road on the right that winds up to the top of the ridgeline. That's where the Western sets are. The turnoff is just past the lake that Thomas Ince built on the left. You can't miss it."

Mathieu stood up to leave. "Thank you for your help, Miss Wosk."

Sylvia handed him her business card. "If you ever change your mind about the movie business, give me a call, Hon. We'll get some headshots taken, and you'll be on your way."

Mathieu smiled and left.

He followed Sylvia's directions to Inceville, riding his

motorcycle along Sunset toward the ocean. When he was a child, he'd been to Inceville once with his father. At that time, Thomas Ince still owned it, and the movie studio straddled both sides of the mouth of Santa Inez Canyon.

To Mathieu's child's eyes, it had been a wonderland. With its Western sets, Scottish town, and sound stages scattered about the canyon and along the ocean road. But Ince was a restless soul and sold Inceville when Henry Culver convinced him to open Triangle Studios in Culver City.

Tragically, Ince died on William Randolph Hearst's yacht in Santa Monica Bay nine years later under mysterious circumstances. The coroner ruled that Ince died of a heart attack. But rumors persisted that Hearst shot Ince by mistake, thinking he was Charlie Chaplin, trying to seduce his lover Marian Davies. Despite the coroner's ruling, most people still chose to believe the rumors. The rumors reinforced the common man's belief that the super-rich could get away with anything, including murder. It was the kind of logic that hard to argue with.

Now Inceville was a shadow of its former self but still fascinating to Mathieu. He admired the skill of the set makers who could create entire worlds out of their imagination. He turned right off of Sunset and rode a short way up a dusty road. He got off his motorcycle and walked toward the Western set a little farther up the hill.

Mathieu felt anxious. This was the first time he was going to question a suspect in the case on his own. He'd prepared himself, but he knew that nothing is ever how you imagine it until you actually confront the suspect. Then you have to think on your feet. He hoped he was ready. He took comfort in the advice one of his mentors at the Police Academy had given him.

"Listen more than you talk," he'd said. "People are uncomfortable with silence. They'll reveal things they hadn't intended to just to break the tension."

As Mathieu approached the Western set, a woman in braids wearing jeans and holding a clipboard stopped him.

Looking at the clipboard, she asked, "What's your name, young man?"

Before Mathieu could answer, she said to herself, "I can't believe those morons at Central Casting sent an actor in a police costume to a Western set."

"I am a policeman," Mathieu said as he showed her his badge and identification.

The woman stared at his ID, then back at his face before realizing he wasn't kidding.

Recovering, she said, "I'm sorry, Officer, but I wouldn't put it past Central Casting. Some of those fools are so dumb they can't walk and chew gum at the same time."

She held out her hand. "I'm Sally McPherson. I'm the production assistant on this shoot. How can I help you?"

"I'm looking for Samuel Johnston."

"What's old Samuel done now?" she laughed.

"I just need to talk to him."

"He's over there in front of the jail. They're filming right now, but I'll walk you up."

"Thanks."

When they got close to where they were filming, Sally and Mathieu stood quietly off to the side. Johnston was in front of the jail, dressed in a black suit, vest, and a bowler hat. He was arguing with an actor wearing a cowboy hat and boots, presumably the sheriff from the badge on his vest. A horse was tied up to the hitching post next to them. The film crew was small, just the director, a cameraman, and a sound man holding a boom.

When the director called "Cut," Sally waved Johnston over to them.

"Samuel, this Officer Mathieu from the LAPD," she said, introducing them. "He'd like to talk to you."

Johnston was an imposing presence in person with his sturdy body and intelligent eyes. He didn't seem surprised to see a policeman as if he'd been expecting it.

"Is there somewhere private we can talk?" Mathieu asked.

"Sure," Johnston said, not resisting. "Sally, we'll be in the saloon. Come get me when they're ready for the next shot."

Johnston led Mathieu along the boardwalk in front of the Western town. Mathieu assumed the buildings were just false fronts. But when Johnston pushed open the saloon's swinging doors, they entered a fully built interior set. There was a long bar with a huge mirror on the wall behind it, and circular oak tables spread throughout the room.

They sat down at one of the tables near the door. Johnston took off his bowler hat and placed it on the table. He mopped his brow with a handkerchief staining it with makeup as he did.

"Why are you here? Did that little wanna be starlet complain?" Johnston asked.

Mathieu didn't say anything. He just kept looking at Johnston.

"She told me she was eighteen years old before I slept with her. But after she didn't get the part I promised, she said she was going to the police. That little trollop would spread her legs for anyone to get a part in a movie."

"That's not why I'm here, Mr. Johnston," Mathieu said. "I'm here because I'm investigating the death of Miss Irene Simpson."

Johnston noticeably tensed on hearing Irene's name.

"How well did you know Miss Simpson?"

"I barely knew her at all."

"But you attended her funeral," Mathieu said as he pulled a photo of Johnston at the gravesite from his notebook and put it on the table.

"That was to comfort Harry."

Mathieu waited for him to say more. When he didn't, Mathieu said, "You realize, Mr. Johnston, that it's a crime to lie to the police during an investigation. If it's found out later that you lied, you could go to jail."

Trying to throw Mathieu a bone, Johnston said, "I used to chat with her a little when I visited Harry at his office."

"Where were you the night she died?"

"I was out on the Ritz in Santa Monica Bay."

"How long did you stay?"

"Till about three in the morning."

Mathieu knew from the coroner's report that Irene had died around midnight. But that information had never been made public.

"Can anyone verify that?"

"There were tons of people who saw me on the boat, including the 'hostess' I slept with."

"Do you remember her name?"

"She called herself Marlene," Johnston said, laughing. "Those tarts love to use movie star names."

"I'd like to ask you again, Mr. Johnston, how well did you know Irene?"

"Is it just me, Officer, or do you treat everyone like a suspect?"

Without responding, Mathieu continued to study Johnston's reaction. It took all his will power not to smile. There was truth in the remark because most policemen did.

"How well did you know Irene?" Mathieu repeated calmly.

Beads of sweat started to form on Johnston's bald head. He took out his handkerchief again and patted his forehead. Johnston shrugged and said, "I took her to dinner a few times."

"Where?"

"Usually, Musso and Franks."

"Did you meet her anywhere else?"

"No," he said, not too convincingly.

Johnston looked like he thought he was getting away with it. Mathieu took a risk and tried to shock him.

"Then why did you give Irene five apartments?" he asked suddenly.

Johnston froze; his mouth dropped open. The young cop wasn't stupid.

"You know about the apartments," he said, amazed.

"Yes. Why did you give them to her?" Mathieu persisted.

"I'd rather not say. But I promise you I didn't kill her," Johnston said. "Whatever happened between Irene and me was consensual and legal. It had nothing to do with her death. I can assure you."

"How did you know Irene was murdered?" Mathieu asked, now suspicious. "It wasn't in the papers."

"Harry confided in me afterward … he was devastated," Johnston said. "Please don't mention the apartments to Chandler. He adored Irene like a daughter. I don't want him to think badly of her."

Or about you, Mathieu thought. "Can you think of anyone who would have wanted to kill her?"

"No," Johnston said, shaking his head. "Irene was damaged, but she was the sweetest person I've ever met. I can't think of anyone who'd want to harm her. She was pure magic."

As Johnston spoke, there was real sadness in his eyes. It seemed genuine to Mathieu. He didn't think Johnston was a good enough actor to fake it.

"Were you in love with her?"

Johnston shrugged. "Everyone was in love with Irene, but no one could ever have her," he said almost to himself.

"Reason enough for some to kill," Mathieu said.

"Maybe, but they'd have to be pretty sick to kill someone as special as Irene," he said in anger.

They were silent for a moment, neither sure what to say next when Sally came in to get Johnston for the next shot. He nodded to her that he'd be there in a minute, and she left.

"Are we through here?" Johnson asked.

"Yes, for now," Mathieu said. "But I may need to talk to you again."

Johnston reached into his coat pocket and pulled out a business card. He handed it to Mathieu. "This is my answering service number. Call if you want to talk. I'll try to help. But please don't mention this to Harry."

Johnston shoved his chair back, scraping the floor as he did. He stood, straightened his coat, and grabbed his hat. Then he pushed through the saloon doors and went outside. The doors continued to swing after he'd left, just like in the movies.

18

The Apartment

The next morning Mathieu called the Ritz's business office in San Pedro, the closest harbor to Santa Monica Bay large enough to accommodate a ship the size of the Ritz. Mathieu needed to check Johnston's alibi for the night Irene was murdered.

When the receptionist answered, Mathieu asked to be put through to the employment office. There was a short delay, then a young woman answered. "Ritz Employment Office, how can I help you?"

"My name is Officer Mathieu from the LAPD. Who am I speaking to?" he asked. That was something else Mathieu had learned at the academy. Always ask a person's name when questioning them. It puts them off balance and implies they'll be held accountable for their answers.

The young woman hesitated then said, "My name is Elizabeth Walker. How can I help you, Officer?"

"Do you have a hostess that works on the Ritz whose first name is Marlene?" he asked.

"Is there some problem, Officer?"

"Not at all. I just need to speak with Marlene to verify some information."

"Very good," she said relieved. "Just a second, please, while I check."

Mathieu could hear the rustling of papers then she came back on the line. "Yes, we have a hostess by that name."

"What's her last name?" Mathieu asked.

"Chambers," she answered.

"Can you verify if Miss Chambers worked the evening of May 7 and the early morning hours of May 8?"

"Let me see," she said as she thumbed through some old timesheets. "Yes, Marlene worked onboard the Ritz all that evening until five the next morning."

"Do you have a contact number for her?"

"We don't normally give that kind of information out."

"I understand. If you'd feel more comfortable, Miss Walker, I'll give you my number here at LAPD headquarters in downtown Los Angeles, and you can call me back."

"That won't be necessary," she said, trying to be conciliatory. "Her phone number is 'WA 6933'. I believe it's an answering service number."

"Thank you for your help Miss Walker, goodbye," Mathieu said.

After hanging up, Mathieu called Marlene's answering service and left his name and number. He didn't identify himself as a policeman; he just asked for Marlene to call him back. He didn't want to spook her.

Now that Mathieu knew Johnston had given Irene five apartments, he needed to see them. Irene's office manager had only known about the two apartments Irene had started to rent. But Mathieu wanted to see the others, the ones Irene used for herself. He was hoping Rose might be able to figure out the names of the apartments. He called her and went back to the Bradbury Building to see her.

When Mathieu entered the office, Rose was on her own again, but this time looked calmer than when he'd seen her on his previous visit.

"How are you feeling, Rose?" he asked as he sat down next to her desk.

"Better," she said, her face brightening. "It's kind of you to ask. Miss Simpson's lawyer called me a few days after you visited. He told me not to worry and to continue working as usual. He said it would take a while to figure out all the details of Irene's estate. At this point, he isn't even sure how much property Irene owned."

"That must be a relief for you not to have to find another job now," Mathieu said.

"Yes," she said. "And I apologize again. I was kind of a wreck when you were here last time."

"There's no need to apologize," he said. "I'm sure it was quite a shock for you."

"The lawyer told me something else interesting," Rose said.

"What's that?"

"Irene made provisions for me in her will."

"Really?" Mathieu asked, surprised.

"Yes. According to the lawyer, her will states that I'm to be paid during the entire period it takes to liquidate her estate. And afterward, I'll be given a year's severance pay. I couldn't believe she was so thoughtful."

"That's quite generous," Mathieu said and meant it. But it also disturbed him. Irene was a young woman, too young to be concerned with wills and contingency plans. And yet, she had made both as if she knew her life might be in danger.

"I need your help," Mathieu said, handing Rose the list of key codes for the three unrented apartments Irene got from Johnston. "These are the codes on three of Irene's key tags. We decided the last time I was here that the first two letters are probably an abbreviation for the apartment's name. But I can't figure these out. Do you have any idea which apartment buildings they might be for?"

Rose studied the codes, then, without saying anything, got up and retrieved a binder from the bookcase behind her desk. She took a while to scan through it, studying the handwritten notes on each page.

She looked up at Mathieu and said, "These are the notes I kept whenever I spoke with Irene on the phone. She was usually busy and hard to get a hold of, so I always wrote down her instructions so I wouldn't have to bother her."

Rose turned the binder around so Mathieu could see it. "This is the last time I spoke with Irene. See here I wrote, 'Irene will let me know in two weeks if she wants to rent out her Gaylord Apartment.'"

Mathieu gave her a quizzical look, not quite sure what Rose was getting at.

"See this code 'GL-SJ.' I think that could be her Gaylord Apartment," she said, smiling with pride at figuring it out.

Mathieu smiled back. "You're a genius, Rose. I think you're right. Where is the Gaylord?"

"It's on Wilshire Boulevard on the north side of the street across from the Ambassador Hotel."

"That's a nice address," Mathieu remarked.

"All Irene's properties are nice," she said. "That's another reason I think it's the Gaylord."

"She didn't give you a key, did she?"

"No, but she said she would when she decided."

Mathieu thought about what to do. He could go back to the Hotel Figueroa and get the key out of the chess set, but he preferred not to disturb the evidence yet. He had another idea on how he could get into her apartment that might work.

"This is great, Rose, thank you," Mathieu said. "I'm going to go over to the Gaylord now. Can you keep working on the other two codes and call me if you come up with anything?"

"Certainly," she said, glad that she could be of help.

It took Mathieu less than fifteen minutes to ride over to the Gaylord. He parked on a side street off Wilshire next to the thirteen-story Italian Renaissance apartment building. Constructed only a few years earlier, it had already attracted an elite clientele.

Mathieu entered the shallow foyer, its walls covered in a light-colored glazed stone. He passed quickly through it into the lobby and walked across the polished marble floor to the concierge's desk. The concierge was on the phone. She was a middle-aged woman with elegantly coiffed gray hair. Mathieu looked up at the ceiling, adorned with an intricate plaster cast design, as he waited for her to finish.

After she hung up, the concierge stood and asked, "How can I help you, Officer?"

There was a hint of smugness in the way she asked the question. Mathieu had experienced it before with waiters and waitresses in elite restaurants. They tended to adopt their affluent clients' attitude when addressing those they assumed were not wealthy.

Mathieu ignored her attitude and said in a matter-of-fact tone, "My name is Officer Mathieu from the LAPD. I'm investigating a suspicious death. What is your name, please?"

He said all of this in a manner designed to put her off balance. It had the desired effect. Her face momentarily turned ashen as she stammered and replied, "Judith Williams."

"Miss or Mrs.?"

"Miss," she replied. "I'm a widow."

Mathieu nodded. "Miss Williams, can you tell me if an Irene Simpson has an apartment here?"

"Why yes, she certainly does," Miss Williams said. "Irene has one of our largest apartments facing Wilshire Boulevard on the tenth floor."

"I'm going to need to see it," he said as he quickly flashed the search warrant that he had for the Hotel Figueroa. The concierge was so flustered she didn't ask to examine it closely.

"Certainly," she said. "I'll have one of our bellmen take you up, Officer."

"Thank you," Mathieu said.

She rang for a bellman who came almost immediately. "Joseph, this is Officer Mathieu. Can you take him up to Irene Simpson's apartment on the tenth floor and let him in, please."

"Of course … please follow me, Officer," Joseph said as he led Mathieu to the elevators.

Joseph looked to be in his early sixties, thin but with perfect posture.

As they rode up in the elevator, Mathieu asked him," How long have you worked here, Joseph?"

"Since it opened in '25," he answered.

"Do you know Miss Simpson?"

"Oh, yes, sir. She's a very nice lady," he said. "And quite a beauty. She puts most of the famous actresses that live here to shame."

"Have you ever seen her enter or leave the hotel with any celebrities?"

"No sir, but in truth, I can't say I'd have noticed there are so many famous people that live and visit here. I've seen Charlie Chaplin here a few times myself."

"How often did Miss Simpson stay here?"

"At most a few nights a month. She traveled a lot for her work."

"Did she have any male visitors at night?"

Joseph seemed reluctant to answer. "Can't say that I noticed, Officer."

The elevator stopped at the tenth floor, and Joseph led Mathieu down the polished corridor to Irene's apartment at the front of the building. Joseph opened Irene's door with his passkey then stood aside to allow Mathieu to enter.

"Thank you for your help, Joseph," Mathieu said. "I'll be sure to close up when I leave."

Realizing he was being dismissed, Joseph said, "As you wish, Officer." He bowed slightly, turned around, and walked back down the corridor to the elevators.

Mathieu entered the apartment. It was huge, over a thousand square feet. The living room was tastefully but sparsely furnished with carpeting, a couch, comfortable chairs, and a coffee table. He went into the adjoining full kitchen, where he noticed a few bottles of expensive French wines on the counter. Mathieu recognized the labels from his father's restaurant. He checked the cupboards; there were wine glasses, plates, cups, but no food.

Mathieu checked out the bathroom next. It was clean and tidy, with thick towels folded over the towel rack. He opened the medicine cabinet. There he found a toothbrush, toothpaste, soap, some lipstick but little else. Then he went into the bedroom.

The bedroom was spacious, but there was no bed.

A red velvet couch sat against the far wall under the window. It was too small to sleep on but big enough for two to sit on. The floor was covered in plush white carpeting with a concentric circle design that radiated from its center.

In the center of the room, there was a lone wooden chair. Mathieu recognized the chair's spare, elegant silhouette; it was a

Le Corbusier Bentwood chair in nude-colored wood. His father had brought several over from France. Its design was devoid of any ornamentation, just the sensuous curves of the wooden legs, back, and armrest as though one was staring at a naked body.

Near the bedroom door were a set of switches that controlled spotlights mounted on the ceiling and walls. Mathieu turned them on. Except for one light over the red velvet couch, all the others pointed to the center of the room, bathing it in a warm, seductive light as if it were a stage.

Mathieu looked in the bedroom closet. The only thing he found was a woman's negligee made of see-through white lace with tiny satin shoulder straps.

On the wall opposite the couch was a floor to ceiling bookcase. The bottom of the bookcase contained cabinets, above which were wall-mounted bookshelves. Mathieu opened the cabinet doors and found a few extra towels and blankets but nothing else. The bookshelves themselves were filled with books on law, real estate, and investing. It was an odd room. On the one hand, it seemed design to seduce. On the other, the only personal touch was the books.

There was a record player on the cabinet countertop, next to which lay a stack of albums. He looked through them; most were by Duke Ellington. There was a record on the turnstile. He turned the player on and lowered the stylus; as he did, the seductive sound of Duke Ellington's "Black and Tan Fantasy" began to fill the room. The song had the Duke's signature "jungle sound," which defined his music, a down-low sensual rhythm.

Mathieu moved toward the center of the room and stood behind the chair. He could feel the warmth from the spotlights on his face. He gazed at the velvet couch, itself lit by a spotlight above it. The circles on the carpeting seemed to form an implied barrier between where he stood and where the couch sat. As he went around in front of the chair, he heard something click under his foot. It felt like a footswitch under the carpet. He stepped on it again and heard it click once more. He turned around and looked back toward the bookcase.

Walking over to it, he knelt down and lifted the edge of the carpeting. He saw a wire running under the carpet up into the bookcase. He looked up and imagined where it might end. On the top shelf, he spotted a red decorative box with a gold leaf Chinese design. He stood on top of the cabinet so that he was now eye level with the box. He could see a tiny opening on the front of it. He lifted the lid. Inside was a small camera. Attached to it was the wire which ran up the bookcase to a cable pull device for the camera's shutter and the film advance.

The camera pointed directly at the red velvet couch across the room.

19

The Break-in

The phone rang, disturbing the desert stillness. The man hesitated for a moment, fear and anxiety rising in his chest, before he picked up the phone.

"Is it done?"

"Yes, sir," said the female voice on the other end of the line.

"Did anyone notice you?"

"No one notices a cleaning woman."

"You wore gloves?"

"Of course, sir."

"Where are you calling from?"

"A phone booth at the main train station downtown."

"When does your train arrive here?"

"At seven."

"I'll have the butler pick you up."

"Thank you, sir," she said, then hung up.

At the Gaylord, Mathieu removed the camera from the red box. He opened the camera back, but there was no film inside. Putting the camera down, he turned the box on its side and looked at the maker's mark. It was the same as the one on the chess set in Irene's room at the Hotel Figueroa.

Mathieu felt anxious. Was it time to tell Bull about the apartments? But how could he without admitting he'd found the keys earlier? He walked around the room, trying to calm himself, and then it came to him. He'd tell Bull the truth, or at least part of it, that Rose had told him about the Gaylord. Having decided that, he took some photos of the room with the Leica and left.

On the ride back to headquarters, he changed his mind and decided to go to the Hotel Figueroa first. He was going to do what he should have done earlier, secure the evidence. What if someone had gotten into Irene's room since he'd been there and removed the chess set? He berated himself for being so stupid as to leave it there. Thinking about that, instead of riding, he went too fast into a corner, and his rear wheel fishtailed on some loose gravel. The bike started to go down, but he quickly turned into the slide, recovered, and continued on. He slowed down the rest of the way and arrived safely.

Mathieu entered the lobby, but this time went straight to the elevators without stopping at the front desk. He took the elevator up to Irene's floor and used the key from the evidence bag to enter her apartment. The room seemed different to him; maybe it had been cleaned. He went to the dresser, opened the bottom drawer, and sighed in relief when he found the chess set was still there. He snapped a few photos of it in the dresser before lifting it out, then wrapped it in a pillowcase and went back downstairs. Outside, he put the pillowcase in his saddlebag and rode back to headquarters.

When Mathieu got back to the detectives' office, it was after six. No one was there. He opened the bottom drawer of his desk, put the chess case inside, and locked the drawer. He was sitting at his desk, considering what to do next when Bull walked in.

"Just the man I wanted to see," Bull said. "Are you making any progress on the Simpson case?"

"Yes, sir. I've been interviewing some of Irene's friends," Mathieu said.

He hesitated for a moment, unsure whether he should tell Bull about the chess set now and what he'd found at the Gaylord apartment.

Bull saved him the trouble. "Good because there's something I want you to do tomorrow."

"What's that?"

"There's been an apartment break-in. I want you to check it out."

"Why?" Mathieu asked, a little confused.

"Because it might fit your theory," Bull said. "Turns out the apartment belongs to Irene Simpson."

"Really? Where is it?"

"It's in Hollywood on Franklin Avenue."

Bull handed him a slip of paper. "It's called 'Casa Laguna.' The building manager's name is Peter Howard. Go take a look around in the morning."

"Yes, sir," Mathieu said.

As Bull went into his office, Mathieu breathed a sigh of relief. Without knowing it, Bull had just done him a huge favor.

Early the next morning, Mathieu arrived at the Casa Laguna apartments. The yellow Spanish-style building, with its red-tiled roof and green, accented windows, was on the corner of Franklin and Kingsley. Mathieu had called ahead. The building manager was anxiously waiting outside for him at the main entrance on Kingsley.

"Thank you for coming, Officer," he said. "My name is Peter Howard. This has been pretty upsetting for the residents. It's usually such a safe neighborhood."

Mathieu introduced himself then asked, "Are you the one that discovered the break-in?"

"Yes, but almost by accident," Howard said. "I was walking along Franklin Avenue and saw a side window had been broken into. I called the police; a patrolman came and took a report. I told him the apartment belonged to Irene Simpson. A couple of hours later, I got a call from your chief. He said he was going to send one of his detectives over today. I didn't expect you to be so young," he said. "Or to be riding a motorcycle."

Mathieu nodded and said gracefully, "I get that reaction a lot. Can you show me the apartment?"

"Of course."

Howard opened the gate and led Mathieu through a beautifully landscaped courtyard with palm trees and a central fountain. Irene's apartment was on the right in the back.

"As you can see, Officer, it would be hard to break into these apartments via the courtyard. A burglar would risk being seen by myself or the other residents. I guess that's why they chose to break the window on the street."

Mathieu nodded. Howard opened the door, and they entered. It was an attractive, spacious, Southwest-style apartment with whitewashed walls and gracefully curving arches connecting the rooms. The main room had a vaulted ceiling two-stories high with exposed beams and a polished wooden floor. A staircase with Spanish tile runners ran up one wall to a landing that looked over the main room and led to the second-story bedroom. The landing's wood banister had thin wrought-iron supports. It was almost see-thru from the ground floor.

Mathieu turned to Howard and said, "I'm sorry, but I'm going to have to ask you to leave now. I need to look around."

"I understand," Howard said, reluctant to leave. "If you need me, my apartment is near the entrance on the left."

"Thanks," Mathieu said. "I may have some questions for you before I leave."

After Howard left, Mathieu walked around the main room, trying to get a feel for the place. It was an entirely different style than the Gaylord. But like it, sparsely and tastefully furnished. And like the Gaylord, revealed little of the owner's personality. There were no personal photos or objects on display. It appeared to have been decorated by a professional, not Irene.

Usually, Mathieu thought, the room would have looked neat and tidy. But whoever had broken in had turned over furniture, emptied drawers, and tossed things on the floor. Whether they found what they were looking for was hard to determine. But Mathieu doubted it. There was something about the frenzied mess that hinted at an unsuccessful search.

He went up the staircase and turned left into the bedroom. As at the Gaylord, there was no bed. But unlike the Gaylord, the bedroom wasn't set up like a stage. In the closet, he found a sheer pink negligee cut high to accentuate a woman's legs. A fresh scent of perfume permeated the room, which surprised Mathieu. Irene hadn't been here in weeks.

Mathieu went back out on the landing, leaned against the banister, and scanned the main room below. He noticed a comfortable couch positioned in such a way that an occupant would have a clear view of anyone on the landing. He glanced at the vaulted ceiling above and saw several spotlights hanging from the beams. The lights pointed to where he was standing. This was the stage.

But where was the camera? Mathieu went back downstairs. He walked around the room, carefully avoiding the objects strewn on the floor. There was a built-in Kiva-style fireplace in one corner of the room, its opening edged in tiles and shielded by a black wrought-iron screen. To the left of the fireplace, mounted high on the wall, was a brightly painted Mayan head-mask. It looked untouched from the search.

Mathieu retrieved an overturned chair and placed it under the head-mask. Standing on the chair, he noticed a thin wire running up from the back of the Mayan-mask to the balcony railing, where it attached to a tiny switch. He removed the mask from the wall and found a miniature camera inside attached to a cable pull. He opened the camera. It was empty. Had the burglar found the camera, removed the film, and put it back? Mathieu thought it was unlikely.

He spent several minutes taking photos of the mask and the rest of the apartment with his Leica. Then he locked the door and walked toward Mr. Howard's apartment. Howard opened the door before Mathieu had a chance to knock.

On a hunch, Mathieu took the newspaper clipping containing Joseph Friedkin's photograph from his notebook. He handed it to Howard.

"Have you ever seen this man visit Miss Simpson?"

Without hesitating, Howard replied, "Oh yes, every time Miss Simpson stayed here, he would come to visit her in the evening."

"Thanks for your help, Mr. Howard," Mathieu said. "You can have someone repair the window. But please don't clean up Miss Simpson's apartment or let anyone else in. We may have to come back."

"Certainly, Officer," Howard said, eager to assist in any way he could.

Outside on the street, Mathieu checked his notebook. He found the key-tag code he was looking for, "CL-JF." "Casa Laguna-Joseph Friedkin."

20

Clearing the Air

When Mathieu got back to headquarters at noon, the detectives' room was empty. He was surprised to see Bull in his office with the door closed. He knocked and heard Bull's voice say, "Come in!"

"What did you find at the Casa Laguna?"

"It was a mess," Mathieu said, sitting down. "But it didn't appear like anything had been stolen."

"Why did they'd break-in then?"

"I think they were looking for something," Mathieu said.

"What makes you think that?"

"Because it looked like a search, not a burglary. And because I found a hidden camera in the room. I think that's what they were looking for."

"Any film in it?"

Mathieu shook his head. He was tired of concealing things from Bull, so he decided to come clean even if it meant losing the case.

"I have something to show you," Mathieu said as he got up and went to his desk. He retrieved the chess set and brought it back to Bull's office. Placing it on Bull's desk, he removed the chess pieces, then pulled the drawer out of the case.

"What's this?"

"A drawer with a hidden compartment filled with the keys to all the apartments Irene owned."

"Where did you find it?"

"In Irene's room at the Hotel Figueroa."

"My guys searched that whole damn apartment and didn't find anything!"

Mathieu shrugged.

"Where was the chess set hidden?"

"In the dresser across from Irene's bed under some blankets."

"When did you find it?"

"The first time I searched her apartment."

Bull looked disappointed, "And you're just telling me this now, Mathieu?"

"I'm sorry, sir," Mathieu said, sitting back down. "I was afraid you'd take the lead away from me. And I didn't know what the keys were for when I first found them. I wanted to do some digging on my own before I told you about it."

"Let me see the keys," Bull said, pointing at the drawer.

Mathieu pressed the corners of the drawer, and the lid to the hidden compartment popped open.

Bull looked at the contents, and his mouth fell open, "Mother of God, how much property did she have?"

"At least twenty-six apartments plus raw land in various developments including Hollywoodland."

Bull whistled. He picked up one of the apartment keys. "What do these codes mean?"

"That took a while to figure out, sir," Mathieu said. "The first two characters are the name of the apartment."

"And the second two?" Bull asked, looking at Mathieu.

"The initials of who gave her the property."

Mathieu pointed at the key for the Gaylord. "I was over at the Gaylord yesterday before you told me about the break-in at the

Casa Laguna. I was there because Irene's office manager helped me figure out some of the apartment names. See the code 'GL-SJ.' 'GL' stands for 'Gaylord.'"

"And the 'SJ?'" Bull asked. "Who's that?"

"An actor named Samuel Johnston."

"Why do you think it's him?"

"Because I saw him at Irene's funeral and took his photo. Chandler's secretary Francine helped me identify him."

"Have you talked to Johnston?"

"Yes. I interviewed him the other day at Inceville. He didn't deny he gave Irene the apartments, but he wouldn't tell me why. He has an alibi for the night of her murder. He was on the Ritz gambling ship sleeping with a 'hostess.' I'm still checking his alibi, but I don't think he killed her."

"Who gave Irene the apartment at Casa Laguna?" Bull asked.

Mathieu picked up the key for the Casa Laguna and handed it to Bull. "See the 'JF,' I think it's Joseph Friedkin. He's a film producer."

"Why him?"

"Again, because Francine helped me with the initials. She was the one that suggested his name. But more importantly, I showed Friedkin's photo to the apartment manager today. He said every time Irene stayed at the Casa Laguna, Friedkin visited her in the evening."

Bull sat back in his chair and tried to digest everything he'd just learned. As disappointed as he was that Mathieu had hidden all this from him, he was equally impressed with his work. Mathieu was bright and resourceful. It was hard to be too upset.

Leaning forward, Bull looked directly at Mathieu and said, "Listen, kid, this was always your line of investigation. You came up with it. I wasn't going to take it away from you. In the future, you're going to have to trust me more."

"And don't ever lie to me again!" he added, banging his fist on the desk. "Are we clear?"

"Yes, sir. Thank you, sir. I'm sorry," Mathieu said, relieved. He didn't want to spoil the moment by bringing up the reward money, so he left it for later.

"What's your theory?" Bull asked.

Mathieu shrugged. "Irene had some kind of hold over these men. I don't know if it was sex or love or blackmail or even influence peddling. But she was in control."

He told Bull about the stage set up, the spotlights, the hidden cameras, and the fact there was no bed in either apartment. He told him about Irene's life at St. Anne's and that she had been abused as a child. That she feared and hated men but realized she had power over them because she was so beautiful.

"She had some kind of plan for herself," Mathieu said. "She was amassing all this real estate for a reason. To be rich or independent or to get some kind of revenge for her childhood. I don't know why she was doing it, but she had a plan. And I'm convinced one of the men she was involved with killed her."

"Why would they kill her?"

"I don't know. Maybe she cut them off. Maybe she blackmailed one of them. Maybe one of the men found out that there were others giving her property, and he killed her out of jealousy."

"Do you think she betrayed Chandler?"

Mathieu shook his head. "I don't think so. Chandler treated her like his daughter. He relied on her. He treated her with respect. He was one of the few men who ever treated her well."

"What are you planning to do next?"

"I thought I'd interview Joseph Friedkin. Unless you think I should do something else first."

"No, that sounds like a good plan," Bull said. "Do you know how to get a hold of him?"

"I'll ask Francine she can help me track him down."

"Alright, get to it," Bull said. "But no more withholding information understood?"

"Yes, sir."

Mathieu left Bull's office and went back to his desk. A few minutes later, his phone rang. He picked it up and said, "Officer Mathieu LAPD."

There was a silence on the line.

"Hello, can I help you?" Mathieu asked.

A woman's voice said hesitantly, "You called me."

"Who is this?"

There was another hesitation, "Marlene Chambers."

In as calm a voice as he could muster, Mathieu said, "Thank you for calling me back, Miss Chambers."

"Am I in some kind of trouble?" she asked.

"Not at all. I just need your help in verifying some information."

"What information?" she asked, relieved but still wary.

"Did you work on the Ritz the night of May 7?"

"Yes."

Mathieu struggled with how to phrase the next question. "Can you verify if you 'entertained' a Samuel Johnston that evening?"

"Is this some kind of trick?"

"No. I just need your help in verifying if you were with him that evening."

"Yes, I was with him."

"Can you tell me approximately what time?"

"From midnight until about two."

"You're sure about that?"

"Yes, he was my last 'client' for the evening. He gave me a big tip, so I took the rest of the night off," she said. "After he left, I went back upstairs, had some drinks with the girls, played a little

Blackjack, and caught the crew launch home around five in the morning."

"Thank you for your honesty, Miss Chambers. You've been very helpful. Goodbye."

Mathieu had one more thing to do. He called Francine, hoping she was back from lunch. He caught her just as she was unlocking her desk. He asked if she knew where Joseph Friedkin lived.

"He has several apartments in Hollywood, a home in Beverly Hills, and I think he just finished building a home in Palm Springs."

"Would you mind calling around for me tomorrow to find out where he is now? I need to speak to him."

"Of course, Theo," Francine said. "If I get ahold of him, when would you like to see him?"

"The day after tomorrow, if possible," he said.

"What should I say it's about?"

"Irene Simpson."

"What if he refuses?" Francine asked.

"Tell him Mr. Chandler would appreciate his cooperation in this matter."

Francine smiled to herself. "You're getting the hang of this, Theo."

"Out of necessity, Francine," Mathieu laughed.

Francine called Mathieu back the next morning. She told him she had located Friedkin. He was out in Palm Springs at his new home.

"I made an appointment for you for tomorrow afternoon," she said. "That should give you enough time to drive out there."

"Thanks, Francine," he said. "How was Friedkin on the phone?"

"He seemed reluctant and a little defensive at first until I told him Mr. Chandler would appreciate it. Then he acquiesced."

"Kind of the reaction I suspected," Mathieu said.

"It's fine. Theo, I'm used to dealing with his type," she said, then added. "I thought after the long ride, you'd want to stay overnight, so I got you a room at the Desert Inn."

"I should pay you for being my travel agent Francine."

"Once your babysitter, always your babysitter," she said, laughing. "And drive safely out there, Theo."

"Don't worry, Francine, I will."

21

Warm Desert Nights

Mathieu left early the next morning. Bull had offered him a squad car. But Mathieu preferred riding his motorcycle, where all his senses were fully tuned in to the wind, weather, and the road.

He headed east on Foothill Blvd with its Route 66 markers. The route paralleled the Southern Pacific railroad tracks that served the citrus growing towns along the right-of-way. As he rode, he could smell the heady scent of orange and lemon groves in the air. The orange groves especially had an almost sensual quality to their aroma. Just past the groves in Azusa, he could still see a dusting of snow on Mount San Antonio from the late spring rains.

Rimmed by mountains and foothills, the LA Basin is vast. From a distance, it looks flat. But it isn't. It slopes upward to the east. Riding in a car tended to flatten the journey out, but on a motorcycle, Mathieu experienced every rise and fall in elevation. In the forty-five minutes it took him to get to Claremont, he'd gained almost a thousand feet.

Thirty minutes later, Mathieu was in San Bernardino, where he stopped to get some gas and shake out his legs. After fueling up, he left Route 66 and headed southeast to Banning Pass. As he rode through the pass, the winds picked up and buffeted the motorcycle, forcing him to wrestle the bike a few times to regain control. Continuing on, the road dropped steeply to the desert floor and the village of Palm Springs.

The tiny hamlet hugged the San Jacinto Mountains' eastern foothills, taking refuge in their shadows from the intense afternoon sun. At midday, a torpor had descended over the village and its handful of streets. Heat rose up from the pavement. A stray dog roamed the main road through town. Here and there, cars were parked at an angle. But there was no one to be seen outside. The place seemed almost deserted.

Before going to see Friedkin, Mathieu headed to the Desert Inn. The entrance to the lush, thirty-five-acre, palm-filled resort was on Main Street. The inn was founded in 1909 by Nellie Coffman, who was often called the Mother of Palm Springs.

Nellie had initially come to the desert for her health. She and her husband began the Desert Inn as a sanatorium. But Nellie had bigger dreams, and after they divorced, she began transforming the inn into a resort. By force of will and passion, she singlehandedly invented desert tourism. Now almost twenty years later, the resort had begun to attract celebrities and the elite, drawn to the solitude and splendor of the desert oasis she had created.

Mathieu rode through the inn's open gates and down a wide pathway toward the main building. The long one-story Spanish style structure was at the back of the property, nestled against the foothills. In front, a garden area provided a grassy oasis shaded by palm trees that gave the feeling of being in a secluded grove. A swimming pool sat off to one side, the sun's reflections dancing off its surface.

As Mathieu got off the motorcycle, he could still feel the vibrations from the long ride. He shook out his legs and walked under the shaded veranda to the office. To his surprise, Nellie

Coffman herself was there to greet him. Nellie reminded him of his grandmother on his father's side. Her smile suggested an unconditional affection and graciousness. Mathieu thought she probably extended that warmth to all her guests as if they were family.

"You must be Officer Mathieu," she said before he had a chance to introduce himself. "I'm Nellie Coffman. Welcome to the Desert Inn."

She handed Mathieu a tall, cold glass of iced tea. "This might help after your long ride, Officer."

The glass was cold to the touch. Mathieu took a generous sip of the tea. "Thank you, Miss Coffman, this is exactly what I needed."

Surprising Mathieu, Nellie said, "Your parents have stayed here a few times."

"I didn't know that," he said.

"You bear a striking resemblance to your father," she said. "You're both very handsome."

Mathieu blushed. "Thank you."

Nellie leaned forward in confidence and whispered, "We have a special reduced rate for policemen. And since we aren't too busy tonight, I've put you in one of our nicest rooms in the back where it's cooler."

"That's extremely kind of you," Mathieu said.

He could tell why Nellie was so successful as an innkeeper; she made everyone who visited feel special.

"May I ask if you have a hotel safe? I need to store some important documents while I'm here."

"Of course, Officer. Your papers will be as secure as the royal jewels in our safe," she said, smiling.

"Thanks."

"I'll have someone show you to your room. I assume you don't have any luggage since you came here on a motorcycle."

Mathieu opened his arms and said, "What you see is what you get. I just have to get my papers from the saddlebags." He retrieved the papers, brought them to Nellie for safekeeping, then followed the bellman to his room.

Mathieu's room was in the northwest corner of the inn. He could see Friedkin's home carved into a rocky ledge just to the north. He checked his watch; it was almost two o'clock. Mathieu washed up quickly then went back to his motorcycle.

He rode north a few blocks on Main Street, then turned left onto a road that went to the base of the foothills. There, he continued on a steep winding driveway up to Friedkin's house.

The house sat on a flat pad that must have been dynamited out of the hilltop. Mathieu parked his motorcycle next to a Bentley, then walked through a narrow opening between two rocky outcroppings. He came out onto a spacious terrace in front of the Spanish-Colonial house with its tiled roof and second-story balcony. A maid, wearing a starched black and white uniform, stood outside the entrance, waiting to greet him.

Mathieu walked up to her. "Hello, my name is Officer Mathieu from the LAPD. I have an appointment to see Mr. Friedkin."

The young maid was attractive, with her almond eyes and lush black hair pinned up in a bun. She looked at Mathieu with suspicion. She didn't attempt to hide her distrust of the police. It was a look he'd seen countless times before as a policeman.

"This way, please," she said as she led him through a wide arched entranceway, easily fifteen feet high, into a great hall. The hall was longer than wide, with a fireplace at the far end of the room, where comfortable chairs were arranged facing it.

"Mr. Friedkin will be with you in a moment," she said,

pointing to some chairs and a long bench facing the terrace and the desert view beyond.

While he waited, Mathieu looked around the great hall. A portrait of Friedkin hung on one wall near the fireplace. The room had a southwest feel to it with its wood-beamed ceiling and richly tiled floor. It reminded him, on a much grander scale, of Irene's apartment at the Casa Laguna.

A few minutes later, Friedkin entered through a carved oak door to the left of the fireplace. He was wearing a suit and tie, even in the desert heat. He was a tall, vibrant looking man in his mid-fifties with a weak handshake and a reedy voice as he greeted Mathieu.

"Please have a seat, Officer," he said, motioning to the chairs that looked out at the terrace.

"Thank you for taking the time to see me, Mr. Friedkin," Mathieu said.

"I'm doing this as a courtesy to Mr. Chandler," Friedkin said in a tone that he probably used with his servants. As if he was doing Mathieu a huge favor.

Mathieu decided to throw him off balance immediately. "I'm here because I'm investigating the murder of Irene Simpson." His bluntness had its effect as he watched Friedkin flinch.

"I thought she died in a car crash," Friedkin said.

"Don't believe everything you read in the papers … or see in the movies," Mathieu replied.

"How was she killed?" Friedkin asked.

"I'm not at liberty to say," Mathieu said. "Where were you on the evening of May 7 and the early hours of May 8?"

"Am I a suspect," Friedkin asked, alarmed.

"No. It's just a routine question."

Friedkin fidgeted with his tie. He took a moment to gather his thoughts, then said, "May 7, I was here. I remember the workmen were just finishing the upstairs bathroom that day."

"Can anyone verify that?"

"My maid and butler can," he said as if that was sufficient.

"Anyone else who isn't on your payroll?"

"Nellie Coffman can," Friedkin said. "I went down for a few drinks at the inn that evening. Afterward, Nellie and I sat out by the pool and talked."

"What was your relationship with Irene Simpson?"

"I didn't have a relationship with Miss Simpson. Why are you asking me these questions, Officer?" he asked defensively. "Are you interrogating me because I'm Jewish? I'm sure many of Mr. Chandler's associates knew Miss Simpson. Maybe even your father. Why don't you ask them and stop bothering me?"

Not taking the bait, Mathieu said bluntly, "I wouldn't care if you were an Eskimo, Mr. Friedkin. This is a murder investigation. Everyone who knew Miss Simpson is being questioned. You came to the top of the list because of a recent break-in at her Casa Laguna apartment."

Friedkin tried not to react, but a nervous tic gave him away.

"What does that have to do with me?" Friedkin asked, trying to bluff his way out of it.

"The building manager positively identified you as having visited Irene Simpson every time she stayed at the Casa Laguna."

"He must have made a mistake. It wasn't me."

"No, he didn't," Mathieu said. "He's quite positive it's you. I showed him your photograph."

Sweat started to form on Friedkin's broad forehead. "Why did you show him my photograph?"

"Because I already suspected you had given Miss Simpson the Casa Laguna apartment plus four others."

Trapped in his own lies, Friedkin stood up and started walking around the room, trying to buy some time to think. He stared out at the desert landscape for a few moments then, without turning around, said. "While this house was being built, I used to picture Irene and myself sitting here together, looking out at that view. I had this fantasy that I could convince her to live here."

Friedkin sighed, sat back down, and shook his head slightly deflated. "I'm just an old fool, Officer," he said as if asking for sympathy. "I was obsessed with Irene. But I would never have harmed her."

"When did you first meet her?" Mathieu asked.

"Four years ago, just after my wife divorced me," he said, mocking himself. "Never marry an actress, Officer. They are the most self-centered creatures on earth. At first, I thought I could use Irene to influence Chandler to invest in my movies. Later on, I fell in love with her."

"Did Irene promise to influence Chandler?" Mathieu asked.

"No," Friedkin said, shaking his head. "Irene was very honest in that way. She never promised anything. She was always clear about her boundaries."

"How did it start?" Mathieu asked.

"Irene discreetly slid me a card one day in Chandler's anteroom. All it had on it was a number. I called her that night. We had a late supper the next evening."

Friedkin said all this as if remembering the excitement and hope of a first date.

"Did it ever turn into a romance?"

"No, not for her," he said with a sigh. "But it was exciting. I don't regret a moment of it. I could afford the gifts, the apartments. They were nothing to me. I'm a rich man. Just being around her was all I needed. I was lonely after my divorce, and she filled a void. Irene had a hard side but also a vulnerable one, that's irresistible in a beautiful woman. You think you're the only man in the world that can save her. And if you do, she will love you for it. But alas, it was not to be."

Mathieu thought about asking Friedkin for more details about their relationship but decided against it. Friedkin seemed sincere in his feelings for Irene.

After a few moments of silence, Friedkin asked, "Did the burglar take anything from the Casa Laguna?"

"It wasn't a burglary. It was a search," Mathieu said. "I don't know if they found anything, but I did."

"What?" Friedkin asked, alarmed.

"A camera," Mathieu replied.

Without thinking, Friedkin asked, "Was there film in it?"

"Yes," Mathieu said, lying.

"What was on the film?"

"I don't know yet. I haven't had time to get it developed. I brought it along with me. I'll send it to the lab when I get back to headquarters."

Friedkin looked like he was going to say something, then changed his mind. "If you don't have any more questions, Officer, I think I'm going to lie down. This has been very upsetting for me."

"Just a few more questions. Do you own a handgun?"

"No. I've never owned any kind of gun."

"Did Irene ever try to blackmail you?"

Friedkin looked shocked. "No, of course not. Why would you think that?"

"No reason, we just have to check all the possibilities," Mathieu said. "One last question, do you have any idea who might have wanted to kill Irene?"

Friedkin shook his head. "No," he said. "But I hope you find him."

Mathieu stood up and handed Friedkin his card. "Thank you for your cooperation, Mr. Friedkin. If you think of anything else that might help, please give me a call."

Friedkin was still staring at the card as Mathieu left.

Before going to dinner, Mathieu asked Nellie about Friedkin's alibi. Nellie confirmed she was with him that evening. She remembered it because one of the pool pumps had failed and she had to have it replaced the next day.

Mathieu ate dinner alone and afterward went to the bar for a beer. He sat there, nursing his drink and thinking about what he'd learned that day. A few minutes later, a beautiful woman with thick dark hair draped over one shoulder strode in. She was wearing high heels and a short black dress. It was Friedkin's maid.

She had cleaned up nicely, Mathieu thought to himself, as she walked toward him. Her body was firm and tight, and most of it was on display, with her plunging neckline and the slit on the side of her dress showing off her tanned legs.

But what Mathieu noticed most was the perfume she was wearing as she sat down next to him. He had smelled it somewhere recently. Remembering where. He smiled to himself.

"Night off?" Mathieu asked.

"Mr. Friedkin went to bed early. Care if I join you?"

Mathieu shrugged. He ordered her a drink.

"My name is Maria," she said, extending her delicate hand.

"Theo," Mathieu said.

"What kind of name is that?"

"French."

Maria leaned forward just enough so Mathieu could see she wasn't wearing a bra. Her drink came, and she leaned back and took a sip of it.

"You look 'mixta,'" she said, staring at him. "Your eyes are too dark for a purebred Frenchmen."

"I'm not a purebred anything," Mathieu replied.

"What are you then?" she asked.

"I have no idea," he said, turning away from her gaze.

"Bad subject?"

"No," Mathieu said, shaking his head. "Just one for which I have no answer."

Changing the subject, Mathieu said, "Seems kind of quiet here. What do you do at night?"

"Not much. There's nothing but celebrities and old people out here."

"Have you worked for Mr. Friedkin very long?"

"Yes, for over seven years. I've been with him longer than his wife was," she said in a mocking tone. "Mr. Friedkin has been very good to me. And no, he doesn't come on to me."

"Do you work for him in Los Angeles?"

"Yes. The butler and I go with him to all his homes."

The conversation between them was strained, each suspicious of the other. Maria broke the ice. She moved closer to Mathieu, pressing her thigh lightly against his. "Neither of us is very good at small talk. I could join you in your room if you'd like," she said, looking into his eyes.

"I would like that," he said.

She responded by pressing her thigh even tighter to his.

"But I suspect you've already been there," he said, smiling.

Her playful smile dropped, and her face hardened.

Mathieu leaned in close as if to kiss her and whispered, "The next time you break into an apartment in Los Angeles, Maria, I wouldn't wear that perfume."

He left her with a speechless expression on her face.

When Mathieu returned to his room and opened the door, he could smell her perfume in the air. He had made it easy for Maria; he'd left the window open. He didn't want Nellie to have to replace it.

22

The Property Deeds

Before leaving the next morning, Mathieu thanked Nellie for her hospitality. She told him he was always welcome, and his policeman's discount would apply for business or pleasure.

"Bring your girlfriend next time," she said as she stood next to his motorcycle and handed him his papers from the safe.

"I'll have to get one first," he said self-mockingly.

"I can't imagine that would be too difficult for you," she said with a warm smile.

Mathieu blushed, started up his Henderson, put it in gear, and waved goodbye to her.

"Drive safe," she said as he pulled away.

The trip back to LA was a blur. The ride seemed to go faster than the ride out. Perhaps it was because it was mostly downhill once he climbed over Banning Pass. But in reality, it went quicker because Mathieu was so absorbed thinking about Irene that he barely noticed the passing landscape.

Mathieu arrived back at LAPD headquarters in the early afternoon. He sat at his desk for a few minutes in a bit of a daze after the long hot ride, then gathered his notes and knocked on Bull's door.

"You look like you got a little sun … did you have a nice vacation?" Bull teased.

"Windblown is more like it," Mathieu responded.

"What was Friedkin like?"

"Typical rich man full of himself. He denied knowing Irene even when I confronted him with the apartment manager's testimony that he'd seen him at the Casa Laguna. But when I told him I knew he'd given Irene five apartments, he finally broke down. He said he was lonely after his divorce. He admitted he gave Irene the apartments and had dreams she would move into his Palm Springs home. He said he was in love with her."

"Does he have an alibi for the night of the murder?"

"Yes. He was in Palm Springs. He spent part of the evening talking to Nellie Coffman, the owner of the Desert Inn. I talked to Miss Coffman, and she confirmed his alibi."

"So no longer a suspect," Bull said.

"Well, yes and no," Mathieu replied.

"What do you mean?"

"He couldn't have murdered Irene himself, but he could have paid someone to do the dirty work for him."

"What makes you think that?"

"Because I'm almost positive that his maid broke into the Casa Laguna apartment and my hotel room. She showed up at the bar last night dressed to kill. I think Friedkin sent her to see what I knew, after I told him I found some film. I confronted her about the break-in at the Casa Laguna."

"What did you say to her?"

"I recognized the perfume she was wearing as she sat next to me. It was very distinctive. I'd noticed it at the Casa Laguna. I advised her not to wear it the next time she broke into an apartment."

"How did she react?"

"Her face fell to the floor," Mathieu said.

"Sounds like Friedkin is really worried about what's on that film."

"Yes, sir. That's what I think also."

"Then you need to find it," Bull said.

"That's not going to be easy, sir," Mathieu said, shaking his head in frustration.

After meeting with Bull, Mathieu went back to his desk. He wondered where Irene had hidden all the photos she had secretly taken. And why did she take them to begin with? Was it for leverage? Or blackmail? Maybe the photos were in Chinatown at Hop Li's. He was thinking about that when the phone rang.

"Officer Mathieu," he said, picking up the phone.

"It's Rose, Irene's office manager," came the timid voice over the phone.

"Hi, Rose! Have you figured out any more of those apartment codes?"

"I have even better news for you," she said. "The lawyer found the legal documents for all the apartment leases and lots that Miss Simpson owned."

"Wow!" Mathieu exclaimed. "That's fantastic."

"And he also found all the transfer deeds."

"So, we have proof who gave them to her?"

"Yes," she said.

"That's the best news I've had in weeks," Mathieu said.

"I thought it would make you happy," she said. "I've typed up a complete list for you if you'd like to come by."

"I'll be there as soon as I can, Rose. Thank you again," he said as he hung up.

Fifteen minutes later, he was at the Bradbury. He was so excited he didn't wait for the elevator. He ran up the stairs two at a time to the third floor and knocked on the door, slightly out of breath.

"Come in, Officer Mathieu, the door is open."

Rose was sitting at her desk with a Cheshire cat's grin on her face as he entered. Mathieu walked over and sat down next to her, close enough so he could see the documents.

"I actually have two lists," she said, sliding the first one over to him. "This is the one for the apartments. It lists the apartment name, address, date of transfer, lease-length, most of which are for over twenty years, by the way, and most importantly, who paid for the lease and transferred it to Irene."

Mathieu picked up the list and studied it. It was a gold mine of information. Now he had hard evidence; no more need to speculate or guess.

The apartments he already knew about were on it. The Gaylord that Samuel Johnson had given Irene and the Casa Laguna that she got from Joseph Friedkin. As he continued on, he spotted the other apartments from Friedkin, including two called the El Cabrillo and Andalusia.

Further down the list was an apartment in Pasadena called the Castle Green from Thaddeus Harrison, the Eugenics freak. In Hollywood, the La Belle Tour on Franklin Avenue came from Jeremy Eckert, the financier. Out in Santa Monica near the Crystal Pier was an apartment in the Horatio Court she got from the USC professor Kevin Patterson. Near the Wilshire Country Club, there was one called the El Royale from the oil tycoon Fredrick Fallon. In total, there were twenty-seven apartments from seven different people.

"This is the second list for the raw land. It's much shorter." Rose said, passing it to him.

"The dates of transfer for the raw land look much more recent," Mathieu said, studying the list.

"I noticed that also," Rose said.

The donor names on the second list were the same as the first, except for his father's. If Rose had noticed, she was kind of enough not to bring it up.

"Did the lawyer also give you a copy of the leases and transfer deeds?" he asked.

"Yes, and I asked him for two copies. One for my records and one to give to you," she said, pointing to a thick folder of documents sitting on her desk.

"I could kiss you, Rose," Mathieu said.

Rose blushed as if she would welcome that.

Mathieu went back and studied the first list again. Of the seven people who gave Irene apartments, there was one name on the list he'd hadn't known about before, Anita Benson.

"Rose, do you know who Anita Benson is?"

"No," she said, shaking her head.

"Can I use your phone? I have to call a friend at the LA Times."

"Certainly," Rose said, moving the phone toward him.

Mathieu dialed Francine's number, and when she answered, he said, "Hi, Francine, it's Theo."

"How's the investigation going?" Francine asked.

"Good, there's been a major breakthrough," he said. "I'm calling because I need your help with a name that has come up. Have you ever heard of Anita Benson?"

"Of course, Miss Benson is a successful screenwriter, one of the highest-paid in Hollywood. According to the Times columnist, even William Faulkner and Aldous Huxley are fans of her writing. Plus, she's beautiful; she started her career as an actress. She has a sultry look you'd like, big dark eyes peeking through her seductive bangs."

"Does she know Chandler?"

"Yes, Mr. Chandler loves her movies. She's a charming, witty woman. She used to make Irene laugh every time she'd drop by the office," Francine said.

"Do you have any contact information for her?

"Let me look through my phone diary, where I keep all of Mr. Chandler's contacts."

"That diary is worth a lot of money, Francine," Mathieu quipped as she searched.

"I've found it," she said, then read him Anita Benson's address and phone number.

"Thanks again for coming to the rescue Francine," Mathieu said before he hung up.

Rose had been observing the easy way Mathieu had been talking on the phone to Francine. Somewhat jealous, she asked, "How long have you known Francine?"

"Since I was about two years old," he said.

Rose gave him a quizzical look.

"She was my babysitter when I was a little boy."

"How nice," she said, relaxing noticeably.

"Thanks again for the lists and the documents Rose, this will be so helpful to the investigation," he said.

"You're welcome," she said, her face beaming. "By the way, when I mentioned your name to Irene's lawyer, he asked if you were Pierre Mathieu's son."

"Yes, I am."

"He thought so," Rose said. "He told me your father recommended him to Irene. Apparently, he's your father's lawyer also."

Mathieu laughed to himself. His father was like a bad penny, showing up everywhere he went.

23

Anita

Anxious to show Bull what he'd learned, Mathieu hurried back to headquarters. But when he got there, Bull's door was shut. He was in a meeting with one of his other detectives. Mathieu sat down at his desk in the otherwise empty room and waited for them to finish. When the door opened and the detective left, Mathieu gathered his papers and rushed in.

"Look what Irene's lawyer found," Mathieu said, laying the apartment list on Bull's desk. "These are all the apartments Irene owns and who gave them to her. It's just as I thought. The donors are a Who's Who list of the Los Angeles elite."

Bull took his time looking at the list then slowly whistled to himself. "Sweet Jesus, what do we have here?" He drummed his fingers on the desk, then leaned forward and put his head in his hands. "Christ, what a minefield. If we fuck this up, we'll both be back walking the beat."

"I thought you'd be happy," Mathieu said, disappointed at his reaction.

"I am ... I am," Bull said. "But it still doesn't mean any of them killed her."

"I know," Mathieu said. "But I'm convinced her death was

personal. She wasn't killed by a stranger. She was followed to that house and murdered by someone who knew her."

"Sit down," Bull said, trying to slow things down. He admired Mathieu's conviction, but he was still wary. "What's your plan?"

"First, I'll have a look at all the apartments and see if I can find any new evidence. I have all the keys. We won't need any warrants. No one else has to know for now."

"And then?"

"I'll talk to everyone on the list I haven't interview yet, starting with the least threatening," Mathieu said.

"Who are?" Bull asked.

"The professor and the woman. I'll talk to them and see how their stories jive with Samuelson's and Friedkin's."

"Okay … but what about Harrison, Fallon, and Eckert?"

"I'll save them for last when I know more. Because even if they're not involved, they're sure to lawyer up and stonewall any attempts to interview them."

"It's still a minefield," Bull said, unconvinced.

"Don't forget Chandler has our backs," Mathieu said, trying to reassure him, "He wants Irene's killer found."

"How can you be so sure?"

Mathieu hesitated and said, "Because Chandler gave me two-thousand dollars in cash last week to use as reward money. I've been waiting for the right time to tell you. Chandler told me not to tell anyone, including you, but you need to know now."

"What did you do with the money?" Bull asked, alarmed.

"I kept three-hundred to use to encourage people to talk and put the rest in a safe deposit box. You can have the key if you want."

"I don't want anything to do with it," Bull said. "Let's just pretend you never told me about it. Okay?"

"Sure … fair enough," Mathieu said.

"But I agree with you if Chandler gave you reward money, then he is serious about finding Irene's killer. And we're certainly going to need his backing when we start to shake up his friends," Bull said. "When are you going to show him the list of donors?"

"After I know more," Mathieu said, omitting the fact he had already told Chandler about Irene's apartments.

"Okay, then you'd better get to work."

"Yes, sir," Mathieu said as he picked up the list and left.

He purposefully hadn't shown Bull the second list with his father's name on it. He feared Bull would take him off the case if he knew his father might be involved. He wanted to delay telling Bull about it as long as possible, hoping it would never be necessary.

It took a day for Mathieu to search the other four apartments Irene got from Friedkin. None had beds in the bedroom, but all had "performance" areas and hidden camera compartments.

Next, Mathieu moved on to the El Royale at Four-Fifty North Rossmoor that Irene had received from Fredrick Fallon, the oil tycoon. Of all the properties he'd seen so far, this was the most jaw-dropping from the street. The twelve-story New York style apartment building, with its Rocco detailing and green neon sign, towered over its surroundings. Mathieu could easily imagine it being on Fifth Avenue in New York rather than in LA.

Entering the lobby did nothing to dispel the feeling of refined, elegant opulence. No expense had been spared here. Thick woven rugs lay on the dark parquet floor, and comfortable seating surrounded a massive fireplace. The two-story-high Spanish-style ceiling was hard to take your eyes off with its intricate hand-painted design. Off to the left was an arched entranceway that led to a marble stairway. The building had an elevator, but Mathieu chose to take the stairs to the fifth floor where Irene's apartment was located.

He used his key to open the door and enter the living room.

The spacious but sparsely furnished room was light and airy. Off to the right was a fireplace. Large French windows, overlooking the Wilshire Country Club, faced west, filling one entire wall. The ceiling, walls, and crown molding were all painted white. It was easy to imagine yourself transported to Paris in this light-filled room.

As Mathieu looked around the living room, he assumed it was the performance space. Without too much searching, he found a camera discretely hidden behind a light sconce. He opened the camera-back, and as with the others that he'd found, it was empty.

He quickly inspected the rest of the apartment. Compared to the main room, the galley kitchen was modest in size. The bathroom was tiled in pink, and the bedroom, as expected, was devoid of a bed. Except for blankets, towels, and a silk robe in the closet, there were few personal items in the apartment.

Mathieu locked up and walked to the elevators. As he waited, he looked over his notes, trying to find something, and then he spotted it. The address Francine had given him for Anita Benson, the screenwriter, was also in the El Royale. When the elevator came, he entered and pressed the button for the twelfth floor where Miss Benson's apartment was located. As long as he was here, he might as well try to question her.

Standing in front of her door, Mathieu knocked and waited. Soon after, a woman with striking dark eyes answered the door in a negligee as if she was expecting someone. When she saw Mathieu standing there in his uniform, her eyes widened. "To what do I owe this pleasure, Officer?" she asked.

"Are you Anita Benson?"

"Yes, I am. Are you my birthday present?"

"Is this your birthday, Miss Benson?"

"Every day is my birthday, young man," she said flirtatiously.

"My name is Officer Mathieu. I'm with the LAPD. I'm investigating the death of Miss Irene Simpson."

Anita didn't react at the mention of Irene's name. She seemed imperturbable. She just continued to stare at Mathieu's face.

"How ironic that they would send a beautiful man to investigate the death of a beautiful woman," she said almost to herself. "Would you like to come in, Officer?"

"Yes, please, if you have the time, Miss Benson," Mathieu said.

"I do for you," she said with a smile.

She left the door open for him as she turned and walked back into the living room.

The room was much like Irene's but lavishly furnished with expensive lamps, chairs, couches, and a white lamb's wool rug in front of the fireplace. But the most notable difference was a large painting of Anita, lying nude on a red velvet couch, hanging on one wall.

She watched Mathieu's face as he stared at the painting. She seemed pleased by his reaction. "Have a seat," she said, pointing to a chair next to the fireplace. "I'll go put something on."

Anita walked across the room toward an open doorway that led to her bedroom. She stopped in the doorway, undid her negligee, and let it drop to the floor. Without a word, she stood there for a moment, totally naked, before entering the bedroom.

She re-emerged a few minutes later, as if nothing had happened, wearing shorts and a halter-top that revealed a toned midriff. She sat on a couch near the fireplace and brought her long gorgeous legs up to her chest.

Looking at Mathieu, she asked, "How can I help you, Officer?"

"How did you meet Miss Simpson?"

"At the LA Times when I'd go to visit Harry. I'd flirt with her a little and make her laugh. One day she slipped me her card. We met for dinner, she explained her terms, I agreed, and the rest, as they say, is history."

"And you gave her two apartments, the Charmont and the Harper House."

"Glady," she said, impressed that he'd done his homework.

"As you can see, money is not an issue for me," she said, waving her arms at the opulent surroundings.

"I'm a damn good writer. The studios throw money at me for a good script. I've learned how to survive in a man's world on my own terms, and so did Irene. I admired her for that."

"Did Irene ever come here?"

"Never, we only met at the apartments I gave her. Her rules."

"Did you know she also had an apartment here?"

Anita hesitated, seemingly surprised. "Of course," she said with a dismissive wave of her hand.

"What was your relationship with Irene?"

"Let's say I introduced her to Sapphic delights."

Mathieu didn't respond.

"Are you shocked that I'm a switch hitter?"

"Not at all," Mathieu said. "Do you think Irene was also?"

"I doubt it. I don't think a dick ever touched her lips except when she was molested as a little girl," Anita said. "But who knows with Irene, she kept her secrets. She certainly knew she was beautiful and used it to her advantage. I'm sure rich men were falling all over each other to give her apartments. Men are such saps," she scoffed.

"So, you knew there were others?"

"Of course."

"Were you jealous?"

"Do I look like the jealous type?" she asked, batting her eyes.

"Were you in love with her?"

"I was in lust with her," she said, "And, by the way, Harry told me how she really died, so you don't have to be coy with me, Officer."

"Where were you the night she was killed?"

"Here."

"Can anyone verify that?"

"Only the gentleman who had his head between my thighs that evening. However, I doubt he'll confirm it since he's a married studio head. We were having a story conference here about a romantic comedy I'm writing. We ended up acting out a love scene from it on the rug," she said with a wink.

"The scene concluded with bodice-ripping and my legs over my head. I can assure you it wouldn't have passed the proposed Hayes Code floating around Hollywood these days."

Mathieu smiled. He admired Anita's unapologetic brazenness.

"Just one more question before I leave. Can you think of anyone who would want to kill Irene?"

"No one specific. But I bet it was some pathetic rich guy who was angry because he couldn't own and control her completely."

Mathieu nodded then stood to leave. "Thank you for your help, Miss Benson."

Anita's eyes took in his long, lean body as he stood in front of her. "Drop by anytime, Officer," she said. "Unlike Irene's apartments, mine has a bed in the bedroom."

"I'm sure it gets put to good use," Mathieu said in a playful tone.

"It does," she responded, unoffended. "And remember to bring your handcuffs along if you stop by. We can play cops and robbers."

They both shared a laugh, then Mathieu turned and walked to the door.

When he got there, Anita stopped him and said in a wistful voice, "For what it's worth, Officer, I think you would have been good for Irene. She could have trusted you."

With a troubled look on his face, Mathieu opened the door and left.

24

An Empty Box of Film

Albert stood near the bow of the S.S. Catalina smoking a cigarette as the ship slowly approached Avalon Harbor at dusk. There were over a thousand passengers on board.

The steamship company had added an extra crossing to accommodate the guests for the world premiere of Cecil B. DeMille's latest film in the newly opened Catalina Casino theatre. The ship's sumptuous salon-deck below was filled with producers, directors, stars, fans, and wannabes. Albert had seen Charlie Chaplin down there earlier when he stopped in for a drink. As usual, Chaplin had been playing grab-ass with a couple of buxom twenty-year-olds.

Albert quickly tired of celebrity watching and spent much of the two-and-a-half-hour crossing on the upper deck. While it was still light, he'd seen a school of dolphins playfully surfing on the bow wave, as if they had been hired to entertain the passengers. He could almost imagine DeMille taking full credit for the spectacle down in the salon.

Now Albert watched as Avalon Bay came slowly into focus as the ship prepared to dock. Lights along the esplanade reflected off the water and outlined the crescent shape of the compact harbor. Off to the right, the twelve-story-high casino shone like a jewel as it stood floodlit against the night sky.

Behind the esplanade, streetlights in the tiny town of Avalon had just come on. High up on Mount Ada to the left, he could see a warm glow coming from the Wrigley Mansion. His employer was dining there with the Wrigleys before the premiere.

After the ship docked, Albert followed the crowd as they walked along the esplanade toward the casino. The moviegoers stopped to mingle near the entrance, but Albert continued on to the end of the breakwater. There he waited for his employer as they had planned.

He had smoked several cigarettes by the time his employer strode up twenty-minutes later.

"How was your crossing, Albert?" his employer asked.

"Fine, sir. Very smooth," Albert replied.

Anxious to hear Albert's report, his employer asked, "Did you find anything in the apartments?"

"Not much, sir. I searched each one carefully. I found hidden compartments in each of them where cameras could have been placed. I found remote cable releases, but I didn't find any cameras, film, or photos."

His employer looked down and sighed, disappointed that the searches had all been for naught.

"But I did find this, sir," Albert said, handing him an empty yellow and red Kodak film box.

"Where did you find it?"

"In a trash can in the bathroom of one of the apartments."

His employer studied it and laughed to himself. "So, she made a mistake."

"Yes, sir," Albert said.

"It's not much, but I was beginning to think she never made mistakes," his employer said to himself as he turned the box over in his hand.

"It's better than you think, sir," Albert said. "Take a look at the bottom of the box. There's a stamp on it from where she bought the film."

His employer moved closer to the light and examined the bottom of the film box. He squinted to read the stamp. "Hop Li's. Is that what it says?"

"Yes, sir," Albert said. "It's a film processing shop in Chinatown."

"That makes sense," his employer said, nodding. "I remember her telling me she had taken Kung Fu lessons in Chinatown." He was silent for a moment, considering what to do next. "You're sure you weren't noticed?"

"Yes, sir. I wore a maintenance uniform. No one gave me a second look. And having the keys made it a cinch to get in."

"And you cleaned the apartments, so there's no trace of me left in them."

"Yes, sir ... exactly as you had instructed."

His employer nodded and said, "Then I need you to give Mr. Li a visit, Albert."

"Yes, sir."

"I want you to use all of your powers of persuasion to get Mr. Li to tell you where the negatives and the photos are. Is that clear? All your powers."

"Understood, sir."

"Good then that's settled," his employer said. "I have to get back to the premiere. The Wrigleys are waiting for me."

"Of course, sir."

"I'm staying with the Wrigleys tonight, but I've made arrangements for you to stay with Zane Grey at his pueblo up on the hill if that's all right with you. In the morning, we'll both take the first ferry back to Wilmington."

"Thank you, sir. As you wish."

"Good work, Albert. I'll see you in the morning," his employer said as he turned and walked away toward the theatre entrance.

After his boss left, Albert stood alone for a few minutes looking across the channel at the hazy glow of lights coming from the coastline. Then he turned and walked back along the esplanade to the center of the harbor.

Soon after passing the yacht club, he turned right at the public showers and walked up Crescent Avenue to Hill Street. Hill Street became Chimes Tower Road, where the road became steeper as it switchbacked up the mountainside. As Albert rounded the last curve, he looked up to his left and saw Zane Grey's beige, two-story adobe home spread out across the ridgeline above him. Albert had been here before.

He liked Zane. He was a man's man and an outdoorsman, unlike his employer. And Albert loved his novels, especially "Riders of the Purple Sage." Grey's heroes were loners like himself. But the real star of his books was the vast expanse of the American West, which Grey described in such exquisite detail that you felt like you were there.

Albert took a set of steep steps up to an outdoor walkway at the base of the adobe structure. When he got there, he opened the door to the lounge and peeked in. The comfortable room with western style furniture and a fireplace was empty. In one corner of the room was a bookshelf filled with Grey's novels and a movie poster of "Riders of the Purple Sage," starring Tom Mix hanging over it.

He closed the door, then walked toward the rear of the house and up some stairs to the pool area. As he walked by the pool, a beautiful young woman emerged from it. She stood on the concrete deck as water dripped off her raven hair and sleek naked body.

Startled, Albert stopped and said, "I'm sorry, Miss. It was so quiet I didn't think anyone was around. I'm looking for Zane."

"Don't worry about it," she said with a smile as she stood stark-naked in front of him and extended her hand. "I'm Brenda … Brenda Montenegro. I'm Zane's friend. Are you, Albert?"

"Yes," he stammered, mesmerized by her glistening bare skin as he took her hand.

Brenda shook his hand, then bent down to pick up a towel and secured it around her slender body as she straightened up.

"Zane's up on the top deck waiting for you," she said as she pointed toward the front of the house. "The one that looks over the harbor. Do you know how to get there?"

Albert nodded yes, not yet quite able to speak in complete sentences.

"Great. I've just had a little swim before going to bed. See you in the morning," Brenda said as she turned and walked away, seemingly unfazed by their encounter.

Albert felt quite the opposite. He couldn't get the vision of her beautiful naked body out of his mind. And didn't want to.

He took a flight of stairs from the pool area up to a narrow porch that ran the length of the second story of the pueblo. He headed toward the front of the house, where he took another set of stairs up to the deck.

Zane Grey was sitting there, with a drink in his hand and his feet up on a low stucco ledge looking out over the town and harbor below. Zane was a handsome man in his late fifties with a full head of silver-grey hair. Depending on his mood and the light, he could look like the dentist he once was or a famous author. Tonight, he looked like a famous author.

"Good evening, Mr. Grey," Albert said as he took in the sparkling view.

"Good to see you again, Albert. Have a seat, and please call me Zane."

"As you wish, sir."

Zane pointed to a bottle of Scotch and some glasses on a small circular table next to his chair. "Pour yourself a drink," he said.

"Where'd you get the Scotch?" Albert asked, thinking Wrigley might be a stickler for obeying the prohibition laws.

"We occasionally have some midnight deliveries on the other side of the island," Zane chuckled. "The road to the interior goes right by my house. It's the one you walked up on."

"Mr. Wrigley doesn't mind?"

"No. Bill's a good guy. I'm grateful to him every day for letting me buy this piece of land from him. He's got his mountaintop view, and I've got mine," Zane said, looking across at Wrigley's mansion on the hillside on the other side of Avalon.

"Must be heaven for you in March when the Chicago Cubs have their Spring Training here," Albert said.

"Oh god, yes," Zane said. "Baseball is my other passion in life besides writing. That's another thing I'm grateful to Bill for bringing his team here to practice."

"I heard you were quite a good baseball player in college," Albert said.

"I was," Zane said in the matter of fact way that good athletes talk about their own talent. "But my father discouraged it, along with discouraging my writing. He made me get a real job, so I studied dentistry and became a dentist. But I guess I had the last laugh in the end. I've done okay as a writer."

Changing the subject, Zane asked, "Is your boss down at the Casino trying to get lucky with a starlet?"

Albert didn't say anything; he knew Zane didn't like his employer.

"Do you think he's ever got laid without having to pay for it? He's such a dislikeable bastard and a racist to boot, him and the whole Chandler gang. 'Keep the White spot White'—what a bunch of bollocks. The Indians were here long before the Spanish arrived, and when the Americans took over, Los Angeles was the mulatto capital of the world. And those pricks are trying to sell it as some kind of white man's paradise."

Albert looked uncomfortable. He didn't know what to say.

Noticing it, Zane said, "Sorry for the rant, Albert. It just pisses me off."

"I understand, sir. But if you dislike him so much, why are you still friends?"

Zane shrugged. "I wouldn't call us friends, Albert. But I've found it's best to keep the peace with your neighbors even if you can't stand them. Besides, as an author, I can't be too choosy about who likes my books," he said, laughing.

"He's always been very fair to me, sir."

"Well, be careful, Albert. Men like him are snakes. They can turn on you in an instant and kill you with their venom. Then leave you to rot."

It was Albert's turn to change the subject. "I met your girlfriend on the way in at the pool."

"So, you've seen Brenda?" Zane asked.

"Yes, sir, quite a lot of her," Albert said with a wry smile.

Zane laughed. "Brenda isn't shy about her body. Her motto is 'if you've got it, flaunt it.' And she certainly has it."

"Yes, she does, sir," Albert said.

"Your wife doesn't object to your girlfriends?" Albert asked.

"I love my wife deeply, and she loves me. Fortunately, she understands my needs. She's a generous woman in that way and many others."

Albert nodded. "Where did you meet Brenda?"

"Hiking in Eaton Canyon."

"In that case, I think I should take up hiking, sir," Albert laughed.

"You should come along with me sometime, Albert."

"I'd like that."

Zane was quiet for a few moments, then said wistfully, "But there's always one that gets away, Albert. The most beautiful woman I've ever seen, I met hiking in Millard Canyon."

"Something tells me you want to tell me about it."

"Yes, I do, Albert, but more for my benefit than yours." Zane laughed. "So, I can relive it all over again."

"Then I'd be happy to indulge you," Albert said, smiling.

Zane began his story.

"The hike to Millard Falls is just a little over a mile from the beginning of the trailhead. But it's slow going because the canyon is steep and narrow. You're continually crisscrossing from one side of the stream to the other, climbing over boulders and downed trees to make your way upstream.

"However, once you get to the falls, you're rewarded with an incredible view. The canyon abruptly ends in a small bowl. The rim of a fifty-foot-high sandstone wall is cut in the middle by a boulder-filled gap where water streams down into a little pool below. Lichen grows on the canyon wall from the constant exposure to the waterfall. The day I was there, it was flowing strong enough so that you could stand under it and cool off.

"But the most beautiful thing I saw that day wasn't the falls, but a young woman rock-climbing on a steep cliff to the right of the falls. She was wearing shorts and a halter-top, her golden blonde hair tied in a ponytail, sweat glistening off her tanned satin-smooth skin. She wore a climbing harness around her hips, secured to a safety line that looped through permanent bolts in the cliff face.

"Her climbing partner was on the ground holding the line. He was a lean, handsome man in his early fifties, fit and athletic. I spoke to him briefly. He had a bit of a French accent.

"Try as I might to be casual, I couldn't take my eyes off the young woman as she climbed. Her face was beautiful, her arms taut, the line of her back and hips curving seductively around her delicious bottom to her long-tapered legs. Looking up at her on the rock face provided a captivating view of her entire body.

"Yet the most mesmerizing thing about her wasn't her body but her smile when she looked down at her climbing partner. It was at once sweet, frightened, and confident at the same time. You could tell she was new to climbing. Her partner provided her with gentle encouragement from below as she struggled to find the next hand or foothold.

"Later, when she descended to the canyon floor, she unhooked the safety line from her harness and gave it to her climbing partner. He attached it to his and started his climb. She held the belay-line and carefully monitored his progress as she looked up at him.

"I approached her then and casually started to talk to her. Her climbing partner took his time carefully threading his way up the cliff. He was the more experienced climber of the two, showing great skill as he ascended. While he climbed, I chatted with the young woman. I learned her name. I asked for her address, which she gave me. I told her who I was trying to impress her, but it didn't seem to. A few days later, I wrote her a quick note, but nothing ever came of it. She never responded."

Zane was quiet for a few moments. A look of sadness came over his face as he said, "About three weeks ago, I read in the newspaper that she died in a car accident. It shook me to the core. That the life of such a beautiful, vibrant young woman could be so tragically snuffed out in an instant."

"What was her name?" Albert asked.

"Irene ... Irene Simpson."

25

Hop Li

The next night the streets of Chinatown were empty as Albert drove down Main Street. It was just past one in the morning, no one was about. The restaurants and shops had closed hours ago. Only the smell of cooking oil lingered in the warm night air.

Albert glided his car to a stop a half-block north of Macy Street and turned off the lights and ignition. He sat there for a moment going over his plan. He got out of the car and grabbed a watch-cap, gloves, flashlight, and screwdriver from the back seat. He put the cap on and turned up his collar to partially hide his face.

He walked east on Macy for one block, where he quickly crossed Alameda. Alameda was also empty. No cars, trains, or people on the street. He walked south until he reached a spur of the main rail line that curved off to the left. He followed the tracks through an empty field for a couple hundred yards until he was directly north of the tiny lane where Hop Li's shop was located. He squatted down beside the tracks and looked toward the shop.

Earlier in the day, Albert had checked out the area after returning from Catalina. He had decided that approaching from the north was the safest route. Hop Li's shop was at the end of the lane close to the tracks. Coming from the north, he wouldn't have to go by the other dwellings on the narrow lane and risk being seen by someone.

He crossed the tracks and ran across the open field until he reached the side of Hop Li's building. There he stopped, put his back against the brick wall, and caught his breath. He peered around the corner. The lane was dark. There were no streetlights, and the lights in the buildings were out. He'd noticed the lock to Hop Li's shop earlier in the day. It was cheap; he was sure he could pry it open it with a screwdriver.

Albert rounded the corner and ducked under the shop's shuttered window as he crept toward the door. He tried the handle. To his surprise, it was unlocked. He pushed the door open and entered. He stopped after a few steps to allow his eyes to adjust to the dark. As he did, he spotted Hop Li lying on the floor, moaning in pain.

Albert stooped down next to him. "What happened? Were you robbed?"

Hop Li shook his head no.

"Then what did they want?"

"Photos."

"Whose photos?"

"Miss Irene's," he said almost, unconscious.

"Irene Simpson's photos?"

Hop Li nodded his head, yes.

"Where are they?"

"Don't know … I told the other man. I don't know. Call an ambulance, please."

"I'm not going to call anyone until you tell me where the photos and negatives are."

"Don't know … I don't have. What's wrong with you people?"

Albert shook him, and blood started dripping from Hop Li's mouth. "Where are the photos?" Albert shouted again in anger.

"Don't know … don't have, please help me," Hop Li said, now delirious as he fainted.

Albert stood, turned his flashlight on, and quickly searched the small shop. It was a mess; everything had been smashed or tossed on the floor. Behind the counter, the door to the darkroom was open. Albert looked inside; broken bottles of developer solution lay on the floor, spilling their pungent-smelling liquid everywhere. Toward the back of the shop, Albert found a room no bigger than a closet. He peered in; there was a mattress on the floor, the bedding and pillows ripped open.

If Irene's photos had ever been in the shop, they were gone now, he thought. Albert switched off his flashlight, stepped over Hop Li's body, and started toward the door. Hop Li cried out once more in pain. Albert stopped, hesitated for a moment, then went to the phone and dialed the emergency number.

Covering the phone, he said, "A man is bleeding in Hop Li's photo store in Chinatown. Send an ambulance." Then he hung up.

Albert took one last look at Hop Li and left. Backtracking through the field to his car, he started it and quickly drove away. His employer wouldn't be happy. Someone had gotten there before him.

Gerard gripped the wheel of the black sedan with his massive hands. It was almost four in the morning. It had taken him over three hours to drive the ninety miles along Route 44 from Los Angeles to Montecito.

He had stopped a few times along the way to clean up and get coffee. The first time was in Newbury Park, before the Conejo Grade, where he got gas and washed Hop Li's blood off his knuckles. The second time was at a diner along the Rincon Road between Ventura and Carpentaria, where he got some coffee to stay awake.

Rounding the curve at Rincon Point, he took one hand off the wheel to wipe the sweat from his broad Welsh forehead. A former boxer, he was used to busting heads, but this night's work was particularly unpleasant. It wasn't a fair fight; he was twice as big as the Chinaman. He'd almost killed him and for nothing. He hadn't found anything. The lady of the house would not be pleased when he reported to her later in the morning.

Two miles before Summerland, Gerard turned right onto El Toro Canyon Road. He took the dusty lane up to East Valley Road, where he turned left. East Valley traversed the foothills along the base of the Santa Ynez mountains that loomed above. Gerard drove for a few miles until he got to the gated entrance of a two-hundred-acre estate on his right.

There he pulled off the road, opened the gate, and drove through. It was another quarter-mile drive on a winding lane through lemon and avocado orchards until he arrived at the main house. To call it a house, of course, was an understatement. Twelve buildings, faced in brick and stone, totaling over twenty-nine-thousand square feet, made up the sprawling Monterey Colonial-style manor.

Gerard drove around to the back of the estate toward the servant's quarters where he parked. He opened the door to his small room and immediately fell on the bed, fully clothed. He hoped he could get a few hours' sleep before meeting her ladyship later in the morning.

Four hours later, shaven and dressed in his chauffeur's uniform, Gerard stood in front of a dark mahogany desk in the library. Seated before him and framed by the French windows behind her, sat her ladyship with her customary stiff bearing.

The library had an understated elegance to it. The room's interior and one other in the manor had been purchased from an estate in England. Where it had been dismantled and shipped to

America, then reassembled and incorporated into the architect's final plans for the building.

Oak-paneled bookcases covered three walls of the spacious room. A comfortable couch sat beneath the bookcase on the east wall, while mahogany chairs and end tables were arranged throughout the room on plush carpeting.

Over the fireplace hung a stone-faced portrait of the matron's father. Reminding everyone that the source of wealth on display came from her ladyship's family and that she was the sole heir. This was her room, her manor, her grand estate, and no one else's.

Even at this early hour, the matron had dressed appropriately for her self-exalted station in life. Her finely coiffed grey hair was perfectly in place. Her regular, though not delicate features made her attractive but not pretty. The ultra-rich in America had few role models to emulate, so many ended up choosing the British Aristocracy. That certainly was the case with her ladyship. And while she didn't go so far as to affect a British accent, she carefully enunciated each word as she spoke to indicate her high-born status.

Gerard began with the good news. "Your information was correct, madam. The Chinaman did develop the film for Miss Simpson."

"It was more intuition than information, Gerard, based on what my useless husband told me about that blonde hussy."

"In any case, it was correct," he said. "However, neither the negatives nor the photos were in the shop. And the Chinaman claimed he didn't know where they were. He said he developed the film for her, but she took everything with her, including the negatives. I tore up the entire shop, searching for them but found nothing."

"And you're sure he wasn't lying."

"Yes," Gerard said. "I beat him pretty bad. I'm not sure he'll survive."

"Who cares. It's just as well if he doesn't," she said dismissively. "Don't let it bother you, Gerard. He's only a Chinaman; they're like vermin. Dozens used to die daily, building the transcontinental railroad. I can assure you my grandfather never lost sleep over them, and neither should you."

"Yes, madam."

"We will press on regardless, Gerard. I still have to clean up the mess my husband made … with your help, of course."

"Yes, madam."

The matron sighed and said to herself. "It's my mistake for picking a husband based solely on the fact he looks good in evening wear."

Gerard could barely keep from smiling as she made fun of her dandy of a husband.

"I recently discovered from one of my friends that the blonde tart had a lawyer," the matron said. "You're going to pay him a visit, Gerard."

"To beat him?" Gerard asked, alarmed. There was no consequence in beating a Chinaman, but beating a lawyer was a different matter.

"No … to bribe him," the matron said, smiling.

Mathieu sat at his desk in the detective's room. He was the only one there; everyone else was still at lunch. He was going over the list of Irene's properties, deciding which apartments to check next, when the phone rang.

"Officer Mathieu," he said, as he answered.

A soft but efficient voice came across the line. "My name is Nurse Claudine Chastain from the French Hospital in Chinatown."

"How can I help you, Nurse?"

"A Chinese man by the name of Hop Li was admitted to the hospital late last night. He was badly beaten and was in surgery for three hours. He's stable now, but he's in and out of consciousness. Among his effects, we found your business card. I thought it best to call you. I know the Chinese are sometimes reluctant to deal with the police," she said.

"Thank you for contacting me," Mathieu said. "I know Hop Li from an investigation I'm currently conducting. When do you think I can talk to him?"

"If he continues to recover, I think by tomorrow afternoon. I can call you then and let you know if you wish."

"Yes, please. I would much appreciate that," Mathieu said. "What ward is he in?"

"Ward C on the third floor," she replied. "I'll be on duty there tomorrow."

"And may I have a number where I can contact you?" Mathieu asked.

She gave him the number, then they said their goodbyes and hung up.

Mathieu assumed the beating wasn't random. He suspected it was related to Irene's case. And he knew it would be challenging to get Hop Li to talk, so he decided to enlist some help.

The next afternoon at three o'clock, Mathieu entered the French Hospital on College Street just past Hill. Nurse Chastain had called him earlier in the day to say Hop Li had regained consciousness. Mathieu had brought along his old Kung Fu instructor Mr. Yang. They took the elevator up to the third floor and found Ward C, where Nurse Chastain was waiting for them.

Nurse Chastain was Mathieu's age, slender and beautiful with long, light brown hair and kind, knowing blue eyes. As

Mathieu took her soft hand, he felt a shock of electricity or at least imagined it. If she felt the same thing, he wasn't sure, but she held his gaze for a moment as she smiled at him. Mathieu recovered, released her hand, and introduced her to Mr. Yang.

"Come this way," Nurse Chastain said as she led them past a row of occupied beds to Hop Li's near the window.

Hop Li observed Mathieu as he approached. He didn't say anything, but his eyes followed Mathieu as he came around to the side of his bed. Hop Li's face was almost unrecognizable with the swelling and bruising. There was an expression of intense pain on it. Mathieu hoped he had been given enough painkillers.

"Hop Li, this is Mr. Yang. I think you know him," Mathieu said respectfully.

Mr. Yang bowed and said something in Chinese. Hop Li nodded, acknowledging his sympathy.

Addressing Mathieu, Nurse Chastain said, "I'll leave you to talk, but please be gentle with him. He's been through a lot." She smiled at Hop Li to reassure him, then left.

Mathieu felt it would be difficult to refuse a request put that way. He sat on one side of Hop Li's bed, Mr. Yang on the other.

"Can you tell me what happened, Hop Li?"

Since the young policeman had shown respect by bringing Mr. Yang along, Hop Li decided not to draw it out. Speaking in obvious pain, he said, "Two men came to my shop looking for Miss Simpson's photos."

"Two men at once?"

Hop Li shook his head. "No ... first one, then another."

"Two men came separately on the same night?" Mathieu asked, confused.

"Yes, the first one came just after midnight. He's the one that beat me. I told him I didn't have photos, but he kept beating me. Then he tore up my shop looking for them. He was angry and kicked me hard in the stomach as I lay on the floor, just before he left."

Mathieu nodded, hoping Hop Li would continue.

"The second man came maybe forty minutes later. He also wanted photos. He shook me hard and yelled at me but didn't beat me. He searched the shop also but didn't find anything. He started to leave. I beg him to call an ambulance. He came back, called an ambulance, then left."

"What did the men look like?"

"First man, a giant, huge hands, square head, short hair. Second man, tall with a long scar on his face."

"When you're feeling better, could you describe them to a sketch artist?"

"I no want to get involved," Hop Li said with a stone face.

Mathieu nodded. "I understand … you've been through a lot."

Taking a moment, Mathieu thought about how to proceed. He'd expected resistance and was surprised how much Hop Li had already told him. But Mathieu had prepared a counteroffer that he didn't think Hop Li could refuse. An offer that would make good use of Chandler's reward money.

"Hop Li, after the nurse called me, I sent a police detail over to your shop to make a report and see if they could find any fingerprints. They told me the shop was badly damaged."

Hop Li nodded. "Yes … real bad."

"I think I can help you with your shop if you can help me," Mathieu said.

Hop Li looked at him with wary eyes.

Mathieu pulled three one-hundred-dollar bills from his shirt pocket. "This is three hundred dollars in reward money to repair your shop. It's yours if you can describe the men who beat you to a sketch artist for me. You don't have to go to police headquarters;

the artist will come here. I'll be with them. When I have the sketches, I'll give you the money."

Hop Li stared at Mathieu then turned to Mr. Yang. They had a long conversation in Chinese. Hop Li seemed resistive at first but slowly, and calmly, Mr. Yang seemed to assuage his fears.

Hop Li turned back to Mathieu. "No tricks?"

"No tricks. You have my word," Mathieu said. "Mr. Yang can vouch for me."

Hop Li again looked at Mr. Yang, who nodded in the affirmative.

Looking back at Mathieu, Hop Li said, "Okay, but I only describe them to artist nothing more."

"I understand that's all I need," Mathieu said. "Thank you, Hop Li."

26

The Sketch Artist

The next day Mathieu returned to the French Hospital with a sketch artist, Audrey Hunter, a bright young woman in her early twenties who knew several languages, including Chinese. Audrey had graduated first in her class at the Chouinard Art Institute two years earlier and was now the LAPD's top sketch artist.

Entering Hop Li's ward, Mathieu hoped to see Nurse Claudine, but she wasn't on duty. Mathieu led Audrey to Hop Li's bed. The swelling on his face had gone down, and he was sitting up. Mathieu introduced them, then let Audrey take charge while he stood off to the side.

"I'm so sorry this happened to you, Hop Li," she began in a kind voice. "I'm going to guide you through the whole process today. And whenever you want to stop, just tell me, and we'll stop. Okay?"

"Okay."

"Let me explain how this works. The point of a police sketch isn't to make an exact portrait of a suspect; that's impossible and not even useful. The point is to try to create a good resemblance to the suspect. So that if someone sees the sketch and later sees the suspect, they will seem familiar to them. Does that make sense?"

Hop Li nodded.

"We'll do one feature at a time, eyes, lips, chin, nose wherever you want to start. I also brought along a facial reference photo book that will help us refine the features. The photos often help to jog the memory. Ready to get started?"

"Yes, I'm ready."

"Good, so before we get to the sketch. Tell me about that night. What did you do before the attacker broke into your shop?"

Audrey's calm manner seemed to relax Hop Li. He began to talk freely with her. "I cook dinner on the stove in the shop, then go into the darkroom. I develop the film I get that day, then make prints and hang them on the clothesline to dry. I finish around eleven. Then I turn out safety light in the darkroom, wash hands, and go to bed."

"What happened next?" she asked.

"I fall asleep, and the next thing I know, a huge man grabs me out of bed and throws me on the floor. He asks me where Miss Irene's photos and negatives are. I tell him I don't know. He didn't believe me. He starts beating me in the face and stomach. I double over in pain on the floor, covering my head with my hands. Then the man starts searching my shop, tossing things on the floor, breaking things. He searched the counter, darkroom, bedroom everywhere but didn't find anything. He was very angry. He stood over me one more time. I thought he was going to beat me again. He says if I'm lying, he'll come back and kill me. Then he kicks me hard in the stomach and leaves."

"Describe him to me," she said gently.

"Big man, huge hands, square head, short hair, tall maybe six foot tall."

"How old?"

Hop Li thought for a moment and said, "Maybe forty."

"Anything else unique?"

"Man had a funny accent."

"What kind?"

Hop Li shrugged. "Maybe English but low class."

Mathieu was impressed with Hop Li's description of the man's accent.

"What was the first thing you noticed about his face?" Audrey asked.

"Huge broad face, big forehead, short hair."

"What shape?"

"Like square block," Hop Li responded.

Audrey began sketching a rough outline of the head. She showed it to Hop Li. "Like this?"

He nodded.

"What about his eyebrows?"

"Almost straight, dark brown."

"And the color of his hair?"

"Same."

"And his nose?"

"Not big but broad like pug nose. Looked like it was broken."

As Hop Li described each feature, Audrey lightly sketched them in on her pad. Every once in a while, she stopped to show him the sketch and get his feedback.

"And his lips?"

"Thin."

"His jawline?"

"Square."

When she had finished with the initial sketch, she showed it to Hop Li. "What needs fixing?" she asked.

"Lips too far away from his nose," he said. "And chin too narrow."

Audrey corrected the nose and chin, then spent some time adding depth to the man's features and highlighting the cheekbones. She took her time, erasing things when she wasn't satisfied and starting over. Hop Li watched her draw, fascinated by her skill. When she felt the sketch was good enough, she held it up for him.

Staring at the sketch in amazement, Hop Li said, "That's him."

"Good," Audrey said, smiling. "Now, tell me about the second man."

"He was tall but leaner. Thinner face, not square like the first man. Wore cap, dark hair, handsome but had big scar on his cheek," Hop Li said as he moved his thumb down his left cheek.

"What kind of scar?"

"Jagged. Like he got cut in a knife fight or maybe the war."

"How old did he look?"

Hop Li shrugged, "Mid-thirties, maybe."

Audrey repeated the process of going one feature at a time, as she'd done for the first sketch. When Hop Li wasn't sure, she showed him the photo reference book. It had an assortment of full-face photos along with closeups of a variety of nose, chin, lip, and eye shapes. Hop Li would study them then point to one he thought was close. It was harder for Hop Li to remember the second man because he'd been in so much pain when he first saw him.

When Audrey finished the second sketch and showed it to Hop Li, his eyes widened in recognition. "You good artist, Miss," he said. "That looks like him."

"Thank you," Audrey said, closing her sketchbook. "I just need you to sign each of these on the back for me, Hop Li."

She handed him the sketches to sign. Hop Li hesitated. "It's okay your signature won't appear on the copies we distribute," she said. "It's just our way of recording that you approved the drawings."

Reassured, he signed them and gave them back to her.

Audrey turned to Mathieu and said, "I think I'm done here."

"Thank you, Audrey," Mathieu said. "I agree with Hop Li. You are an amazing artist. Can you have some copies of the sketches made for me and sent to my office?"

"Certainly," she said, rising and putting her things away. She turned to Hop Li and said, "I hope you get well very soon."

Mathieu escorted Audrey to the door, thanking her again for her help. Then he went back to the side of Hop Li's bed.

Mathieu reached into his pocket and handed Hop Li an envelope. "Your three hundred dollars are in here," he said in a low voice. "Will it be safe with you here?"

"Yes, I will pin to underwear," Hop Li said, then added. "You good man, Officer, you keep your word."

"Thanks, Hop Li," Mathieu said, as he stood to leave. "These sketches are going to help me find the men who beat you. I hope you heal quickly, so you can get back to your shop." Then Mathieu turned and walked away.

Mathieu was so preoccupied thinking about the sketches that he almost bumped into Nurse Claudine in the hallway.

"I'm sorry," he said, his face lighting up when he saw her.

"Hello again, Officer," she said, in a detached manner.

Mathieu's heart sank; he'd had been hoping for a warmer welcome. Perhaps he'd misread her the previous day.

"Did you interview Hop Li again?"

"Yes," Mathieu said, matching her distant tone.

"Did it upset him?"

"No," he said, shaking his head. "He was fine. The sketch artist was gentle with him. Hop Li did well."

She nodded. "Good."

"Tough day?" Mathieu asked, sensing something was wrong.

"Yes, a young patient died … a little girl."

"I'm sorry," he said.

She shrugged. "Comes with the job. Yours, too, I guess."

Mathieu nodded, not knowing what to say. He had hoped to ask her to join him for coffee, but that seemed inappropriate now. Besides, he sensed she wasn't as interested in him as he had imagined.

"Well, I have to get back to headquarters," Mathieu said. "I'm sorry about the little girl."

As he turned to leave, she asked? "Will you be back tomorrow?"

"No," he said. "We finished up today. But thanks again for contacting me. I doubt if Mr. Li would have contacted the police on his own."

"I was glad to help," she said, noticing his manner had become more formal.

There was an awkward silence between them. "Well, goodbye, it's been nice to meet you, Nurse Chastain," Mathieu said, then started to walk away.

"Do you have time for a coffee?" she asked, stopping him. "I could use some company."

Turning back to her but not getting his hopes up, he said, "Sure if you'd like to, Nurse Chastain."

"I would like to," she said. "And please ... call me, Claudine."

"Okay," he said, still cautious. "My name's Theo."

"Nice to meet you, Theo," she said, smiling for the first time. "We can go to the cafeteria on the first floor. The coffee's terrible there, but at least it's close."

Sitting alone together at a table in the cafeteria, they were still awkward with each other. Both of them stared at their coffees, stirring the scolding hot liquid in hopes it would cool down.

Mathieu broke the silence first. "How long had the little girl been in the hospital?"

Claudine sighed. "About a month."

"So, you got to know her?"

"Yes," she said, wiping a tear from her eye. "She was such a sweet little girl."

"How old was she?"

"Three."

"What was wrong with her?"

"Her heart ... it was a birth defect. There wasn't a lot we could do. They tried an experimental procedure today, but she died on the operating room table."

"Her parents must be devastated," he said.

"Yes, they are," she said. "I tried to comfort them, but I was such a wreck, I don't think I helped."

"Doesn't seem fair," Mathieu said.

"No, it's not," she said. "You must see it also."

He nodded.

"What kind of case are you working on now?" she asked.

"The murder of a young woman," he said flatly.

"How was she killed?"

"She was shot twice just below the heart ... died instantly."

"How old?"

"Twenty-nine," he said.

"That's too young also," she said.

"Yes, it is," Mathieu said as he took a sip of his coffee. "You were right about this coffee ... it is awful."

"I told you it would be," she said, as they shared their first laugh together. Looking at him, she said, "I once had an excellent cup of coffee nearby, though."

"Where was that?" he asked.

"At Mathieu's Restaurant," she said.

Mathieu laughed to himself and shook his head.

"Are you related to the owner?"

"Yes," he said, nodding his head. "He's my father."

"I thought so. I was there last year with my mother on Bastille

Day. After dinner, we were having our coffees, and your father came up to the table and introduced himself. We chatted a bit, he offered us some brandy on the house. He noticed that I wasn't wearing a wedding ring and asked me if I had a boyfriend," she said with a mischievous smile.

Mathieu started to cringe, "Oh god, how embarrassing."

Claudine leaned forward and said, "It gets better. I told him I didn't, and he said, 'You should meet my son.'"

"He didn't."

"Yes, he did," Claudine said, enjoying Mathieu's discomfort. "He told me his son was a policeman, and he was quite handsome. He seemed very proud of you."

Mathieu buried his face in his hands and said, "How humiliating."

"I thought it was kind of sweet."

Shaking his head in dismay, Mathieu said, "I can't believe he tried to set us up on a date. What did you say?"

"I thanked him but said I was busy with my work. He said you were also, so it might work out between us."

"I'm so sorry that happened. I had no idea he did things like that."

Claudine lightly brushed Mathieu's hand with hers.

"I'm not sorry he did," she said.

Mathieu welcomed the touch. He looked at her hand, now withdrawn, then at her face, and a thought came to his mind. He smiled to himself.

"What is it?" she asked, noticing the change in his expression.

"Did you recognize my name when you saw my card in Hop Li's things?"

"Maybe," she blushed.

"Maybe?"

"I'm not going to tell you," she said with a nervous laugh. "You'll just have to wonder if we met by accident."

"I don't care how we met," he said, looking into her eyes.

"Neither do I," she said, glancing down at her cup.

Lightening the mood, Mathieu asked, "But what are we going to do about this awful coffee?"

"We'll just have to imagine we're marooned on a desert island, and this is the best coffee in the world," she said with a big smile.

"In that case," Mathieu said. "A Votre Sante!"

27

Death at the Beach

Irene Simpson's lawyer sat at his desk with a self-satisfied smile on his face. For the second time that week, he'd sold a list of all of Irene's properties to a willing buyer. Best of all, he didn't have to seek them out; both buyers had approached him.

He had also supplied them with the address of Miss Simpson's primary residence in Santa Monica. And as lawyers often do, he found a way to rationalize it to himself. Even though he was handling Miss Simpson's estate, what he'd sold was public information, easily obtainable with a little work. He'd done the research, so why not profit from it.

Four days later, Mathieu was sitting at his desk when the phone rang. Lifting the handset, he said, "Office Mathieu LAPD."

"Officer Mathieu, I'm Detective Peter Barnes with the Santa Monica Police."

"How can I help you, Detective?" Mathieu asked.

"We had a break-in at an apartment in Santa Monica yesterday. The apartment belongs to Miss Irene Simpson. I understand you're investigating her death."

"Yes, I am … thanks for calling me," Mathieu said, "Have you finished with the crime scene?"

"Yes, we have," Barnes said.

"Do you mind if I check the apartment out then?" Mathieu asked.

"Not at all. That's why I called you. Do you need a key?"

"No, thank you. I have keys to all of her apartments."

"All?" Barnes asked.

"Yes, she had quite a few."

There was silence on the line.

"What's wrong, Detective Barnes?"

"It was more than a simple break-in."

"What do you mean?" Mathieu asked.

"Her neighbor was killed when he confronted the burglar," Barnes replied.

"Who was her neighbor?"

"Professor Kevin Patterson from USC."

"Wow!" Mathieu exclaimed.

"You know about Professor Patterson?"

"Yes, I do," Mathieu said. "He's on my list of suspects. Look, I think it's best if we meet up at her apartment. I need to bring you up to speed. It's a complicated case. It might help both of us."

"Sure, I'd welcome that," Detective Barnes said.

"Where's the apartment?" Mathieu asked.

"140 Hollister Ave in Ocean Park," Barnes said. "It's called the Horatio West Court."

"Yes, I remember that one from the list," Mathieu said. "How about this afternoon at one."

"That's fine. I'll see you there then," Barnes said.

South of Pico, Ocean Park was Santa Monica's poor stepchild, lowbrow, and tacky with a Coney Island feel to it. Built on sand dunes, the neighborhood consisted of small summer cottages and a string of amusement piers along the beach. It wasn't upscale like the other areas where Irene owned apartments. What surprised Mathieu was that she had accepted an apartment in that area at all.

Mathieu got there early. He wanted to get a feel for the place before Barnes arrived. Horatio Court was unlike any of Irene's other properties. It was a cluster of six small cube-shaped units on a modest-sized lot a half a block from the beach. The detached two-story units were painted white with green trimmed-windows and arched-entryways.

Irene's unit was in front, facing Hollister Avenue. Across the street was the three-story Maryland Apartment building. At the end of the street, the Crystal Amusement Pier jutted out over the sand and into Santa Monica Bay. Just north of it was the "Inkwell," one of the few beaches where blacks were allowed to congregate.

Mathieu unlocked the door to Irene's unit and entered the small living room. The police had left the room the way they found it. It was obvious it had been searched; books and papers were strewn across the floor. There was a chalk outline on the carpet where Professor Patterson's body had been found. Mathieu spotted a bloodstain on the corner of the piano. It was likely that's how Patterson had been killed.

Despite the mess, the room's overall feeling was warm and cozy, unlike Irene's other apartments. The others had felt sterile, but this one felt like her home.

To the left of the door was a floor to ceiling bookcase. Next to it, a cushioned window-seat that looked out on the courtyard and street. The window-seat had storage underneath that held some records and a record player. The front wall had a small built-in fireplace A rocking chair sat next to it on the hexagonal-shaped Spanish floor tiles. To the right of the fireplace was another bookcase and a comfortable Mission-style chair in the corner.

The center of the room had a colorful woven rug. A black upright piano stood against the wall across from the door.

Mathieu suspected this was where Irene had been able to be herself. The personal items in the room reinforced that feeling.

On the narrow mantlepiece above the fireplace was a framed photo of a little girl hugging a nun. Mathieu picked it up and examined it. The nun in the photograph looked like a younger and thinner version of Sister Mary Catherine. And the little girl hugging the nun was Irene, already stunningly beautiful. He put the photo down and explored the rest of the first floor. There was a galley kitchen off the main room and a bathroom near the stairs. By the look of the mess, both rooms had been searched.

He climbed the stairs to the second floor, where there were two bedrooms. The smaller one, off to the right, had been converted into an office with a desk and file cabinets. The file cabinets had all been ransacked, file folders and papers littered the floor.

At the end of the hallway, the larger bedroom faced the ocean and overlooked the courtyard and street. It was a wonderful light-filled room. Windows ringed the upper third of three of its walls, like a watchtower. White lace curtains let in light but also provided privacy.

Beneath the ocean-facing windows, there was a large bed with thick, cozy blankets and fluffy pillows. The closet was full of brightly colored summer dresses and casual shoes. The dresser drawers were open but empty. Their contents, shorts, blouses, swimwear, sweaters, and underwear lay strewn across Irene's bed.

Finished with the bedroom, Mathieu went back downstairs. He stopped under the archway to the main room. He stood there for a few moments trying to take it all in. He walked over to the bookcase and scanned the contents. Books on Art and Architecture filled the top shelf. On the shelf below it, novels by the Bronte sisters, including "Wuthering Heights" and "Jane

Eyre," took pride of place. Irene seemed to have had a wide range of interests.

Mathieu crossed to the other side of the room and sat down at the piano bench. There was some sheet music on the stand, which he scanned through. He found a piece he knew, a piano solo for Gershwin's "Rhapsody in Blue." As he was looking at it, he heard a knock on the door. He got up to answer it. Standing on the porch was a big-boned man in his early forties with short blonde hair and watchful but friendly brown eyes.

"I'm Detective Peter Barnes," he said, reaching out his big hand.

Returning his handshake, Mathieu said, "Officer Theo Mathieu. I got here a little early to get a feel for the place. Come in."

The room was immediately smaller, with the two men in it.

"You're a motorcycle patrolman. How did you get assigned to a murder investigation?" Barnes asked.

"I was the one who found Irene's body with two bullets in her chest. When I went through her personal effects, I discovered she was Harry Chandler's personal secretary at the LA Times."

"Jesus!" Barnes said in disbelief. "Harry Chandler?"

"Yeah," Mathieu said. "The other thing to know is I'm Chandler's godson. Mr. Chandler requested I be assigned to the case so I could keep him informed."

"Fuck … that sounds political as shit," Barnes said.

"Yes, it is," Mathieu said.

"Who are you reporting to at the LAPD?"

"Chief Detective Inspector William Braden."

"Bull Braden?"

"Yes."

"I've heard he's a tough bastard."

"He's actually been pretty fair to me … probably because I'm Chandler's godson," Mathieu said with a sheepish smile.

"Why don't you fill me in on the details of your case," Barnes said as he sat down on the window seat.

Mathieu went back to the piano bench and sat across from him. "I'll try to make it as brief as possible. I found Irene's dead body in a black musician's house. She was naked, shot twice just below the chest. The musician's name is Paul Thornton. Bull and his detectives immediately suspected him. They beat the hell out of him, trying to get him to confess. But he had an airtight alibi for the night she was murdered. He was in San Francisco playing a gig."

Mathieu passed Barnes the photo of Irene he got from Francine.

Barnes stared at the photo for a few moments, then passed it back. "I've never seen a more beautiful woman," he said with a look of sadness.

"Neither have I."

"What was she doing at Thornton's house if he was out of town?"

"He'd given her a key," Mathieu said. "Thornton met Irene one night at the Dunbar. She drove him home and asked him to play for her. While he was playing, she started taking off all her clothes and dancing for him."

"Jesus … lucky guy!"

"Yeah," Mathieu said. "He gave her a key because she wouldn't tell him how to get ahold of her. After that, she'd just show up unannounced."

"Was he sleeping with her?" Barnes asked.

"Not according to him."

"Do you believe him?"

"Yes, because he was embarrassed to admit it," Mathieu said.

"Why not? She was beautiful."

"Because Irene wouldn't let him touch her," Mathieu said.

"Her father sexually abused her as a child. Her mother gave her up for adoption to protect her. But she was never adopted because she was terrified of men."

Barnes shook his head in disgust. "What happened next with the case?"

"Bull's detectives rounded up a few more Negro suspects and beat them senseless. But to no avail, they all had alibis. Then the case went cold. Because of my relationship with Chandler, Bull has given me free rein to investigate Irene's life. I found out she'd been given expensive cars and apartments by several rich and powerful men in Los Angeles, including Patterson."

"Was she a high-priced call girl?" Barnes asked.

"I don't think so," Mathieu said, shaking his head. "I think it's more complicated than that."

"What do you think was going on then?" Barnes asked.

"I'm not sure. Obviously, there was a sexual aspect to her relationship with her 'patrons.' But I'm not sure she ever slept with any of them," Mathieu said. "For one thing, there were no beds in any of the apartments she was given. And the men I've interviewed so far only admit to her dancing nude for them, nothing else."

"If she wasn't sleeping with them, maybe she had some other kind of leverage over them," Barnes said.

"Maybe … but you saw her photo. She was stunning, and she knew it," Mathieu said. "So even if she was just dancing naked for them, she would have had an incredible sexual hold over them."

"That's true," Barnes conceded.

"And I think it was more than just the sexual aspect," Mathieu said. "All the men I've questioned so far were totally enchanted with her. One of them even wanted to marry her. I think she picked men, who despite their wealth, were needy and weak in some way. Men she could easily control. Men who could never have a woman like her any other way. And remember, they're all super-rich. The apartments and cars they gave her meant nothing to them."

"So, who are your main suspects?"

"Everyone who gave her apartments. The ones I've interviewed so far all have alibis for the night of the murder. But their alibis could be meaningless. Men who are that rich can afford to pay someone else to do their dirty work."

"How many more do you have to interview?"

"Three, and they're the richest and most powerful on the list."

Barnes nodded knowingly. "So careful as it goes?"

"Yeah," Mathieu said. "There's one other thing you should know. Irene put hidden cameras in every apartment where she 'entertained.' The cameras were pointed at the men who were watching her dance."

"Was she blackmailing her patrons with the photos?" Barnes asked. "Do you think that's why she was killed?"

"I don't think so," Mathieu said, shaking his head. "That doesn't seem to have been her style. I think the photos were just insurance for her. But my guess is that's what this break-in was about. Somebody was looking for those photos. Maybe more than one person."

"Why do you think there might be more than one person looking?"

"Because a shop owner in Chinatown named Hop Li, who developed Irene's film, was recently beaten. Two separate men came to his shop on the same night, looking for the photos and negatives. The first man almost beat him to death. Here are the sketches of the two men plus fingerprint cards from the crime scene."

Mathieu stood up, crossed the room, and handed them to Barnes.

"The guy with the square head is the one that beat Hop Li. We found a lot of prints, besides Hop Li's, in the shop. But in the darkroom, we only found one other set of prints besides Hop Li's. I think they might belong to 'square-head.' Because the second man who came that night, the one with the scar on his face, was wearing gloves so they can't be his prints."

"So, if 'square-heads' prints match the ones we found here, he might be our murder suspect," Barnes said.

"Yeah, that's what I'm thinking," Mathieu said.

"That's nice work, Officer," Barnes said, "I hope you get promoted to detective when this is all over."

Mathieu shrugged. "Maybe … if I don't screw it up."

"These sketches and the fingerprint cards will be really helpful to me," Barnes said. "We'll do house to house interviews with the neighbors to see if anyone saw either of these two men. And I'll have their sketches checked against our mugshot book."

"Oh, before I forget, here's Irene's fingerprint card," Mathieu said, handing it to Barnes.

"Thanks, I'll give it to the forensic team for comparison," Barnes said.

Changing the subject, Mathieu asked, "Can you tell me what happened here the night of the break-in?"

"The night shift got a call early yesterday morning about a disturbance here," Barnes said. "When the squad car arrived, they found Professor Patterson's dead body lying on the floor. It appears that he'd been shoved and hit his head on the edge of the piano. The coroner said he died instantly. He was a pretty, frail old man."

"What was he doing here?" Mathieu asked.

"He lived right across the courtyard," Barnes said, pointing to the unit directly across from Irene's.

"I guess he heard the burglar and came to investigate. When

we questioned the neighbors, they said Irene and the professor were good friends. They said they used to hang out together, almost like a father and daughter."

Mathieu nodded, trying to take it all in. "Did anyone see anything?"

"No, just some shouting and a car driving away."

"Did you get any fingerprints?"

"Yes, the forensic team is analyzing them now. We found a woman's prints, presumably Irene's, everywhere. We found Professor Patterson's prints in the downstairs' rooms, but none upstairs. And we found an unidentified male's prints all over the apartment. Hopefully, they will match these," Barnes said, holding up the fingerprint card for 'square-head' that Mathieu had given him.

"I'm sure the burglar was looking for the photos," Mathieu said almost to himself. "And I have a feeling Irene kept them here. This is the only one of her apartments that has any personal items in it. The question is, did the burglar find them, or are they still here?"

"We don't get many murders in Santa Monica, but we do get a fair number of burglaries," Barnes said. "This doesn't look like a successful one to me."

"Why not?" Mathieu asked.

"Because everything looks too hastily searched. In my experience, that means they didn't find what they were looking for."

Mathieu nodded, looking around. "Yeah, I think you might be right."

Barnes stood up. "Here's my card. I'm going back to the station. I'll call you if I get a match on the fingerprints."

"Thanks," Mathieu said. "I really appreciate that you called me, Peter. It's been a big help. I'm going to stay around for a little while and see if I can find anything. If that's okay with you?"

"Sure," Barnes said. "And come back anytime you want to look around."

"Thanks, I probably will."

They shook hands, and Barnes left.

Mathieu stood in the center of the room and asked himself, where would Irene have hidden the photos?

28

Traces of Her

If Mathieu was going to find the photos, he'd have to think like Irene. He knew she'd been careful and deliberate in everything she did. But what had motivated her? Personal riches and revenge seemed too banal for her. He suspected she'd had bigger plans, but what were they?

And what about her character? He didn't think Irene had been a prostitute or blackmailer like Bull did. She hadn't even appeared to be that interested in money. If she'd only wanted wealth and riches, why would she make the least of her apartments her home?

He knew for sure Irene wouldn't have left anything out in the open related to her clients. She would have hidden it and artfully like she had with the keys. With that in mind, he began his search.

Mathieu started with the smallest room, the bathroom, to get it out of the way. All the usual things were there, soap, towels, shampoo, toothpaste, and a toothbrush. The medicine cabinet was empty except for a tin of aspirin. He began to remove the trap from beneath the sink but changed his mind. It wouldn't be practical to hide anything there, so he moved on to the kitchen.

Methodically he removed everything from each shelf and drawer. He put all the contents on the counter and inspected them. Before putting them back, he removed the drawers and checked for false bottoms. He did the same with the shelves. He tapped on the bottom and sides of the kitchen cabinets listening for hollow spots. Satisfied, there was nothing to be found, he put everything back in its place.

On the counter next to the stove was a binder. Handed printed on the cover, it read, "The Professor's Cookbook." Mathieu scanned the pages, each presumably written in the Professor's neat hand. There were recipes for Buckwheat Pancakes, Codfish Patties, Lamb Stew, Cream of Celery Soup, Baked Apples, and Blueberry Pie.

But the most endearing aspect of each recipe were the comments written in the upper right corner. Printed in a delicate feminine script, they said things like "Irene's favorite" or "Please make for Sunday brunch Professor."

Putting the binder aside, Mathieu opened the French doors that led to a small enclosed patio at the front of the unit. With high walls for privacy, the deck was sparsely furnished with an umbrella and lounge chair.

The lounge chair still had a towel laying on it, as if Irene would return any minute. The poignancy of the scene caught Mathieu off guard. The finality of her death came rushing back to him in an instant. He could see her dead body lying on the floor. Overwhelmed, he turned and went back inside to seek refuge from the haunting memory.

He stood in the living room for a moment until his breathing returned to normal. Then he knelt down and methodically started to gather up the papers and books strewn on the floor. He sorted everything into neat little stacks by category. When he finished, he picked up one pile at a time and took it to the piano bench, where he started to look through the items.

The first stack had some nineteenth-century English novels

and a copy of Zane Grey's "Riders of the Purple Sage," which by the look of the pages had been carefully read. A Western seemed a strange choice for Irene, mixed among the Bronte sisters' books. But then Mathieu remembered the central character of the novel was Jane Withersteen. A strong-willed woman fighting for independence in a male-dominated Mormon community in the Old West.

Also mixed amongst the books were several on architecture. Mathieu opened the cover of one and saw a handwritten note, "Irene, some good ideas in this book for our project," signed "The Professor." Mathieu recalled that Patterson had been a Professor of Architecture at USC. The note intrigued him. What was their project?

Mathieu picked up the second pile, which included mail, a phone book, and a flyer for a summer festival on the pier. Mingled in with those were several editions of Time and Cosmopolitan magazine, and of course, the LA Times. A large sheet of paper slipped from the pile and fell to the floor. Mathieu picked it up and unfolded it.

It was an architectural sketch of a building. It was hard to tell what it is was for, perhaps a school or hospital wing. Mathieu looked at the signature on the drawing; it was Professor Patterson's. Was this their project?

Finished looking through the books and papers, Mathieu went upstairs to Irene's office. Scattered on the floor amongst the bills and bank statements were several U.S. Treasury Bond certificates. They were redeemable certificates, and yet the burglar hadn't taken them. Mathieu looked at her recent bank statement, and his mouth fell open.

Irene had over fifty-thousand dollars in her account, all held in Treasury Certificates. Her bank was the same as his, the Farmers and Merchants Bank at Fourth and Main downtown.

Irene's wealth was staggering, but she had chosen to make this tiny apartment her home.

On the floor, he found copies of some letters to her business manager Rose. One letter instructed Rose to rent an apartment in Hollywood. Another one to sell an apartment on California Street in Pasadena.

The typewriter on the desk had a half-finished letter in its carriage. Mathieu sat down to read it.

"Dear Sister Mary Catherine. I'm sorry I haven't written in such a long time. But please know that I love you above all others and think of you every day ..."

The letter abruptly ended there as if Irene wasn't sure what to say next. Standing up, Mathieu scanned the office one last time, then moved on to the bedroom.

Most of Irene's clothes had been thrown on the bed, except for the dresses hanging in the closet. He turned her blouses and slacks upside down, shaking them out, emptying pockets, and searching for anything hidden within. He picked up a sheer pink blouse, catching a whiff of her perfume as he did.

And again, the image of her dead body came flooding back into his mind. He was beginning to understand why so many detectives committed suicide. The job wore on you emotionally if you allowed yourself to get too close to the victim. And yet you had to, in order to do your job.

When he'd finished going through the clothes on the bed, he went over to the closet. He pushed the dresses to one side to look at the closet floor. He spied something there he recognized. He stooped to pick it up. It was a leather climbing harness his father had given him when he was fifteen.

It looked like it had been taken in slightly to fit Irene's waist. But Mathieu was sure it was the same one. There was a white stain on the cinch strap that he remembered. It brought back memories of climbing with his father. Maybe the best memories of his childhood. Back before he discovered his father had lied to him about who his real mother was. Something he still didn't know the answer to.

Discovering the harness, Mathieu assumed his father must have taken Irene climbing. It was yet another mystery about his father's relationship with her. He took the climbing harness with him as he left the room and went downstairs. He would confront his father with it later when the time was right.

Downstairs Mathieu stood in the center of the main room. He turned around slowly, scanning the room as he did. He was looking for places he hadn't checked. He walked to the fireplace and tapped on the mantle to see if it was hollow. It wasn't. But as he looked to his right, he noticed something.

On the bottom shelf of the bookcase next to the fireplace, Mathieu spotted something that looked familiar. Almost hidden from view by the Mission-style chair in front of it was a chest set. The same kind Mathieu had found at the Hotel Figueroa that contained Irene's apartment keys.

He pulled the chess set out of the bookcase, sat down in the chair, and put it on his lap. He removed the drawer, found the release latches, pressed them, and the lid to the hidden compartment popped open. He reached in and removed some cards and letters.

There were several Birthday and Christmas cards from the Professor. One read, "Happy Birthday, Irene, you've given me vitality, hope, and a sense of purpose after my wife died. I'm excited about our project together. Love the Professor, p.s. Look in the fridge. I've baked you something special for your Birthday."

Yet another reference to their project together. But what exactly was it? It wasn't at all clear. Besides the greeting cards, there was a letter from the author Zane Grey. Intrigued, Mathieu opened it and began to read. The letter described the first time he'd ever seen Irene.

"After making my way up the narrow canyon, boulder-hopping, and stream-crossing along the way, I came to the end. There a waterfall, fed by generous spring rains, was in full flow cascading down the sandstone cliff, bouncing and dancing as it hit the canyon floor. It was a magnificent sight but paled to what I saw next. To the right of the waterfall, a beautiful young woman, wearing a safety harness, made her way up the cliff face. Her climbing partner stood below, holding her belay line, looking up at her, and providing gentle instructions. The look on his face was much like the look on mine. One of genuine awe at the sight of this beautiful creature climbing the rock-face above us."

Mathieu wondered if his father was the climbing partner. A few lines later seemed to confirm it.

"I was impressed by the skill and patience of your French climbing partner. I wonder if it would be too forward of me to ask about your relationship with him. Forgive my curiosity, but if, as I surmise, it is only platonic, then please write me back. Zane."

It was the only letter from Zane Grey in the drawer, which probably meant Irene never wrote him back. Did that mean Irene's relationship with his father hadn't been platonic, or did it mean something else?

29

Aunt Bessie

The next day Mathieu got a call from Paul Thornton. He said a neighbor of his recently told him she had seen an expensive car in front of his house the night Irene was shot. He suggested Mathieu talk to her. Mathieu agreed and rode over to Paul's house, where they met up. As they walked down the street to see her, Paul explained about his neighbor.

"We all call her Aunt Bessie," Paul said. "You'll see she's a little eccentric, but everyone loves her. She has trouble sleeping. So, some nights she just sits in the dark on her porch and keeps watch over the neighborhood."

Aunt Bessie was sitting on the porch, waiting for them when they arrived. As soon as Mathieu stepped on the porch and saw her, he wished he hadn't let Paul talk him into this. She was wearing glasses as thick as Coke bottles and had a confused look on her face. Mathieu was sure this was going to be a total waste of time. His impatience showed on his face. But he liked Paul, so he tried to hide it.

It was difficult to guess Aunt Bessie's age. Her stiff movements suggested she was a woman in her late sixties. But her unlined skin had the creamy smoothness of a woman twenty years younger.

Introducing them, Paul said, "Aunt Bessie, this is Officer

Mathieu. He's the policeman I told you about. He's a good man. He believed me and helped clear my name after the beating."

Aunt Bessie looked up at Mathieu through her thick glasses. Her impassive stare suggested she would take her time deciding whether he was a good man or not.

"Mathieu?" she asked, pondering his last name. "Where are your people from?"

"France," he answered.

"They come in through New Orleans?"

"Yes, mam."

She scrutinized Mathieu's face. "You're something besides French, child. You're not as fair-skinned as most Frenchmen. Where are your momma's people from?"

"I don't know," he answered, his impatience growing.

"You don't know where your momma comes from?"

"No, mam. I don't know who my momma is," he said flatly.

"That's sorrowful, child," Aunt Bessie said.

Mathieu shrugged. Uncomfortable talking about his mother with her, he changed the subject, "Can you tell me about the car you saw that night?"

"It was a black, four-and-a-half liter 1929 dual-cowl Bentley Tourer," she said without hesitation.

Surprised by her surety, Mathieu asked, "How can you be so certain?"

"Help me up, child," she said, extending her hand to Mathieu.

He took her hand. She stood up with some difficulty. She straightened her dress and winked at Paul as if sharing a secret. "Come inside. I want to show you something, child," she said to Mathieu.

Bessie led them inside. It was a modest house but immaculately clean. She stood in the front room and raised her hands like a preacher as she pointed toward the walls. They were papered with magazine photos of automobiles.

"This is the Bentley room," she said with obvious pride.

"The dining room is the Packard room, the bedroom is the Cadillac room, and the bathroom the Model T room," she said with a wry smile. "Have a look around."

Mathieu took a quick survey of the tiny house. Each room's walls were covered with photos of a different automobile brand clipped from magazines and newspapers. Mathieu returned to the main room and smiled. "Very impressive," he said.

"My late husband was a mechanic," Bessie said by way of explanation. "I used to help him in the shop. I love the smell of motor oil as much as I love the smell of Gumbo cooking on the stove. This is my shrine to him."

Bessie made her way to the couch and sat down. She motioned to two chairs in front of it for Mathieu and Paul to sit on. Mathieu was still skeptical but decided to give it a try since he was here.

"Can you tell me about that night?" he asked. "Tell me everything you heard or saw. The smallest detail might help."

Bessie began her story. "It was warm that night, and I don't sleep well in the heat. So, I came out on the porch and sat on the swing. It was quiet and peaceful with a bit of a breeze. I was rocking gently on the swing. I started to get a little drowsy when I heard the throaty purr of a Bentley. I opened my eyes just in time to see a polished black Bentley float by. Lordy, what a sight! We don't get many Bentleys on this street, child," she laughed.

"Why are you so sure it was a Bentley?" Mathieu asked, still not convinced.

"See those photos on the wall behind you?" Bessie said, pointing to the front wall.

Turning around, Mathieu said, "Yes, mam."

"Go take a look."

Mathieu did as she requested, studying the photos that seemed to be the newest because of the paper's sheen.

"Look at the shape of the front fender as it curves over the front wheel then angles down to the running board. And see where the spare is mounted just in front of the front door?"

"Yes, mam, I see it."

"That's what the car looked like. That's the distinctive front fender line of the four-and-a-half liter. There's nothing else like it. It's like a long teardrop. Vanden Plas is the coachbuilder for Bentley's luxury cars. The body is made mostly out of cloth and wood to save weight. But the engine is from their racing cars. So, the power to weight ratio is outstanding. That car is as fast as the wind!"

"It is a handsome car," Mathieu conceded.

"There's one other thing that convinced me it was the four-and-a-half liter," she said.

"What's that?" he asked.

"See the photos of the front and rear of the car right next to the side view?"

"Yes, mam."

"Do you see how all four wheels toe-in at the bottom?"

"Yes."

"That's another clue that it's a Bentley four-and-a-half liter."

Impressed by Aunt Bessie's knowledge of cars, Mathieu returned to his seat and asked, "What happened next?"

"The Bentley glided by and stopped three houses up in front of Mr. Paul's. The driver turned the lights off but left the engine running. Then the right rear passenger door opened, and someone got out and walked towards Mr. Paul's porch."

"Could you see what they looked like?"

"No," Aunt Bessie said, shaking her head. "There was a bit

of a moon that night, but the car door was blocking the light. Everything was in the shadows."

"What about when they walked up to the porch. Could you see them then?"

"No. I could only see the car parked on the street and the back door open. The trees and bushes of the house next to Mr. Paul's blocked the rest of my view."

"Then what happened?"

"Like I said, I heard them walk toward Mr. Paul's house. They had a real determined stride like they were angry or something. Then I heard them knocking on the door. Real loud like."

"Could you tell if it was a man or woman from the sound of their walk?"

"No, I could only tell they were in a hurry."

"Did they call out when they knocked on the door?"

"No," Bessie said.

Mathieu nodded, encouraging her to go on with her story.

"A minute later, I heard the front door open, then a scream and two gunshots. It sounded like a woman's voice who screamed. I was terrified but decided it was safest if I just stayed still. Nobody can see a black woman sitting on a pitch-black porch at night," she said.

"And then?"

"It was deadly quiet for a few minutes. Then I heard someone slam the front door and leave the house. This time it sounded like they were running. I heard a car door shut, then the Bentley pulled out, turned around, and came back this way with the lights off. I crouched down a little. The driver gunned it, and the car came speeding past my house and out of sight in a couple of seconds."

"Did you get a look at the passenger or the driver's face as they went by?"

"No," she said, shaking her head. "It was all a blur. They were going too fast."

"Are you the one that called the police?"

"Yes, after I calmed down. My heart was racing, and my knees were shaking. But then I realized that car wasn't coming back. So, I went inside and called the police, then came back out on the porch. About twenty minutes later, I see you pull up on your motorcycle. It looked like you were riding a 1929 Henderson KJ Streamline. Am I right?" she asked.

"Yes, mam," Mathieu said, smiling.

"I've heard they can do a hundred miles per hour. Is that true?"

"Yes, it is."

"You ever go that fast on one?"

"Yes, mam," Mathieu said, smiling. "Just recently, when I rode out to Palm Springs for this case."

"That's amazing for a forty horsepower straight-four," she said in admiration.

"After you got off your motorcycle, I saw you walk toward the house. I heard you knock, then call out 'Police!' Then I heard you open the door. You came back maybe fifteen minutes later, went to your motorcycle, and called in on your radio. A half-hour later, a Buick Phaeton pulled up, and two men got out. One was tall, the other kind of stocky. I could see them because they got something out of the trunk before going up to the house. Later on, some more police cars and an ambulance came. I'd gone inside by then and was watching from the side window. I didn't get much sleep that night."

"Did anyone from the police question you that night or later on?"

Bessie shook her head. "Nope. And I'm not sure I would have

answered the door if they had. We Negroes tend to avoid the police. The beating Mr. Paul took a few days later is why."

Mathieu nodded. "I appreciate that you offered to talk to me today. What you've told me has given me a lot to go on." He stood up to go. "I won't take up any more of your time. Thank you again," he said with a newfound respect for her.

Aunt Bessie looked up at Mathieu and said, "You come back anytime with Mr. Paul, and I'll make both of you some of my Gumbo. You two both need some fattening up."

Mathieu and Paul left and walked back to his house, where Mathieu thanked Paul and returned to the station.

Thanks to Aunt Bessie, Mathieu had a clear idea of what happened that night and some tangible clues about the killer. Even with her thick glasses, she had seen and heard everything. She knew the make and model of every car and motorcycle that pulled up to Paul's house that night. Mathieu had learned a lesson. His first impression of her had been totally wrong.

Soon after he arrived back at headquarters, Mathieu got a call from Detective Barnes. "We checked the prints we found at Horatio Court against the fingerprint card you gave me; they don't match 'square-heads' prints," Barnes said.

"That's disappointing," Mathieu said.

"Yeah, but it gets more interesting."

"How so?"

"Besides the unknown male prints, they also discovered an unknown woman's prints all over the house."

"Not Irene's?"

"No."

"So, the person that killed Professor Patterson could be a man or a woman?"

"Yeah, that's what the lab boys think now. The unknown woman has large hands. That's why they were confused at first."

30

The Finely Tailored Mr. Fallon

Aunt Bessie's eyewitness testimony was invaluable to Mathieu. Now he knew what had happened the night of Irene's murder before he arrived on the scene. He knew the make and model of the car used and that two people were involved, a driver and a shooter. And given that the car was a Bentley, he knew one other thing, the killer was wealthy.

He decided it was time to interview the last three suspects on his list, Harrison, Eckert, and Fallon, the wealthiest of them all. He chose to start with Fallon because he'd already searched the El Royale apartment that Irene had received from him.

Mathieu called the number that Francine had given him. It turned out to be Fallon's office in Beverly Hills. He identified himself to the secretary and asked to be put through. When she asked why he said he was investigating the death of one of Mr. Fallon's friends. Expecting to be stonewalled, he was surprised when Fallon picked up.

"Fredrick Fallon here," he said. "Who am I speaking to?"

"My name is Officer Mathieu with the LAPD."

"My secretary said you are investigating the death of a friend of mine. Who is that?" Fallon asked.

"Irene Simpson."

There was silence on the line for a minute. "Ah, I see," Fallon said. "What do you need from me, Officer?"

"I need to meet with you to discuss your relationship with Miss Simpson," Mathieu said.

Clearing his throat, Fallon said, "I hardly knew her."

With an edge to his voice Mathieu said, "Mr. Fallon, I'm going to save us both a lot of time. I already know about the expensive apartments you gave Miss Simpson."

"I see," Fallon said, stalling for time. "In that case, I'd suggest we meet at the Beverly Hills Hotel this afternoon around three," he said. "Will that work for you, Officer?"

"That will be fine," Mathieu said. "Where in the hotel?"

"In the main lobby, I'll be sitting at one of the tables off to the side," he said. "The lobby is quiet in the late afternoon."

Mathieu got to the Beverly Hills Hotel promptly at three. The hotel stood on a knoll, just north of Sunset Boulevard, affording a clear view of the city below. The long T-shaped mission-style building dominated the landscape with its red tile roof and bell towers. It was the hotel that created a city. Just as all roads had led to Rome in the Roman Empire, all roads led to the Beverly Hills Hotel, where five streets intersected in front of it.

Mathieu rode up the curved entranceway lined with palm trees at the corner of Sunset and Crescent. He parked his motorcycle behind a line of expensive vehicles and walked toward the portico, where he entered the lobby. The lobby, with its sturdy columns and comfortable furniture, was stately but not overwhelming. Mathieu walked down the wide carpeted main aisle toward the front desk.

Off to his left, he noticed a finely tailored man sitting alone near a low round table. The man caught Mathieu's eye, raised his hand as if signaling for a drink, and waved him over. As Mathieu approached him, the man stood up and extended his hand.

"Fredrick Fallon," he said. "I presume you're Officer Mathieu. I wasn't expecting someone so young."

Mathieu ignored the comment and shook his hand. Fallon motioned to the chairs surrounding the small table, and they both sat down.

"I don't suppose I can offer you a drink, Officer," Fallon asked.

"No, thank you," Mathieu said, maintaining a professional manner. "Thanks for agreeing to see me so quickly,"

Mathieu took a pen and notepad from his satchel while he observed Fallon. There was something about wealth that made people look more attractive than they really were. That certainly was true of Fredrick Fallon as he sat there in his expensive suit exuding a confident carefree attitude. He was tall, thin, and impeccably groomed, without a crease to be found anywhere in his attire.

With no preamble, Mathieu asked, "What was your relationship with Irene Simpson?"

"I was her client," Fallon responded with a casual air.

"And as her client, what did she do for you?"

"She made me feel alive."

"By doing what exactly?"

"That's none of your business."

"It might be given that this is a murder investigation." Mathieu countered.

Startled, Fallon said, "I thought she died in a car crash."

"No, she was murdered," Mathieu said with little emotion.

"Am I suspect?" Fallon asked, revealing a small crack in his composure.

"You're a person of interest," Mathieu responded, making no attempt to ease his discomfort.

"How was she killed?" Fallon asked.

"She was shot twice in the chest," Mathieu said.

"Oh my god," Fallon said, rubbing his hand over his face. "Did she suffer?"

"No, she died instantly," Mathieu said.

Fallon sighed and said to himself, "There's some comfort in that, I suppose."

"I'd like to ask you again, Mr. Fallon, what did Miss Simpson do for you?"

"I wasn't being facetious when I said Irene made me feel alive," Fallon said.

"In what way?" Mathieu asked.

Fallon looked directly at Mathieu. "One of the worst things that can happen to you in life is getting everything you want at a young age, Officer. It saps you of all ambition, all yearning. You start to wonder if that's all there is in life. There's a feeling of profound emptiness. Can you understand what I'm saying?"

Mathieu nodded, "I think so."

"Through shrewd investment in oil exploration, I became wealthy before I was thirty," Fallon said. "And then I married an older woman even richer than I was. It was a marriage born out of the consolidation of wealth, not love. Look at all the opulence around us. Beverly Hills used to be a lima bean field. You couldn't give land away in this area before this hotel was built; it was in the middle of nowhere. But money attracts money, like flies to shit. As soon as this luxury hotel was built, the rich flocked here like sheep to buy land and build their expensive homes, so they could see and be seen."

"From beanfield to wealthy playground in less than ten years," Fallon scoffed. "But being wealthy can be an empty life. I started taking mistresses. With my money, I can get almost any woman to sleep with me. And yet, I was still unhappy. Until I met Irene."

"Did you meet her at Chandler's office?" Mathieu asked.

"Yes, like her other 'clients,' I assume," Fallon said.

"You knew there were others?" Mathieu asked. "You weren't jealous?"

Fallon shook his head. "No, it made it even more of a challenge. The best thing about Irene was I knew I could never have her. Sure, I could see her naked body, but I could never touch her or sleep with her. I could never possess her or take her away with me to a desert island. She was unattainable. She gave me something to strive for that I knew I'd couldn't have. And it wasn't just her beauty. She was sweet and smart and sexy yet kind. I'd never met anyone like her; I needed her to go on living. Why would I kill her?"

"Peer pressure?" Mathieu suggested.

"Maybe a reason for my wife to kill her but not for me," Fallon said. "My wife cares about that sort of thing, keeping up appearances in society and such. I could care less."

"Where were you the night of her death?"

"Probably out on the Ritz. I go there a lot with my chauffeur," Fallon said as he brushed some invisible lint off his trousers. Then with a perplexed look on his face, he said, "Wait … what night was it?"

"May 7."

"No. I was here at the hotel that night attending a party," Fallon said.

"Can you give me the name of someone who can verify that?"

"The hotel manager can," Fallon said. "He helped me up to my room. I got so drunk I couldn't drive the two miles to my home that night."

"I thought you had a chauffeur."

"It was his birthday. He had the night off. That's why I remember it."

Mathieu unnerved Fallon with his next question. "Do you mind if I take your fingerprints?"

"Here in the lobby?" he asked in a shocked manner that belied his casualness.

"No, I can send someone to your office in the next few days," Mathieu said. "It will be handled privately. It's just for elimination purposes."

Fallon seemed relieved by the offer and agreed.

"Is your wife aware of your affairs?" Mathieu asked.

"Yes."

"How does she feel about them?"

"She tolerates them as long as they're discreet and don't cause a scandal. My wife's major interest in me is that I look good in a suit as her escort," Fallon said in a self-mocking way.

"Was she aware of your relationship with Irene?"

"Yes."

Fallon hesitated for a moment, then asked, "During your investigation, have you found any photos Irene took?"

"Not yet," Mathieu said, implying he would. "Did Irene ever try to blackmail you with the photos?"

Fallon shook his head. "No, that wasn't her style. She told me she took them only to ensure that none of her clients would ever reveal their relationship with her."

"So, she told you about the photos?" Mathieu asked.

"Yes, after she took them and had them safely hidden away. The photos wouldn't have been very effective insurance if she hadn't told her clients about them, would they?"

Mathieu nodded. "I don't suppose you know where they are?"

"Not a clue," Fallon said, laughing. "Though I'm sure my wife would love to know."

As if it was preplanned, a few minutes later, an exquisitely dressed woman approached the table.

Ignoring Mathieu, she said to Fallon, "Fredrick, we have to leave now for the premier at the Biltmore."

"Certainly, dear," he said in a solicitous tone. "Do you have a check on you, dear? I need to cash one at the front desk to have some money for this evening."

His wife sighed, sat down, and took a checkbook and a pen from her purse. She started to sign the check, but her pen didn't work.

"You can use mine if you'd like, Mrs. Fallon," Mathieu said, reaching across the table and offering her his pen.

"Thank you, Officer," she said with barely concealed disdain as she took it.

Mrs. Fallon signed the check and handed the pen back to Mathieu. As she did, Mathieu noticed she had rather large hands for a woman. Both Fallon and his wife stood. Fallon nodded goodbye to Mathieu, and the couple left. After they'd gone, Mathieu wrapped the pen in a napkin and put it in his satchel, then he got up and left the hotel.

Once outside, Mathieu walked back along the line of cars to his motorcycle. He passed a broad-chested chauffeur leaning against a vehicle smoking a cigarette. The man looked familiar. When Mathieu got to his motorbike, he took the Leica out of his saddlebag. As the man turned his head, Mathieu discreetly snapped a photo of him and the car. The chauffeur looked like "square-head," the man who had attacked Hop Li.

A bellhop called out to the chauffeur, telling him Mrs. Fallon wanted the car brought up. The chauffeur dropped his cigarette on the driveway, crushing it with his massive foot, then got into the vehicle and drove to the portico entrance just as the Fallons exited the hotel. The bellman opened the rear door for them, they got in, and the vehicle drove off.

It was a black four-and-a-half liter 1929 dual-cowl Bentley Tourer. It looked exactly like the photos on Aunt Bessie's living room wall.

31

A Feeling of Being Followed

Ever since Mathieu interviewed Fallon, he had the feeling he was being followed. But when he'd look around, he wouldn't see anyone tailing him. In the end, Mathieu dismissed it as paranoia. He shouldn't have.

While waiting for the Santa Monica police to compare Mrs. Fallon's prints on the pen with those found at the crime scene, Mathieu stopped by Hop Li's shop. He showed him the photo of Mrs. Fallon's chauffeur. Hop Li confirmed that it was "square-head," the man who had beaten him.

Next, Mathieu decided to visit the apartments in Pasadena that Thaddeus Harrison had given Irene. He knew Harrison and Chandler were close business partners, so he'd been putting it off, but he couldn't any longer. All Irene's "patrons" had to be checked out regardless of their relationship with Chandler. Mathieu rode up to Pasadena and stopped in front of the Castle Green apartments on South Raymond Street.

In scope and grandeur, the six-story Moorish-Victorian apartment building was an imposing structure. Built of brick, stone, and steel, with fanciful turrets, it once had provided luxurious accommodations for the vacationing Eastern elite. The grounds took up an entire square block between Fair Oaks and South Raymond Avenue, with Central Park lying to the south.

At one time, Castle Green had been part of an even grander complex of three buildings called the Hotel Green. Back then, it had been a playground for the rich wishing to escape the harsh winters back east. A bridge once connected it to the main hotel building on the east side of Raymond. The bridge had been a popular viewing spot for the Rose Parade as it proceeded under it down Raymond Avenue. But in 1924, Castle Green was turned into private apartments, and the rest of the buildings were sold off.

Now the bridge terminated at Raymond Avenue, where Mathieu parked his motorcycle. He walked underneath the bridge to the entrance. While Castle Green looked like a Moorish Castle on the outside, inside, it looked more like a Victorian mansion, with its wood-paneled walls, heavy drapes, and luxurious carpeting.

Mathieu walked through the main drawing room to the central stairwell. Once there, he climbed the white marble steps to the fifth floor. Irene's apartment was located in one of the 'turrets' on the building's southeast side.

As soon as he entered the apartment, he knew something was wrong. The smell of disinfectant was so strong he was sure it had been wiped clean. Mathieu's guess was Harrison had employed someone to remove all evidence of his presence from the apartment after Irene's death. In the process, they had removed all traces of Irene's presence also. What was left were spotlessly clean, mostly empty rooms, and little else.

The main room of the turret-shaped apartment had windows facing south and east. Like the building's exterior, the room was shaped like a semi-circle. The circular shape and low ceilings made it feel claustrophobic. Lace curtains adorned the oak-frame windows. Below the east window sat a small couch. Mathieu assumed this is where Irene had "entertained." He found an inlay in the wainscoting above the south-facing window that had probably held a camera. But it was empty now.

In the bedroom, as with the other apartments, there was no bed. Nor were there any clothes or personal items in the closets or dressers. Similarly, there were no personal effects in the bathroom. Mathieu didn't linger long in the apartment. It was clear there was nothing to be found. He locked it and left.

Next, Mathieu headed to the Brookmore Apartments on North Marengo, which she'd also received from Harrison. The Brookmore was a handsome four-story brick building that sat in the middle of the block. The brick exterior was modest in contrast to the fine detailing of the woodwork in the main lobby.

Irene's apartment was on the top floor. And as at the Castle Green, the smell of disinfectant was overwhelming when Mathieu unlocked the door. So much so that he immediately opened a window to let in some fresh air. The apartment wasn't as opulent as some of Irene's other properties. At best, it could be described as cozy, or it would have felt that way with some personal items in it. But like the Castle Green, it had been stripped bare. Mathieu dutifully checked all the rooms but didn't find anything of interest. He left discouraged that he hadn't learned anything new. But on his way downstairs, he changed his mind.

Perhaps Harrison had made a mistake by cleaning the apartments so thoroughly. None of the other suspects had gone to such lengths to remove any trace of their presence in Irene's apartments. It didn't mean he was the killer, of course, but Harrison had moved closer to the top of the list with his attempt to eliminate evidence.

Hungry and in need of some time to think, Mathieu rode to an all-night diner on the western edge of Colorado Boulevard and got something to eat. When he came out, it was dark. To brighten his mood, he decided to take Arroyo Boulevard south toward downtown. It would be a chance to have a little fun, riding fast down the winding lane as it hugged the edge of the Arroyo Seco streambed.

He drove a short way on Orange Grove Boulevard, then turned left onto a small lane that wound its way under the Colorado Street bridge and connected with Arroyo Boulevard.

The narrow twisting road was dark and quiet. Mathieu opened up the throttle, leaning into the curves as he headed south. He wasn't thinking about the case or anything else, just enjoying the feeling of riding. Because of the roar of the motorcycle engine, he didn't hear a car approach him from behind with its lights off.

As Mathieu rounded a curve just before the San Rafael bridge, he heard an engine rev, then saw a flash of lights behind him. An instant later, the car rammed into him, sending his motorcycle into a slide. He tried to turn into it, but it was too late. The motorcycle skidded off the road and flipped, tossing Mathieu over the handlebars. He tumbled down the steep ravine, hit his head on a rock, and blacked out.

He could feel he was lying on his back, but everything was black, and his body ached all over. He tried to move but couldn't. Maybe he was dead, he thought. While considering that possibility, Mathieu heard someone hovering above him. As they came closer to his face, he could smell their sweet, warm breath.

Then he felt a soft kiss on his lips. He struggled to open his eyes, but they seemed glued shut. Slowly he opened them, and an out-of-focus vision of a woman's face came into view. As his eyes adjusted to the brightness, he could see her more clearly. It wasn't an angel; it was better. It was Nurse Claudine.

Smiling in relief that Mathieu was finally conscious, Claudine said, "You didn't have to almost get yourself killed to see me. You could have just asked me out."

"Where am I?"

"Frenchtown Hospital."

"How long have I been here?"

"Two days," she said. "Your boss has been here every day, and so has your father. And Harry Chandler's secretary Francine came every day also."

"Is anything broken?" Mathieu asked, fearful of the answer that might come.

"No, but you're all scratched up, and you hit your head pretty hard."

Relieved by the news, Mathieu asked, "Do you kiss all of your patients to wake them up?"

"Yes, it's the latest therapy for head injuries," she said, playing along.

"Is it effective?"

"Yes, it seems to work every time," she said, kissing him again.

Mathieu was released two days later after tests cleared him of any permanent damage. In Bull's office, Mathieu told him what had happened the night of the accident and ended by saying, "I'm pretty sure it was a police car that pushed me off the road?"

"Why do you think that?" Bull asked, alarmed.

"I could see spotlights on both sides of the car in my rearview mirrors just before they rammed me," Mathieu said.

Bull was silent for a long time. Mathieu watched him consider the options.

"What are you thinking?" Mathieu asked.

"That perhaps the Pasadena police are protecting one of their own," Bull said. "It wouldn't be the first time the rich and powerful used the police to do their dirty work."

Bull didn't like anyone harming his men, but what he said next surprised Mathieu. "The next time you go up there, take one of the Buick Phaetons. From now on, you're a detective, not a motorcycle cop."

Mathieu was speechless, unsure what to say, then finally eked out, "Thank you, sir."

"Don't thank me, kid. If someone's trying to kill you, then you must be onto something. By the way, you're going to need a suit if you're going to be a detective," he said as he handed him his tailor's business card.

32

Interview at the Courthouse

Mathieu endured some playful ribbing from the other detectives when he showed up wearing his suit for the first time. The suit would take some time to get used to. He felt like he was dressed for a wedding, not work. Bull asked him to write a report on what had happened when he'd been forced off the road. The phone rang while he was still working on it.

"Officer Mathieu," he started to say, then corrected himself and said, "Detective Mathieu LAPD."

"Well, that was a quick promotion, Mathieu," came Barnes' reply over the phone. "Congratulations!"

"Thanks, Peter, came as a surprise to me also," Mathieu said. "It seems all it took was for me to get run off the road and end up in the hospital."

"What do you mean?"

Mathieu filled Barnes in on what had happened in Pasadena and the aftermath.

"Are you okay?" Barnes asked.

"Yeah, I'm fine, thanks," Mathieu said. "Why are you calling?"

"I have some good news," Barnes said. "We got a match on the prints. The woman's prints we found at Irene's apartment at

Horatio Court match the prints on the pen you gave me that Mrs. Fallon used at the Beverly Hills Hotel."

"You're kidding me," Mathieu said. "What are you going to do next?"

"I have an interview set up with Mrs. Fallon at the Santa Barbara County Courthouse on Wednesday," Barnes said. "I arranged it with a friend of mine who's the Sheriff of Santa Barbara County. Want to come along?"

"Of course," Mathieu said. "Can you arrange with your friend to make another arrest that day?"

"Sure, who?" Barnes asked, confused.

"Mrs. Fallon's chauffeur," Mathieu answered.

"On what charge?" Barnes asked.

"Assault ... I took a photo of him at the Beverly Hills Hotel the day I interviewed Mrs. Fallon's husband. I showed it to Hop Li. He positively identified him as the man who beat him up."

"Looks like it's going to be a productive day then."

"I hope so," Mathieu said. "Do you want me to pick you up?"

"I don't want to ride on the back of your motorcycle Mathieu," Barnes responded good-naturedly.

"Don't worry. Bull doesn't want me riding motorcycles for a while. I'll pick you up in a detective's car. Will eight o'clock work?"

"Sure," Barnes said. "That should give us plenty of time. See you Wednesday morning."

On Wednesday, Mathieu and Barnes arrived at the Santa Barbara Courthouse on Anacapa Street just after eleven. Getting out of the car after the long drive, Barnes stretched his long body, then gazed up at the magnificently designed building. The courthouse and its outdoor grounds took up an entire city block. It had just re-opened.

The old courthouse and most of downtown Santa Barbara had been destroyed in the 1925 earthquake. After the tragedy, the city fathers decided to rebuild the city in the Spanish Colonial Revival-style. The courthouse and all the commercial buildings along State Street had been rebuilt since then. Barnes had to admit they'd done an incredible job.

So did Mathieu as he admired the stunning building. "The last time I was up here, I was only seventeen," Mathieu said. "My father brought me up here to help search for people trapped in the rubble. It's hard to believe it's the same city."

"Yeah," Barnes said, shaking his head. "I was up here also helping to keep order and arrest looters. Santa Barbara didn't have enough policemen to handle the problem by themselves."

Barnes looked around and spotted his friend, Jim Walters, waiting for them under the two-story-high arched entrance near the bell tower. In his early fifties, Walters was tall and thin with a full head of dark hair that was beginning to gray at the temples. Mathieu thought he had the kind of face that would look good on an election poster. Walters waved to them, and they walked over to meet him.

"Hi, Jim," Barnes said, extending his hand. "How long has it been?"

"Four years, Peter."

"Has it been that long?" Barnes asked. "Are these your new digs?"

"Yeah, can you believe this place?" Walters said with visible pride.

"Jim, this is Detective Mathieu from the LAPD. He's the young man I told you about who's investigating the murder of Irene Simpson in Los Angeles. Theo, this is Jim Walters, the Sheriff of Santa Barbara County."

"It's a pleasure to meet you, Sheriff," Mathieu said. "Thanks for your help in arranging this."

"You're welcome, Detective," Walters said as he took a moment to appraise Mathieu. "You're pretty young to be a detective … you must be doing something right."

Mathieu shrugged. "It's a long story, Sheriff. But thanks for the compliment."

Barnes asked, "Are we all set for Mrs. Fallon to arrive, Jim?"

"Yes, she'll be here at noon with her lawyer. I have an interview room reserved on the second floor."

Turning to Mathieu, Walters said, "We'll wait until Mrs. Fallon is inside, then I'll have a couple of my deputies arrest her chauffeur."

"Understood. Thank you, sir," Mathieu said, nodding his head.

"Do you have all the paperwork, Detective?" Walters asked him.

"Yes, Sheriff," Mathieu said as he handed Walters a folder with the arrest warrant. "Inside, there's a fingerprint card from the Chinatown crime scene, the witness statement, and a police sketch. We should be able to tell pretty quickly if we have the right man or not."

Walters opened the folder and scanned the contents, silently nodding to himself that everything looked in order. Then turning to Barnes, he asked, "And you, Peter, are we covered for the burglary and murder in Santa Monica?"

"Yeah, Jim, here's a copy of my report, plus fingerprints from the crime scene and Mrs. Fallon's prints that Detective Mathieu obtained. We should recheck her prints to be sure. But I feel confident she was at the crime scene based on what we have here."

Walters smiled. "If nothing else, it will intimidate her when we take her prints."

"Yeah, it usually does with civilians," Barnes said.

"Let's go inside then," Walters said. "No use standing out here like we're Mrs. Fallon's greeting party. From what I hear, she's pretty full of herself as it is."

Walter's led the way as they walked under the massive stone archway to the courtyard's sunken gardens. They stopped to admire the manicured lawn, then backtracked under the arch to the main entrance. The interior of the courthouse had the same understated elegance as the exterior. Their footsteps echoed off the polished Spanish floor tiles as they walked three abreast along the main corridor under magnificent white-stucco arches. At the end of the hallway, they took the stairs up to the second floor.

Mathieu looked around in awe. "This makes the LAPD headquarters look like a warehouse," he said.

"We have a few job openings if you're interested, Detective," Walters said.

Mathieu smiled but didn't respond. Despite its beauty, after two days in Santa Barbara, he knew he'd be bored to death.

Once settled in the interview room, Barnes, Walters, and Mathieu sat on one side of a long heavy oak table. The other side, they left open for Mrs. Fallon and her lawyer. Promptly at noon, a sheriff's deputy escorted them into the room, followed by a court stenographer who took her place along the back wall.

Mrs. Fallon's lawyer pulled a chair out for her, and she sat down without a word of acknowledgment to the others in the room. Her lawyer, impeccably dressed in a light-gray suit, was a poster child for the WASP elite. The only thing missing to define his social status was his Yale Rowing sweater. Tall and lean with blue-eyes and short blond hair, he reached across the table to shake hands. "Steven Jefferies, Yale Law '25," he said, quickly establishing his bona-fides.

When everyone was settled and in place, Sheriff Walters

began the interview. He glanced at the clock, then nodded to the court stenographer and said, "For the record, it is 12:15 p.m. Wednesday, July 7, 1929. This is a formal interview at the Santa Barbara County Courthouse regarding a burglary and murder committed in Santa Monica, California, on June 21, 1929. Present are Mrs. Edith Fallon along with her Attorney Steven Jefferies. Also present are Detective Peter Barnes of the Santa Monica PD, Detective Theo Mathieu of the LAPD, and myself Jim Walters, Sheriff of Santa Barbara County."

The solemn manner in which Sheriff Walters began the proceedings had a chilling effect on the room. No one made a sound. The air seemed to crackle with tension.

"Before we begin questioning," Walters said. "We will need to take your fingerprints, Mrs. Fallon."

Jeffries immediately objected. "We're told this was to be an interview, not an arrest."

"That's correct, Counselor," Walters said. "However, we need to take Mrs. Fallon's fingerprints to rule out any possible involvement on her part. If we're able to do that, then no further questioning will be necessary, and we can adjourn."

Jeffries nodded his assent but remained wary.

Walters instructed the deputy present to take Mrs. Fallon's fingerprints. The deputy brought a pad, roller, and fingerprint card to the table. Mrs. Fallon was impassive as she slowly removed her white gloves. The deputy then inked and rolled each of her fingers and transferred the images to the fingerprint card.

When he finished, he gave Mrs. Fallon a moist towel to wipe the ink off her fingers. Then he removed his equipment and went back to his desk to compare the fingerprints to those from the crime scene. A few minutes later, he looked up and nodded at Sheriff Walters that the prints were a match.

"My deputy informs me that Mrs. Fallon's prints match those

found at the crime scene, so we will continue with the interview," Walters said. "I will now turn the proceedings over to Detective Barnes of the Santa Monica PD to begin questioning."

Nodding to Walters, Detective Barnes began in a matter of fact tone.

"Mrs. Fallon, during the investigation of a burglary and the murder of Professor Kevin Patterson on June 21 at the Santa Monica apartment of Miss Irene Simpson at 140 Hollister Avenue, we discovered your fingerprints. Can you explain why they were there and what occasioned you to be at Miss Simpson's apartment?" Barnes asked.

Mrs. Fallon cupped her hand over her mouth and whispered to her attorney. He nodded in the affirmative that she had to answer the question.

Mrs. Fallon cleared her throat and began in a confident, unruffled voice. "I paid Miss Simpson a social call."

"Are you aware that Miss Simpson is dead? That she was murdered on May 7 of this year?"

"Yes."

"When did you pay her this social call?"

"Before her death, obviously," she said with some haughtiness.

"When exactly?"

Mrs. Fallon shrugged. "Sometime in February, I believe."

"And what was the purpose of your visit to Miss Simpson?"

"It was personal."

Barnes responded to her stonewalling in a firm but polite tone. "Mrs. Fallon, I'd like to remind you that this is a murder investigation. Whether it was personal or not is irrelevant. I repeat, what was the purpose of your visit to Miss Simpson?"

"We discussed a charity event the LA Times was putting on," she answered. "Harry Chandler, Miss Simpson's boss, had reached out to my husband for a donation. Miss Simpson invited me to her apartment to go over the details."

"So, if I understand you correctly, you met with Miss Simpson at her apartment in February of this year to discuss a charity event. Is that correct?"

"Yes," Mrs. Fallon replied.

"Had you ever been to her apartment in Santa Monica before that?"

"No."

"Have you ever been to her apartment in Santa Monica since that meeting in February?"

"No."

Sliding a piece of paper across the table to Mrs. Fallon, Barnes said, "This is a floorplan of Miss Simpson's apartment at Horatio Court in Santa Monica. As you can see, there are two diagrams, one for the downstairs and one for the upstairs. I'd like you to take a moment and mark with a pencil all of the rooms you were in during your visit last February."

"That was a long time ago," Mrs. Fallon objected.

"To the best of your recollection," Barnes said. "Take your time."

"Is this really necessary, Detective?" her lawyer asked.

"Yes, is it, Counselor."

Mathieu watched the back and forth between Barnes and Mrs. Fallon like an observant student. Even though he'd conducted many interviews during the investigation, this was his first in a formal setting. The setting itself gave it its own gravitas, its own code of behavior. Barnes had maintained a calm, polite manner, even in the face of obvious lies from Mrs. Fallon. So far, he hadn't challenged any of them. He'd let them roll off of him as if they were true.

But Mathieu sensed Barnes was setting a trap for her. By not challenging her lies initially, she might grow overconfident and let her guard down. Mathieu was anxious to see how it played out.

When Mrs. Fallon finished marking the diagrams, she showed it to her lawyer, then passed it back to Barnes.

"Thank you, Mrs. Fallon," Barnes said. "For the record, you've marked the living room, kitchen, and bathroom, which are all downstairs, but no other rooms upstairs or down. Is that correct?"

Mrs. Fallon nodded.

"I'm sorry, Mrs. Fallon, we need a verbal response for the stenographer."

"Yes, that's correct," she said.

"Where did you sit in the living room?"

"I sat in a Mission-style chair near the fireplace."

"When you were in the living room, did you have occasion to look through the bookcases, or the record albums or play the piano?"

"Certainly not," she said, annoyed by the question.

"Where did Miss Simpson sit in the living room when you visited her?"

"On the window seat across from the chair."

"Thank you. And what did you do in the kitchen?"

"I helped Miss Simpson carry some teacups into the living room."

"That's all. You didn't get anything out of the refrigerator, or drawers or cabinets in the kitchen?"

"Of course not," she replied.

Barnes took a moment to look through his folder. Finding what he was looking for, he slid two documents across to Mrs. Fallon and her lawyer.

"For the record, these documents are marked 'Exhibit A-1 and

A-2.' As you can see, Mrs. Fallon, 'Exhibit A-1' is identical to the diagrams you just marked," Barnes said.

Mrs. Fallon didn't respond, but her icy glare masked a fear that was starting to grow inside her. She had expected the police to be fools, but they weren't.

Continuing, Barnes said, "The red marks on the diagram are every room where your fingerprints were found in Miss Simpson's apartment. Downstairs your prints were found in the living room, the kitchen, the bathroom, and the outside patio. Upstairs your prints were found in the office and main bedroom."

Pointing to the second diagram, Barnes said, 'Exhibit A-2' is a list of every surface in every room where your fingerprints were found. In the living room, these include the chairs, the piano and piano bench, the bookcases, the window seat storage area, and almost every book in the room. In the kitchen, they include the refrigerator, the stove, and every drawer and cabinet. On the patio, fresh prints of yours were found on the deck chair. In the upstairs office, they were found on the desk, typewriter, file cabinets, and file folders. In the main bedroom, your prints were found on the closet, dresser, and dresser drawers. They were also found on the headboard and several pieces of jewelry."

Jeffries said, "I object to this line of questioning. As you know, Detective, there is no accurate way to tell the exact age of a fingerprint."

"Exact age, no," Barnes conceded. "However, the approximate age can be estimated by various factors, including the presence of sweat marks and the easy adherence of fingerprint powder to the prints. All of these factors were noted in the examiner's analysis of Mrs. Fallon's prints. The examiner's technical analysis leads to the conclusion they were recent prints. Also, common sense tells us that most of these prints, supposedly left in February, would not have survived until now because Miss Simpson's housekeeper came every week until her death in May. And finally, the heavy rains in April would have wiped away Mrs. Fallon's prints on the patio."

Jeffries had no good rejoinder but lodged an objection anyway. "Nevertheless, you cannot prove the fingerprints were left the night Professor Patterson was killed."

"That's why we need Mrs. Fallon's assistance in clearing up the matter."

Barnes was silent for a moment as he waited for Mrs. Fallon to respond. When she didn't, he asked, "Mrs. Fallon, how do you account for the discrepancy between the rooms you indicated and the ones where your prints were found?"

"I don't have to," she said with pent up anger and petulance.

"True, you don't have to. But it would be in your best interest if you did Mrs. Fallon," Barnes said in a calm voice. "As I believe your lawyer would advise you."

She looked at her lawyer, who reluctantly nodded his head in agreement. No amount of Yale Law School education was going to get her out of this. She was trapped, and she knew it. But she remained silent, trying to buy time to think up an answer.

Trying a different approach, Barnes asked, "Let me ask you this, Mrs. Fallon, what were you looking for in Miss Simpson's apartment?"

Mrs. Fallon hesitated for a moment, then, trying to appease him with a lie, said, "Some letters."

"What kind of letters?"

"Love letters between my husband and Miss Simpson."

"And did you find them?"

"No."

"When were you looking for these letters, Mrs. Fallon?" Barnes asked. "And don't tell me in February because we now know that's impossible."

Before she could answer, a deputy came into the room and handed a note to Sheriff Walters. He looked it over then passed it to Barnes.

Barnes studied the note, whispered something to Mathieu, and nodded for him to take over.

"Mrs. Fallon, I'm Detective Mathieu from the LAPD. We met briefly when I interviewed your husband recently at the Beverly Hills Hotel. I'm here investigating the murder of Irene Simpson and the beating of a shop owner, Hop Li, in Chinatown. I've just been informed that your chauffeur, Gerard Clocker, has been arrested on the latter charges. His fingerprints were found at the Chinatown crime scene, and his photo has been positively identified by the victim. Mr. Clocker has pleaded guilty to those charges and agreed to cooperate in this investigation in order to get a reduced sentence. He has provided us with new details on the break-in at Miss Simpson's apartment. I'll turn the questioning on that matter back to Detective Barnes."

Without preamble, Barnes asked, "I'll ask you again, Mrs. Fallon, when did you search Miss Simpson's apartment?"

Looking defeated, Mrs. Fallon finally decided to cooperate. In a less haughty voice, she began. "I broke into Miss Simpson's apartment two nights before you say Professor Patterson was killed. My chauffeur kept guard outside while I searched the apartment. I was looking for love letters between my husband and Miss Simpson. I was trying to avoid a scandal should they be discovered. That's all. I never saw Professor Patterson, and I certainly didn't kill him. I didn't find the letters, and we left without incident. That's all I have to say."

Except for lying about the love letters, Barnes was inclined to believe her. And the chauffeur's testimony tended to collaborate the rest of her story. "Thank you for clearing that up, Mrs. Fallon," he said. "Are you prepared to sign a statement to that effect?"

"Yes," she said with great reluctance.

"Then I'll turn the proceedings over to Sheriff Walters to proceed with the booking process," Barnes said.

Sheriff Walters looked directly at Mrs. Fallon and said, "After you sign your statement, you will be taken to the county jail where you will be booked on one felony count of burglary. I will recommend you be immediately released on bail if there are no objections from Detective Barnes."

"I have no objections to that, Sheriff," Barnes said.

"Thank you, Peter," Walters said.

Getting one last dig in, Walters turned to Jeffries and said, "Counselor, seeing as Mrs. Fallon's chauffeur has been arrested, I assume you can give Mrs. Fallon a ride home from the county jail."

"Yes, I can, Sheriff," Jeffries said, now reduced in status to her chauffeur.

Mathieu spoke up, "If I may, Sheriff, I'd like to ask two more questions before we adjourn."

"Go ahead, Detective," Walters said.

"Mrs. Fallon, where were you the night Miss Simpson was killed?"

Prepared for the question, she said, "At a fundraiser in Montecito ... for this courthouse as it turns out."

"And can someone verify that?"

"The Chairman of the fundraiser can."

"Thank you," Mathieu said. "One last question. Do you own a 1929 Bentley Tourer?"

"I don't, but my husband does," she said with a smirk. "It's his favorite car."

33

Thaddeus Harrison

During the long drive back to Los Angeles, Mathieu and Barnes had plenty of time to discuss what happened at the courthouse.

"How do you feel about today?" Mathieu asked Barnes.

"Disappointed. Mrs. Fallon won't spend a day in jail," Barnes replied, shaking his head in frustration.

"But her chauffeur will," Mathieu said. "And I'm glad he confessed because Hop Li would have never testified against him in court."

Barnes looked at Mathieu and smiled. "You got lucky then."

"We both did," Mathieu said. "His confession helped get Mrs. Fallon to talk. At least you can eliminate her as a suspect in Patterson's death."

"True … but we both still have killers to catch," Barnes said.

Mathieu glanced over at Barnes. "Have you ever wondered if our killers might be connected?"

"What do you mean?"

"Well," Mathieu said. "Both 'square-head' and 'scar-face' showed up at Hop Li's on the same night. Maybe, they showed up at Horatio Court within a day or two of each other also."

"It's possible," Barnes said, warming to the idea.

"And if that's the case, maybe 'scar-face' killed Patterson," Mathieu said.

"If he did, I think it was probably an accident," Barnes replied.

"That's what I think also," Mathieu said. "Remember he called an ambulance for Hop Li. He could have left him to bleed to death. Maybe Patterson surprised 'scar-face,' and he pushed him too hard, and Patterson hit his head on the piano."

Mathieu fell silent for a minute as he considered a new possibility.

Barnes looked over at him and asked, "What are you thinking?"

"What if 'scar-face' is a veteran," Mathieu said.

"Why do you think that?" Barnes asked.

"Because Hop Li said the scar on his face looked like a battle wound. Maybe he was wounded in WWI. Doesn't the Army fingerprint every soldier to help identify them if they're killed in action?" Mathieu asked.

"Yes."

"Then I wonder if the VA might have his prints? We could ask them to compare the prints you found at Horatio Court to any WWI vets that have jagged scars on their left cheek."

"That's a long shot, and the VA is hard to deal with," Barnes said.

"Yeah, but it's worth a try, isn't it?"

"Maybe," Barnes said, shrugging his shoulders. "I have a friend that works at the VA Hospital on Sawtelle. I could ask him to check the prints."

"You have a lot of friends, Peter," Mathieu said with a smile.

"Helps in our line of work."

Changing the subject, Barnes asked, "Did you believe Mrs. Fallon's story about the love letters?"

"Not for a second," Mathieu said. "She wouldn't have gone to all that trouble for some letters. It doesn't make any sense. Besides, we already know her chauffeur was looking for photos at Hop Li's. Did you believe her?"

"No, I was just playing dumb. It's a good tactic sometimes."

"By the way, I learned a lot from watching you today."

"Thanks," Barnes said, looking over at Mathieu. "What did you think about the remark she made at the end about the Bentley Tourer. Do you think she was trying to throw her husband under the bus?"

"Probably," Mathieu said, laughing. "I think she's so pissed off that she got caught cleaning up his mess that she wants him to suffer too. But Fallon's alibi for the night that Irene was killed checks out. I talked to the manager of the Beverly Hills Hotel and the concierge on duty that night. Both of them verified his story. Fallon was so drunk he could barely stand up. The manager and concierge had to help him up to his room. Fallon puked all over the hallway before they even got there. They opened the door for him, got him a towel, and Fallon fell face first on the bed fully clothed. In the morning, the maid found him in the same position. He hadn't moved."

Back at headquarters the next day, Mathieu decided to call Thaddeus Harrison. He'd been uneasy about something ever since the motorcycle accident. Was it just a coincidence it occurred the same day he'd searched the apartments in Pasadena that Harrison had given Irene? It was time to talk to the man himself.

He dialed the number for Harrison's office. When the secretary answered, he said, "This is Detective Mathieu with the LAPD. I'd like to make an appointment to speak with Mr. Harrison."

"What is it concerning?" she asked.

"Irene Simpson," he responded.

"One moment, please," she said while she put him on hold.

She came back a few minutes later and said, "I'm sorry, Detective, Mr. Harrison doesn't know an Irene Simpson."

Irritated, Mathieu said, "Tell Mr. Harrison it's regarding the apartments he gave Miss Simpson."

Mathieu listed each one, its address, and the date of transfer. "If Mr. Harrison would prefer, we can conduct the interview at LAPD Headquarters. I'll send some officers over to escort him here."

There was another shorter delay. When the secretary came back, she was more solicitous, "Mr. Harrison can see you this afternoon at one if that is alright with you, Detective."

"That will be fine."

"Do you know our address?"

"Yes," Mathieu said, hanging up.

Harrison's office was in the Braly Block, Los Angeles' first skyscraper. The twelve-story building used to be the tallest in downtown but was dwarfed now by City Hall. Constructed in 1904, the neo-classical structure had been ahead of its time with its fireproof steel frame and built-in wiring. The Braly was located in a section of Spring Street known as the "Wall Street of the West" for its concentration of banks and financial institutions.

Mathieu left headquarters and walked south on Main Street. He was more anxious about this interview than the others he'd done. Harrison was a heavyweight by reputation. A ruthless but successful businessman with enormous wealth.

As Mathieu walked along, he thought about how to handle Harrison. He'd learned a lot from watching Barnes conduct his interview in Santa Barbara. It tracked well with what he'd once learned from a friend of his father, who was a trial lawyer. As a teenager, Mathieu used to sit in the courtroom and watch him question witnesses. It made a lasting impression on him. He almost became a lawyer because of it before choosing police work instead. The lawyer had discussed his technique with the young Mathieu.

"Always remain calm and polite even in the face of a hostile witness. Keep an even tone in your voice and a blank expression on your face. Project a gravitas and respect for the legal institution you represent. Never respond to a witnesses' question. If the witness gives an incomplete or evasive answer, ask it again in a slightly different way."

Mathieu thought about all this as he neared Harrison's office at Fourth and Spring. Unlike the lawyer, Mathieu didn't suffer fools easily. He found it hard to control his anger in the face of lies and evasions. He knew it would take all his patience to remain calm and polite.

A bus honked at Mathieu as he started to cross Fourth Street, bringing him back to the present. After crossing, he entered the Braly building and consulted the directory. Harrison's company occupied the top two floors. Harrison's office itself took up the entire twelfth floor. Mathieu took the elevator there and exited into an alcove where a lone secretary sat. He recognized her voice from the phone call. She was as icy in person as she had been on the phone.

Mathieu had arrived a few minutes early, but she stood as he came in and said, "Please follow me, Detective."

The secretary led him toward two massive oak doors that were easily twelve feet high. She opened them, then stood aside and motioned for Mathieu to enter. After he did, she shut the doors behind him. The sound of their closing echoed throughout the massive room. Mathieu was momentarily stunned but tried not to show it.

The office was meant to intimidate. Except for four interior support pillars, it was entirely open. At the far end of the room, Harrison sat alone at a huge desk, silhouetted by five arched windows behind him.

To get to Harrison, Mathieu had to walk the entire length of the room. It felt like a perp walk. The only sound he heard as he approached Harrison was his own footsteps on the polished wood floor. The sound stopped when Mathieu stood in front of Harrison's desk. Harrison didn't look up at him. He made Mathieu wait, pretending to be engrossed in some papers on his desk.

Mathieu understood the game; he grabbed a nearby chair and dragged it across the floor to the front of Harrison's desk. He did it in such a way as to make a grating sound on the floor, which forced Harrison to look up at him.

Without waiting for a greeting, Mathieu sat down in front of him and said, "I'm Detective Mathieu from the LAPD. I'm investigating the murder of Irene Simpson. I'm here to ask you some questions about your relationship with Miss Simpson."

Harrison stared impassively at Mathieu behind his thick glasses. He was in his late fifties, thin and wiry with a stern face. He put his papers down and looked at Mathieu for a long moment without saying anything, then asked, "How can I help you, Detective?"

Mathieu responded, "I'm interviewing everyone who gave apartments and property to Miss Simpson. You're one of many who did. Can you tell me what the nature of your relationship was with Miss Simpson?"

If Harrison was bothered by being labeled one of many, he didn't show it. Without blinking, he said, "I was trying to recruit Miss Simpson to help with California's Eugenics movement. Do you know anything about the Human Betterment Foundation, Detective?"

"A little, but I'd welcome any information you'd like to share," Mathieu said in a calm voice. He had expected Harrison to stonewall him, so the fact that he wanted to talk was encouraging.

"It was founded last year in Pasadena," Harrison said. "I'm one of the charter members, along with distinguished scientists such as Lewis Terman from Stanford, who created the IQ test. Nobel prize-winning physicist Robert Millikan from Caltech, and David Starr Jordan chancellor of Stanford University."

Harrison allowed a moment for the cavalcade of distinguished names to make their impression, then added. "Your godfather Harry Chandler is also a member."

By dropping Chandler's name, Harrison was indicating he'd done his homework. He was also implying that he might have some leverage over Mathieu.

Playing along, Mathieu asked, "What's your organization's charter?"

"To foster and aid constructive educational forces for the protection and betterment of the human family in body, mind, character, and citizenship," Harrison said as if reciting from a catechism.

"By doing what exactly?" Mathieu asked.

"Educating the populace about eugenics and advocating for the use of sterilization. As you may know, California is one of only three states that allows forced sterilization of prisoners and the feeble-minded. We're at the forefront of this progressive movement. We've performed more forced sterilizations than any other state," he said. "Some people simply shouldn't be allowed to breed," he added.

"And who decides who gets sterilized? Your little group?" Mathieu asked evenly.

"Of course not," Harrison said. "The latest scientific methods are used to evaluate those who should be sterilized. Including standardized IQ tests."

At the mention of IQ tests, Mathieu audibly scoffed. A professor he had admired in college told him IQ tests had been specifically designed to skew the results in favor of white people.

"I can see you don't approve," Harrison said.

"I don't approve of men acting like gods."

"Man has been doing selective breeding for thousands of years, Detective. We've selectively bred crops, cattle, horses, dogs, you name it. Why not humans if it betters the lot?"

Mathieu could see he was being sucked into a debate on eugenics instead of Irene's murder. Catching himself, he asked, "What specifically did you want Miss Simpson to do for your foundation?"

"Several things," Harrison said. "First, I wanted to feature her and her photo in an article about the ideal modern woman. The article would highlight how proper breeding could improve the quality of future generations in this country."

"A master race?"

"If you like."

"You said several things. What else?"

"We prepared a poster using her image."

"May I see it?"

"Certainly, I have it right here."

Mathieu stood while Harrison grabbed the poster from behind his desk and handed it to him.

The black and white poster was set in a dense pine forest. It was backlit, giving the image a dream-like quality. On the right side of the poster sat a beautiful young woman next to a tree. It was Irene. She was dressed in a simple peasant's dress wearing a white cloth headdress, her lush blonde hair cascading down past her shoulders. In her lap was an apron full of ripe fruit. She had a serene but blank look on her face as she gazed out toward the camera.

On the left side of the poster stood a strong, virile young man. He was cradling a wicker basket with his left arm, and with his outstretched right hand, he was dropping seeds on the ground. A banner in bold font ran across the top of the poster reading, "Only Healthy Seed Must Be Sown!"

The message was obvious, too obvious. But it was saved from triteness by Irene's incredible beauty and the enigmatic look on her face, and the fact she wasn't looking at the man at all. Her expression wasn't one of joy or longing but rather of reluctant acceptance. Mathieu couldn't take his eyes off her. It was one of the few photos he'd seen of her alive. Her expression perplexed him. It was hard to get a sense of how she'd felt about being involved in this. He was soon to find out.

"Did you ever use this poster?" Mathieu asked.

"No," Harrison said.

"Why not?"

"Because Irene changed her mind."

"Why?"

"That was my mistake," Harrison said. "I gave her some literature to read about eugenics after the photo session. She called me the next day and said she was withdrawing from the project and didn't want to be involved. She said I had misled her. And I probably had. But I knew she would be perfect for the project. When she called, she reminded me that she hadn't signed a release. She threatened to sue me if I used her image or name in any way. I had this copy printed for myself, but it's never been used publicly. However, the session wasn't a total loss. I had another poster made featuring the young man from the photo."

Harrison grabbed the second poster from behind his desk and handed it to Mathieu.

The large placard looked more like an Army recruitment poster. The young man's pose from the original photo had been turned into an illustration in garish shades of orange, gold, and red. The same banner ran across the top. But across the bottom, it read, "Check the seeds of hereditary disease and unfitness by Eugenics." It was pedestrian in execution and lacked the impact of the original one with Irene.

Mathieu returned to his seat and continued the questioning, this time with a harder edge to his voice.

"Why didn't you take the apartments back?"

"I was hoping she might change her mind," Harrison said. "I don't give up easily."

"Were you hoping for anything else?"

"Such as?"

"You've been referring to selective breeding, perhaps that."

"Don't be insulting, Detective."

"Didn't you find Miss Simpson attractive?"

"Of course, I did."

"Were you hoping for a romantic relationship with her?"

Now defensive, Harrison didn't answer.

"Let me ask you this, Mr. Harrison, where were you the night Miss Simpson was murdered?"

"On the Ritz."

"Can anyone verify that?"

"The management of the Ritz can. They keep a detailed passenger log every evening."

"Anyone else?"

"My chauffeur was with me on the Ritz also."

"And how can I contact him?"

"Call my home and ask for Mr. Stewart. My secretary will give you the number when you leave."

"Stewart with a T," Mathieu asked?

"Yes."

"What time did you leave the Ritz?"

"Around one in the morning."

"And what happened after you got to shore?"

"My chauffeur drove me home. I had a little nightcap, then went to bed."

"Thank you. One more thing. What kind of automobiles do you own?"

Harrison didn't show any surprise at being asked and listed them with evident pride.

"Any others?"

"Yes, I forgot a 1929 Bentley Tourer," he said. "Any other questions, Detective?"

"Not at the moment. Thank you for your time, Mr. Harrison," Mathieu said as he stood to leave. He could see Harrison visibly relax, thinking the interview was over.

He turned to go, then turned back and asked. "One more question, Mr. Harrison. What would you say if I told you some photos of you have turned up that indicate a far more intimate relationship with Miss Simpson than you've admitted to?"

Mathieu knew he was taking a risk, but he wanted to see how Harrison would react. He got what he wanted; the question caught him off-guard. Harrison froze for a moment. Then like any good poker player, he composed himself before responding. "That sounds more like a hypothetical question than a real one, Detective."

Mathieu smiled back at him.

"The next time I see your father, I'm going to tell him you weren't very cordial during your visit."

"I doubt if that will come as a big surprise to him, Mr. Harrison. Good day, sir."

When Mathieu was gone, Harrison pressed the intercom and said to his secretary, "Get Harry Chandler on the phone."

34

Pure Bred

When one of their own was threatened, news spread through the LA elite like a brushfire driven by Santa Ana winds. By the time Mathieu got back to headquarters, there were two messages on his desk. One from Jeremy Eckert's office requesting an interview and a second from Francine asking Mathieu to call her back. Fortunately, none from his father, who knew from bitter experience, not to interfere in his son's life.

Mathieu called Francine back first, but before she could say anything, he said, "Let me guess, Thaddeus Harrison just called Mr. Chandler."

Sheepishly Francine replied, "Yes, he did, Theo. Mr. Chandler would like you to back off your investigation of Mr. Harrison. He said Harrison is one of his most trusted business partners, and he's sure he would have never hurt Irene."

Mathieu held his temper. He knew Francine was caught in the middle. "Please tell Mr. Chandler I can't do that," he said, then hung up.

After hanging up, Mathieu pounded on his desk and muttered, "God damn it!" The outburst startled the other detectives in the room, who looked over at him. He sat there silently for a minute, then stormed out of the office.

He walked to his bank and retrieved Chandler's reward money from his safe deposit box. Next, he went to the teller window and withdrew enough money from his savings to cover what he'd given to Hop Li. Then he wrote a hasty note, stuffed it in the envelope with the cash, and left the bank. He walked with mounting anger to the LA Times building, not seeing or hearing anything along the way. He took the lift up to Chandler's office and went straight to Francine's desk.

Surprised to see him, Francine asked, "Theo, what are you doing here?"

Handing her the envelope, he said, "Please count the money, Francine, and give me a receipt."

She looked up at him with sadness. "You're not angry at me, are you, Theo?"

"Of course not, you're just caught in the middle," he said. "We both are."

Francine did as he requested and handed him the receipt.

"Thanks," he said. "Please give the envelope to Mr. Chandler. Tell him the note inside will explain everything." Seeing the distress on her face, Mathieu added, "It's okay, Francine, we'll have tea together soon at the Biltmore. Don't worry." Then without another word, he left.

Upset, Francine took the envelope to Chandler's office, put it on his desk, and said, "This is from Theo, Mr. Chandler. He's returned your reward money. There's a note inside he'd like you to read."

"Thank you, Francine, you may go," he said, dismissing her.

After she left, Chandler stared at the envelope for a moment before opening it.

The first paragraph of the note was curt and formal in tone. "Dear Mr. Chandler, enclosed is the reward money you provided to aid in finding the person or persons responsible for Miss Irene

Simpson's death. I replaced the money I used to encourage a witness to come forward and testify from my own funds. Given your recent message, it is no longer appropriate to have this reward money in my possession."

Chandler read on with foreboding. "As a sworn officer of the law, my duty is to pursue the truth to the best of my ability without outside influence or prejudice. A policeman has a sacred duty to seek justice for the victim of a crime, especially in a murder case, and to bring those responsible to justice."

Signed, "Detective Theo Mathieu LAPD."

Chandler sat back in his chair and let the note fall from his hand. He'd miscalculated; he should have known better. Theo had always been headstrong and honest to a fault. What had he expected him to do? Give in or give up? Now he had driven a wedge between himself and Theo, who he loved like a son. Chandler shook his head in disgust at himself. He wasn't sure what to do next. Money and power couldn't fix this.

Mathieu had calmed down by the time he got back to headquarters. He was glad he'd given the reward money back. He was no longer beholding to Chandler. He felt good about the break but also knew he was on his own now. He was unlikely to get any help in the future from Chandler on the case. But he was alright with that. He'd broken off relations with his father and survived. He could do it with his godfather also.

Next, he returned the call from Jeremy Eckert.

"Mr. Eckert's office," came the seductive sound of a young woman's voice as the phone was answered. "How may I help you?"

"This is Detective Mathieu from the LAPD. Someone from your office left me a message that Mr. Eckert would like to set up an interview regarding Irene Simpson."

"Oh yes, Detective, that was me who left the message," came the breathless reply. "You sound pretty young to be a detective."

Ignoring her comment, Mathieu asked, "When can Mr. Eckert meet with me?"

"Mr. Eckert would like to meet you at his ranch in Ojai tomorrow afternoon. Would that be alright with you?" she asked.

Yet another long drive, Mathieu thought to himself. But it would be foolish not to take Eckert up on his offer. "That'll be fine," he said. "What are the directions to the ranch?" Eckert's secretary provided them as Mathieu wrote them down in his notebook.

The next day, as Mathieu approached Ojai, he turned onto Del Norte Lane, just after the Maricopa Highway cutoff, and headed north. He drove for about a mile on the rutted tree-lined road until he got to a sign that read, "Private Keep Out." Ignoring the warning, he proceeded past the open gate where the lane narrowed, and the tree cover thickened. Off to the left, surrounded by mature oak trees, he spotted the "ranch house." Mathieu laughed to himself, like Harrison's office, it was designed to intimidate.

Set on over twenty acres, it was what they called a "gentleman's ranch." The dominant feature of the two-story white brick structure was a Spanish-style watchtower that connected two of its three buildings. The cluster of buildings enclosed a courtyard and fountain at the front of the property.

Mathieu parked his car in the shade of an oak tree near the entrance. Getting out, he could hear the sound of a horse being exercised behind the house. Walking across the courtyard, he gazed up at the beautiful covered balcony that ran the building's length. When Mathieu got to the watchtower, he walked through an open passageway that led to the stables. As he came out in back, he heard a man's voice yell, "Detective, over here!

He followed the sound of the voice to the paddock area, where he spotted a man dressed in jeans and a white shirt sitting astride a magnificent thoroughbred. The man waved him over. As Mathieu got close to the enclosure, the man dismounted, tied his horse to a post, and vaulted over the fence.

The man extended his hand and said, "Jeremy Eckert, thanks for coming up to the ranch, Detective." His grip was firm and meant to send a message that he was in charge.

Eckert was a little taller than Mathieu, with a lean, strong frame. He was tan and fit with a full head of dark brown hair streaked with grey. He looked to be in his early fifties but had the animation of someone much younger.

"You must be tired after your long drive, Detective. Let's go inside and have some iced tea. It will be easier to talk there."

Without waiting for a reply, Eckert strode toward the house. Mathieu followed a few steps behind, noticing that Eckert had a slight limp.

Once inside, they settled in the great room, beside a massive unlit fireplace. The walls were thick here, providing cooling relief from the stifling sun and heat outside. Ojai Valley was romanticized as an idyllic paradise, but it was a steaming cauldron this time of year. The temperature was often twenty degrees hotter than in Ventura, which was only twenty miles away on the coast.

Mathieu asked Eckert about the limp he'd noticed. "It's nothing," Eckert said, trying to dismiss it. "Just a riding accident."

Changing subjects, Eckert said, "Yesterday, I heard that you're investigating Irene Simpson's death. I figured you'd get around to me sooner or later, so I thought I'd contact you."

"Why did you think that?"

"Because I gave her an expensive apartment," Eckert said.

Eckert seemed almost too anxious to answer questions about Irene. And Mathieu wanted to learn some things about him first. So, he made him wait by asking, "What business are you in?"

"Stock market investing," he said with pride. "I'm known as the 'West Coast Wizard of Wall Street' for my stock-picking prowess."

Unimpressed, Mathieu nodded, hoping Eckert would continue.

"In addition, I run a hedge fund in favors."

Mathieu looked quizzical.

"I buy, sell and trade favors among the California elite," he said unashamedly. "I'm kind of a broker for the trading of favors. There's no one in power that doesn't owe me a favor, Detective, including your godfather."

Eckert said all this as if it was the most natural thing in the world.

"You looked surprised, Detective. The rich are some of the most corrupt people on earth. Almost all of them have made their fortunes by screwing someone else over. Your godfather and his partners made a killing screwing people over with his San Fernando Valley land deal. Wealth confers de facto respectability only after the fact. It's kind of like putting makeup on a pig. So, I'm not ashamed of what I do. It's all very Darwinian, kill, or be killed."

"Why are you telling me all this?" Mathieu asked.

Dropping the mask, Eckert said, "Because I want to be eliminated from your investigation into Miss Simpson's death. It's bad for business."

"Do you have an alibi for the night Miss Simpson was killed?"

"Yes, I was hosting a charity event here."

"And I assume you can provide me with the names of those who can corroborate that."

"Of course, some very influential names."

Mathieu nodded in acknowledgment. "However, even if you were here, it doesn't mean you couldn't have been involved in her death."

"What are you implying?"

"I'm not implying anything," Mathieu said. "But you just told me you trade in favors. What kind of favor would you have to trade for murder? Hypothetically I mean."

"Much more than I would have to trade to get you kicked off the force, Detective."

Not taking the bait, Mathieu asked, "What was your interest in Miss Simpson?"

"I gave her a luxury apartment and promised her many more if she would have my child," Eckert said. "She refused, so I looked elsewhere."

"You wanted to marry her?"

"No, I just wanted her to have my child," Eckert said. "Look, I believe in the same things the eugenics folks do regarding improving the race through genetics. But while they focus their efforts on forced sterilization. I focus mine on selective breeding. My goal is to sire two hundred children from the most beautiful and healthy women in California. I'm well on my way to achieving that. And I encourage my rich friends to do the same."

"By doing what?" Mathieu asked, attempting to hide his disgust.

"By hosting the charity event, I mentioned earlier. It's called the 'Festival of Virgins', and it's held here annually at the ranch in May," Eckert said. "It's an invitation-only event for select members of the Sundowners Club."

"I'm not sure I understand," Mathieu said.

"It's pretty simple. We recruit the most beautiful and intelligent young women from across the state. They're offered a stipend for life if they agree to have a child with one of our members. Our members are selected based on wealth, health, and good genetics."

Mathieu didn't know how to respond to what he'd just heard.

"Does that shock you?" Eckert asked. "It's all very legal. All of the girls are at least eighteen. They're not paid to sleep with our members. They do that willingly. They're paid when they bear their child."

"How does this festival work exactly?"

"Each year, we select twelve young women, one for every month in the year. They come here to the ranch. And on the night of the event, the field behind the house is decorated and lit with candles. The young women parade around a Maypole dressed in gossamer white gowns with a nametag for their month. Twelve of our members stand in a ring around the field with nametags for their number. Each member selects his top three candidates. Each woman does the same. If there's a match, then they are free to mate here or elsewhere. If a woman doesn't choose anyone or if there's no match, she's free to enjoy the party and leave. A legal contract is drawn up, ensuring that the woman will be paid her annual stipend when she has a member's child."

Mathieu looked skeptical.

"It's all very legal, Detective. No one is being forced to do anything they don't want to do."

Recovering his composure somewhat, Mathieu asked, "When can you provide me with the list of people who can corroborate you were here the night of Miss Simpson's death?"

"My secretary will get that to you by Monday," Eckert replied.

"Then that's all I need for now. Thank you for your time, Mr. Eckert," Mathieu said as he rose to leave.

"I can cause you a lot of trouble, Detective," Eckert said with menace in his voice.

"You've made that abundantly clear, Mr. Eckert. Let's hope

for both of our sakes that won't be necessary," Mathieu said as he turned and left.

Back in the car, Mathieu retraced his route and headed south toward Ventura and the coast. He was so disturbed by Eckert's depravity he couldn't get away from Ojai fast enough. When he got to the mouth of the Ventura River, he found a place to park near the beach. He sprinted across the sand to the ocean, where he removed his clothes and dove naked into the water, hoping to cleanse his mind and body from what he'd just learned.

35

Climbing with Pierre

Mathieu felt adrift. It was hard for him to shake the moral cynicism of Eckert and Harrison. He sought some kind of normalcy, even if that normalcy was fraught with its own problems.

It was time to talk to his father. He'd put it off too long. Whatever his conflicts were with him, he knew him to be essentially a decent man. He knew his father didn't kill Irene, but he still needed to understand his relationship with her.

Maybe his father could provide some clues to unlock the mystery of Irene and her death. But it would be a minefield. He and his father could barely go ten minutes without disagreeing about something meaningful, trivial, or petty.

He called his father the day after he returned from Ojai. He invited him to go climbing in Millard Canyon. Pierre hadn't heard from his son for over a year, when he relented and visited on Christmas Eve. Pierre was surprised by Theo's call but didn't say so. They agreed to meet at the trailhead at noon the following Monday.

Mathieu rode his motorbike to the trailhead, arriving before his father did. He was leaning against a tree, checking his climbing gear when Pierre drove up and parked. Pierre grabbed his rucksack from the back seat and walked over to him.

"It's good to see you, Theo," Pierre said, eyeing his son. "You've put on some muscle."

Theo hesitated, carefully parsing the comment, looking for the smallest slight or criticism. Deciding this one was neutral, he replied, "Helps in my line of work."

It was all the response he could muster.

They stood there awkwardly, each silently appraising the other. His father looked fit but had aged a little since Mathieu had seen him last. Or maybe it was just the harsh sun. In either case, it caused Mathieu a pang of guilt.

They had never been good at small talk with each other. The slightest miscue could set off an argument. Pierre thought about asking his son about the case but decided against it. If Theo wanted to talk about it, he'd bring it up. Chandler had already called him upset after falling out with his son. He had asked for advice on how to fix it. Pierre told him he was the last person in the world to give advice on that subject.

Finally breaking the silence, Pierre said, "Looks like a good day for climbing, son. Shall we head up to the falls?"

Pierre led as they boulder and stream hopped their way up the canyon. Mathieu felt like he was ten years old again, following along in his wake. His father had always displayed an athletic grace in the way he navigated the wilderness. He was sure-footed with perfect balance as he jumped from rock to rock or crossed a narrow log. And he was fearless. He'd lost none of that skill. Mathieu looked on in reluctant admiration as he tried to keep up. After about twenty minutes, they arrived at the base of the falls. There was still a good flow of water because of the heavy spring rains.

Grabbing the safety rope, Mathieu backtracked about fifteen yards down the canyon. There he scampered up a side trail that took him to the top of the cliff. He hiked along the cliff-edge to the falls, where he threaded the safety rope through two permanent bolts attached to the cliff's edge. He let one end of the rope drop down to the canyon bottom, where his father took hold of it. Then he threw the other end of the line with the safety clip attached down.

His father yelled, "I've got it. Come on down."

Mathieu retraced his steps along the cliff-edge. When he arrived at the canyon floor, his father already had his harness on and was clipped in. He handed Mathieu the safety line and said, "I'll go up first."

There was a deep cut in the canyon wall where the waterfall cascaded down the cliff-face. At its crest, a huge chockstone was stuck in the mouth of the falls. It probably hadn't budged in eons, but it would have crushed anyone standing below it if it did. Which was where Mathieu stood now, holding the safety line.

The best route up the rock face was just to the right of the falls. For the first thirty feet of the ascent, it was heavily eroded with plenty of good hand and footholds. Mathieu watched as his father skillfully made his way up the cliff. Two-thirds of the way up, he stopped and leaned back in the harness. Here the cliff-face jutted out over six feet, making continuing on difficult. The rock face was smooth here; hand and footholds were few and far between.

As Pierre pondered the route up, Mathieu yelled at him, "I found my old climbing harness in Irene Simpson's apartment. Did you take her climbing here?"

Disappointed, Pierre looked down at his son and said, "Yes, I did. So what?"

"Were you having an affair with her?"

Holding his temper, Pierre said, "That's not a question worth answering, Theo."

"So, you're not going to tell me?"

"No, I'm not. It's none of your business."

"Why did you give her property in the Hollywood Hills?"

Surprised his son knew about the gift, Pierre said, "Is that why you invited me here? To interrogate me? I hear you're a good cop, Theo, but things aren't always what they seem."

"Then educate me, tell me how things are."

"What are you going to do, Theo? Let me fall if I don't answer your questions?"

As if to test him, Pierre pushed away from the rock face until he was suspended in mid-air, his whole weight hanging in the harness. Mathieu held the line taut. Pierre didn't drop an inch.

"Well, at least we've got that settled ... you're not going to let me die."

Pierre swung himself back to the rock face and continued to try to climb over the overhang. He tried several more times, then gave up and rappelled down to the canyon floor.

In silence, Pierre unhooked the safety line and handed it to his son. Mathieu hooked in, and without saying a word, started up the cliff-face. Three-quarters of the way up, on the most dangerous part of the ascent, Mathieu unhooked from the safety line and stuffed it into a crevice. The rope went slack in his father's hand.

"What are you doing, Theo?"

Mathieu didn't answer but continued climbing this time without the safety rope.

Alarmed, Pierre shouted, "Stop this craziness, Theo!"

Mathieu slipped as a foothold gave way, but he caught himself just in time.

"Please stop this, son," Pierre pleaded.

"Then tell me why you gave her the property," Mathieu yelled back.

"Alright ... alright!" Pierre said, relenting, eager now to do anything to stop his son from this reckless gambit. "Hook in and come down, and I'll tell you what you want to know."

Mathieu grabbed the line, hooked in, and rappelled down the cliff-face in three bounding hops.

Now that his son was safe, Pierre vacillated between anger and relief. "That was a stupid stunt, Theo. You could have been killed. Why do you always have to be so pigheaded?"

Mathieu walked away, putting distance between himself and his father, to avoid a physical confrontation. Without looking at his father, he removed his climbing harness, stuffed it in his rucksack, and sat down on a rock facing the falls.

Staring at the ground, Mathieu said, "You promised to tell me the story."

Pierre moved closer to him and leaned against a boulder. They stayed that way in silence for several minutes, both coming down from the adrenaline rush of what had just happened.

Pierre took a deep breath and began his story. "Years ago, before you were born, Irene's mother worked at the restaurant for a little while. It was a few years after she had given Irene up for adoption. She had finally run away from her abusive husband. She was afraid he'd find her, and she needed a job. So, I gave her a job in the kitchen where she'd be out of sight."

"What was her name?" Mathieu asked.

"Julia … Julia Simpson," Pierre answered with a faraway look as if he was trying to picture her in his mind.

"What was she like?"

"She was sweet but troubled, and like her daughter stunning. She was from Columbia in Central America. She had light brown hair and brown eyes."

"But Irene was blond with blue eyes."

"She must have gotten that from her father, who was a fair-skinned Scot, but a brute. Julia had been through a lot with her husband. She felt guilty about giving up Irene for adoption, but she had no choice. She told me the story about her husband's sexual abuse of Irene."

"How long did she work at the restaurant?"

"A little over a year until her husband caught up to her again. One day she told me she had to leave. So, I gave her some money to start a new life."

"Where did she go?"

"I don't know. I think San Francisco. I put her in touch with a lawyer there who could help her change her name."

"Did you ever hear from her again?"

"No," Pierre said, shaking his head.

"Years later, I went to Chandler's office one day, and I spotted Irene. He had just hired her. I noticed the resemblance to her mother immediately. I got to know her, told her what little I knew about her mother. It was obvious she was scarred by her father's sexual abuse, so I tried to help her any way I could. She told me she wanted to be financially independent. That she had a dream of helping young girls that had been in her situation. I had an extra lot in the Hollywood Hills that I didn't need. I'd already made plenty of money off that deal, so I gave it to her. I think I did it just as much for her mother as I did for Irene. That's the whole story, Theo."

Mathieu had a feeling there was more to it, but this was the wrong time to push his father. He could tell Irene's death had affected him, so he let it go. Mathieu kicked the dirt in front of him. His father's seeming openness made him feel guilty about scaring him with his stupid stunt on the cliff. He also felt guilty about suspecting him of having had an affair with Irene.

"Thanks for telling me, Papa," Mathieu said. "I apologize for pushing, but this case has taken over my life."

Pierre hesitated for a moment, then asked in a quiet voice, "Do you want to talk about it?"

"Yes," Mathieu said, finally realizing he needed to.

And then, all of a sudden, it just poured out of him. He told his father about finding Irene's dead body the night of the murder. He told him about the police's initial suspicion of the black musician and the beating. He explained why he didn't believe it, why he had suspected someone rich and powerful was involved. He described how he'd found the hidden keys and discovered who gave her properties. He told him about the interviews and the motorcycle accident. He confided to his father how he'd kept his name out of the investigation, even though he knew about the lot Pierre had given Irene in the Hollywood Hills.

Pierre listened in silence and with a father's pride as his son told the story. Theo's skill and resourcefulness astonished him. Though, in a way, it shouldn't have. He'd been that way since he was a child. It touched him that Theo had kept his name out of the investigation. It reassured him that he had trusted and respected him enough to do that.

This was the first time Theo had shared anything personal with him in a long time. Pierre knew what he said next would color their relationship for years. He chose his words carefully.

"I'm really proud of you, Theo," he said. "That's incredible detective work."

Mathieu looked at his father with surprise. Praise from him was rare.

"Thanks, Papa," he said with a cautious smile. "But I'm stuck. There are too many suspects, and any one of them could have done it or paid someone to do it."

Neither of them said anything for a few minutes, neither wanting to break the rare peace between them. And then his father asked, "Have you found her diary?"

"What diary?" Mathieu asked, looking up at his father.

"Irene told me she kept a diary."

36

The Diary

If his father was right about the diary, Irene would finally have a voice. Everything he knew so far about her had come from the people he had interviewed. But how much of that was their own fantasies, lies, and projections?

And Mathieu was just as guilty. He'd built up his own vision of Irene. He was almost afraid to find out who she really was. But his job was to pursue the truth wherever it led. And that's what he intended to do. But first, he had to find the diary, if it existed.

The next day, Mathieu called Barnes and asked him if it was alright to search Irene's apartment again. Barnes gave him the go-ahead and said he might have an answer from the VA later in the day about the fingerprints. After hanging up, Mathieu left the office and headed back to Horatio Court.

The apartment smelled stale as Mathieu entered the living room. He went over to the patio doors off the kitchen and opened them to let in some fresh air. He walked back to the living room and looked around. It didn't look like anyone had been here since his last visit. He decided to reverse the order of his search this time and start upstairs. He climbed the staircase and entered Irene's office. The floor was still littered with papers and folders from the break-in.

He gathered up each item on the floor and sorted them into neat piles. He put the stacks against the wall near the door. Then he emptied Irene's desk and file cabinets of their contents and did the same with what he found there. Finished sorting, he picked up one stack at a time and took it to her desk.

There he sat down and scanned each item, looking for anything that looked like it might be personal or from a diary. When he finished going through a stack, he put it on the floor near the window. It was tedious work and took over an hour to examine everything. But in the end, he found nothing of interest. It was all related to Irene's businesses or investments, but nothing personal.

Next, he went into Irene's bedroom. He had searched the clothes in the room thoroughly on his first visit. This time he concentrated on the furniture. He carefully examined the headboard for any hidden compartments. With his fingers, he tapped the entire length of it, looking for hollow spots.

Then he moved on to the dresser, where he removed the drawers and searched the inside of it with his flashlight, looking for anything taped to the sides. Next, he knelt down and checked under the bed. Again, he came up empty. He sat on the floor for a minute and gazed around the room, looking for likely hiding spots. Convinced there was nothing to be found, he went back downstairs.

Mathieu sat on the piano bench and glanced around the room. This was where he'd found Irene's letters hidden in the chest set. Maybe it was also where she'd hidden her diary. But where? He'd searched the room carefully the first time. He'd looked through all the papers and books and bookcases.

He went over to the fireplace and removed the grate. He took off his suit coat and shirt and felt around with his right arm inside the chimney for any hidden recesses. All he got for his trouble was soot all over his arm and hand. He went into the kitchen and washed it off, then came back into the living room.

To clear his mind, Mathieu sat down at the piano again and started fiddling with the keyboard. He ran through some chords, then began playing scales. As he got to the highest octave, the last three notes sounded dead. He tried again and got the same result.

Mathieu stood and tried to open the piano lid, but it didn't budge. He felt along the front edge for a latch. Not finding one, he ran his fingers around to the right side until he felt something metal. He pressed it, and the lid unlocked. Lifting it, he looked inside and smiled to himself.

Tucked inside, against the piano's sidewall, was a small black binder and two manila envelopes. Mathieu reached in and pulled them out. Irene's diary was in the binder, with section dividers for different topics, including a whole section on her clients.

Skimming through the binder, it seemed more like a memoir than a diary to him, written by a woman struggling to come to terms with her own contradictions. She had recorded her life, what she did, and how she did it. Almost expecting that someday someone would read it, and it would justify her actions.

Mathieu put the diary aside for a moment and opened the first manila envelope. He pulled out a stack of photographs, laid them on the piano, and started looking through them.

In the bulk of the photos, the camera was positioned above and behind a beautiful young woman dancing. Her lush hair cascaded down her naked back. She was stunning. In most of the photographs, she was totally naked. In the rest, she wore only panties. None of them showed her face, but Mathieu was sure it was Irene.

What was clearly visible in all the photos was the face of the man watching her. The lighting and focus were such that each man's face was clearly identifiable. It was a rogue's gallery of her clients. Some were fully dressed, others half-dressed, but all had an expression of rapt enchantment as if they had never seen such sensuous beauty.

A few of the photos were almost comical. Fallon sitting in his boxer shorts, wearing socks, shoes, a shirt, and a tie, while smoking a cigarette with his legs crossed. He looked like he was at a private club waiting for his pants to be pressed. Others were harder to look at. Harrison seated in his underwear, looking like a scarecrow with his scrawny legs and arms.

But they were all there, every one of the men he'd interviewed who had given Irene apartments. Thankfully there were no photos of his father.

Mathieu put the photos back and opened the second envelope marked "Special Project." Inside was a complete set of architectural drawings for a building. It looked similar to the sketches he'd found the first time he'd searched the apartment. But these were finished drawings for both the exterior and interior of a two-story structure. He checked the signatures; they were all signed by Professor Patterson. There was no indication as to the purpose of the building, but Mathieu thought he knew.

He picked up the diary again and went over and sat down next to the fireplace. It was time to hear Irene's voice. He couldn't put it off any longer. He was both excited and anxious. Excited because it might help crack the case. Anxious because it might destroy the image he had of her. He began to read, hoping Irene would provide a clue to her own murder.

In her diary, she was unapologetic about her beauty and what she was doing. In one passage, she wrote, "As a child, my beauty was a curse. I was robbed of my childhood because of it. As a woman, it's my power, and I will use it for good to seek my revenge against men."

Moving on to the section about her clients, Mathieu started with the first one he had interviewed, Samuel Johnston. Her description of Johnston was terse and clinical, like a doctor describing a patient's condition.

"Samuel is the easiest to control and least threatening of all my clients. I've totally captivated him. He hangs on my every move when I dance for him. He may play tough guys in the movies, but he's utterly devoid of courage. Plus, he's so anxious to stay in Mr. Chandler's good graces, he always behaves himself. I doubt he would ever reveal our arrangement. He's good for at least three more apartments."

Her assessment of Joseph Friedkin was kinder. "Joseph is an old-fashioned gentleman. I almost feel sorry for him. He has this hope that I'll marry him and take the place of his actress ex-wife who left him. As a movie producer, he's used to having beautiful, glamorous women vying for his attention.

"And I know he's been building his house in Palm Springs for me. He talks about it all the time, about how he can picture us living there together. Now that it's complete, he showed me the photos. Indeed, it is magnificent. I've tried not to give him any hope about marriage. But he's held on to it.

"He's lonely after his wife left him for someone even wealthier. Like most actresses, she's fickle, flitting from one man to another, desperate to secure her financial future, painfully aware her beauty has an expiration date. As mine will also if I live that long. That's why I plan on accumulating enough money for my project while I still have sexual power over men. But I can't take any more apartments from Joseph now that I've made it clear I will never marry him. It wouldn't be fair to him. He needs to forget about me and move on."

Her appraisal of Fredrick Fallon was short and to the point. "Fredrick wants me because he can't have me. I intend to never disappoint him on that score. Given his enormous wealth, he can afford to be generous to me; it means nothing to him. And because his wife is so society-conscious, he'll never reveal our relationship for fear of scandal. In that respect, his wife is my ally. There's a certain irony in that. Fredrick is as close to a money tree as it gets. I feel no guilt in taking his gifts. Their proceeds will ultimately be put to good use."

Later on, she wrote, "All these men project their own fantasies on my naked body. They don't really want me. They want their fantasy. All I have to do is try and not shatter their illusions."

But it was what she wrote about Jeremy Eckert that caught Mathieu's attention and troubled him.

"Eckert is a creep. When I refused to have his child, he tried to rape me. It took all of my martial arts training to fight him off. Here I was totally naked, trying to repel this huge man. He shoved me to the floor and held me down. As he started to unzip his pants, I kicked him in the groin and rolled away from him. I grabbed one of my Escrima fighting sticks from the corner. When he came at me again, I crouched low and swung hard at his shin, breaking it. Screaming in pain, he yelled, 'You, filthy bitch ... you, whore I'll kill you.' I quickly dressed and left the apartment, leaving the door unlocked. I went downstairs, found his chauffeur, and told him his boss needed some help. Then I drove off. I never saw him again and hope I never do."

Her final comment about Thaddeus Harrison was equally troublesome. "Thaddeus has changed recently. He seems angry at me. Like he's found out something about me that he doesn't like. I can't think what it is. But it's a little scary. I wonder if it's time to end our relationship. But he's still addicted to me. He can't help himself. Sometimes I have to laugh though, if he knew my mother was Columbian, not white, he would never have asked me to be in that poster for his creepy Eugenics society."

Besides the section on her clients, there were other sections in the diary on topics she was interested in like, climbing, photography, and jazz. There was a section for her friends, including Paul Thornton, Professor Patterson, and Mathieu's father.

About his father, Irene wrote, "Pierre has always been very supportive. He recognized the resemblance with my mother the first time he saw me. When I told him my story, he knew I was her daughter. He told me my mother had worked at his restaurant for a short time. She had expressed a lot of guilt about giving me up for adoption, but she felt she had no choice. It was the only way to protect me from being abused further by my father. It brought me some peace to learn that. He told me my mother fled to San Francisco when my father caught up with her again. I don't think Pierre told me everything about his relationship with my mother, but I decided not to press him on it. It was clear from the way he spoke of her that he was very fond of her."

Further on, Mathieu found an entry that caught him off guard. "Pierre brought his young son into the office today for the first time. It was his thirteenth birthday, and Harry had a present for him. His name is Theo. And what a sweet, precious little boy he is with his shy smile and dark, brooding eyes. He'll be a handsome young man someday. When I first saw him, there was a flicker of recognition as if he reminded me of someone. It must have shown on my face because he asked me if I was okay. It was such an endearing moment. It made me ache. His wide eyes staring at me, making sure I was alright. I hope he never loses that sensitivity, but I also hope he gains the toughness to deal with the harshness of this world."

Her portrayal of him as a little boy troubled Mathieu. He wondered if he'd become too tough, too insensitive. While he pondered that, the phone rang. The sound startled him. He got up, crossed the room, and picked up the receiver. He put it to his ear, but he didn't say anything. He just waited.

"Mathieu is that you?" came Barnes' voice over the phone.

"Yes, Peter, it's me," Mathieu said, relieved. "The sound of the phone spooked me."

"We got a match on the prints from Irene's apartment from the VA," Barnes said.

"Who do they belong to?" Mathieu asked.

"Albert Stewart."

"You mean Thaddeus Harrison's chauffeur?" Mathieu asked.

"Yes."

"So, he could be Professor Patterson's killer."

"Yeah," Barnes said. "And maybe Irene's also."

"Then, it's time to pay him a visit," Mathieu said.

"I think we should tail him first," Barnes said.

"Why?"

"To get a feel for the guy, observe him a little before we bring him in for questioning. Do you know what night he gets off?"

"Mondays," Mathieu said. "At least that's what he told me when I called him to check Harrison's alibi."

"Monday night it is then," Barnes said. "My car or yours for the stakeout?"

"Yours," Mathieu said.

"Great, then I'll bring my personal car," Barnes said. "We don't want to call any attention to ourselves after what happened to you in Pasadena."

37

Breakthrough at the Dunbar

Barnes and Mathieu arrived in Pasadena on Monday evening, just after sunset. They parked on a tree-lined side street off Orange Grove Boulevard with a clear view of Harrison's mansion. Barnes turned off the ignition and lights, then reached back, pulled a thermos of coffee from the back seat, and offered it to Mathieu.

"No, thanks … I'm good for now."

"I wonder how long we'll have to wait?" Barnes asked.

"I don't think too long," Mathieu said. "Especially if it's Albert's only night off."

"Yeah, good point."

And true enough, twenty minutes later, they watched as Albert drove his Model T down the mansion's long driveway and turned right onto Orange Grove. As he went past them, Mathieu said, "Did you see the scar on his left cheek?"

"Yeah," Barnes said. "I think he's our man."

Mathieu nodded in agreement.

There wasn't any traffic, so they gave Albert a couple blocks lead before they pulled out and followed him. Albert made his way south to Chinatown, then continued on Alameda until Sixth Street, where he turned onto Central Avenue. He didn't seem to be in a hurry and was oblivious to being followed.

After turning onto Central, Mathieu said, "I wonder if he's going to 'Little Harlem.'"

"Could be. Maybe Albert's a jazz lover."

"That would be an irony, wouldn't it? Considering how racist his boss is."

"Yes, it would," Barnes laughed.

As they approached Forty-Second Street, they watched Albert slow down, pull over to the curb and stop. Barnes continued on for a half-block, where he did the same. Turning off his lights, Barnes watched through the rearview mirror as Albert got out of his car, locked it, and crossed the street.

Central Avenue was known as "Little Harlem," with three jazz clubs, the Dunbar, Alabam, and Last Word, within walking distance of each other. The Dunbar was the hub, located in the recently constructed Summerville Hotel at Forty-Second and Central.

The hotel had been built so black people would have a decent place to stay in Los Angeles. And it had soon become "the hotel" for prominent black visitors and musicians. But it was the Dunbar jazz club located within it that would make the hotel a legend. Over the years, all the greats would play there, Duke Ellington, Billie Holliday, Louis Armstrong, Count Basie, and others.

Barnes and Mathieu stayed in the car as they watched Albert walk toward the hotel's main entrance. After he entered, they got out and followed him inside. They were both wearing civilian clothes. Mathieu had on a leather jacket, starched-shirt, and freshly-pressed-slacks. But as they entered, he soon realized he was underdressed for the occasion. The other patrons milling about in the lobby were turned out in their finest evening wear.

Mathieu glanced up at the spectacular art-deco chandelier and the mezzanine above where tables with fine china on white tablecloths were arranged behind delicate arches. They stopped at the front desk, mentioned Thornton's name, bought their tickets, and went into the club.

They found seats in the back under the mezzanine, where they had a clear view of Albert in the first row. The room was intimate; there were no bad seats. Mathieu noticed a smattering of white faces in the mostly black audience. But as on his previous visits, Mathieu felt welcomed as a fellow jazz lover by the crowd.

The quartet's instruments, piano, sax, bass, and drums, sat on the polished wood stage framed by the white curtain behind them. The house lights dimmed, and the spotlights came on. An announcer intoned, "And now ladies and gentlemen, the Dunbar is proud to welcome one of L.A.'s own 'The Paul Thornton Quartet.'"

The crowd applauded as the curtain opened. The four musicians, led by Thornton, stepped forward, bowed to the audience, then took their places at their instruments. Thornton held his sax in front of him, looked at the other band members, then started tapping his foot. As his body began to sway to the rhythm, he whispered, "five, six, seven, eight," and they were off.

For the next two hours, the quartet played non-stop, first the old standards and later their new pieces. The audience was appreciative and vocal. With the kind of back and forth that one came to expect in a black audience, active participants, never mere spectators.

As the quartet played, Mathieu observed Albert. He seemed caught up in the music like the rest of the audience, nodding his head, tapping his foot, and applauding with gusto after each song. He looked relaxed like he'd been here many times before.

Allowing himself to be immersed in the music also, Mathieu softened his focus and let his mind wander for a few minutes. He let the sound envelop him, possess him, carry him along. He forgot about the case and just rode the wave of the rhythm and the beat.

He closed his eyes, losing all sense of time. He imagined being on stage playing with the band. He felt the music resonate inside his body, anticipating every chord change before it happened. And then suddenly, it came to him. The whole sequence of events unspooled like a movie in his head. He could imagine everything that had happened. He should have been elated; he'd just solved the case. But he was depressed, almost devasted. Irene's death had been caused by a fluke coincidence. Mathieu opened his eyes slowly, a look of sadness on his face.

Barnes noticed the change. "What's wrong?"

"This is where it all began," Mathieu said, his eyes now transfixed on Albert.

"What do you mean?" Barnes asked.

"This is where Albert first saw Irene with Thornton," he said as he turned to look at Barnes. A chill ran down Mathieu's spine as he said it. Saying it out loud made it real.

Realizing his distress, Barnes asked, "Are you okay?"

Mathieu shook his head. "Not really."

"What do you want to do?" Barnes asked.

"We'll wait till the set ends, then we'll arrest him," Mathieu said in a flat voice. He felt numb. He needed some time to recover. He was in no hurry for the music to end.

At the end of the two-hour set, the musicians drenched in sweat were rewarded with a raucous standing ovation. Leaving the stage, Thornton made his way through the crowd, shaking hands, signing autographs, and posing for photographs. After Thornton left the auditorium, the audience started to file out. Albert remained in his seat, finishing a cigarette, seemingly in no hurry to leave.

Mathieu and Barnes stood up and approached him. Out of instinct, they surrounded him on opposite sides. Stopping in front of Albert, Mathieu pulled out his badge.

He leaned in close to Albert's face and said in a calm voice, "Mr. Stewart, my name is Detective Mathieu from the LAPD." Motioning towards Barnes, he added. "And behind you is Detective Barnes from the Santa Monica Police."

Albert had a shocked look on his face as if he'd just woken up from a bad dream.

"I'm going to ask you to stand up and come with us," Mathieu said. "Don't make a fuss. Just be cool. We're going to walk out of here together." The tone in his voice made it clear he was deadly serious. To punctuate that, Mathieu opened his jacket so Albert could see the gun in his shoulder holster.

"Are you going to cause us any problems?" Mathieu asked.

Albert shook his head, still in a daze as he stood up.

Mathieu grabbed one of his arms, and Barnes took the other as they sandwiched Albert between them and led him out of the club. Out on the sidewalk, they handcuffed Albert's arms behind his back and then crossed the street to Barnes' car.

Mathieu got into the back seat with Albert, as Barnes got behind the wheel.

Looking in the rearview mirror, Barnes asked, "Your stationhouse or mine?"

"Mine," Mathieu said. "It's closer."

No one spoke during the fifteen-minute ride to LAPD headquarters. When they entered the station house, Mathieu asked the desk clerk to get a stenographer and send her to the detective's interview room on the third floor.

Barnes and Mathieu were sitting across the table from Albert in the interview room when the stenographer arrived. Mathieu turned the questioning over to Barnes.

Barnes stared at Albert and said, "I'm curious, Mr. Stewart, why you haven't asked us why we brought you in for questioning?"

"You cops usually don't need a reason," Albert replied. "Maybe you don't like the scar on my face."

And indeed, in the interrogation room's harsh light, Albert's jagged scar looked even worse than Hop Li had described it.

"In this instance, we do have a reason, Mr. Stewart," Barnes said. "We found your fingerprints in an apartment in Santa Monica, owned by Irene Simpson, where Professor Kevin Patterson was murdered on the night of June 21 of this year."

"I don't know anything about that," Albert said, dismissing the implied accusation.

"Then how do you explain your fingerprints being in her apartment?" Barnes asked.

"I don't have to explain it," Albert said.

"That's true. You don't have to," Barnes said calmly. "But if you don't want to be convicted of his murder, you might want to rethink that."

You could see Albert doing the math in his head. Calculating how many years he'd get for burglary versus the possibility they had enough evidence to convict him of murder.

"Okay, so I was there," Albert said with a shrug. "I was searching for some embarrassing photos of my boss in her apartment. But I didn't find any, so I left. I didn't see anybody, and I didn't kill anybody."

Barnes smiled the smile of a poker player laying down a winning hand as he said, "You're going to have to do better than that, Albert. We found your thumbprint on Professor Patterson's watch-face."

"You're bluffing."

Even Mathieu wasn't sure if it was a bluff. It was the first he'd heard of a fingerprint on Patterson's watch.

"Am I?" Barnes asked. "Because if I'm not, you're going to hang for his murder, Albert. So, I'm giving you one chance to confess to manslaughter. But if you'd rather hang, that's okay with me."

Albert stared at Barnes, wondering if he should call his bluff. But Barnes didn't blink as he returned his stare.

"It's was an accident," Albert said. "The old man came in while I was searching the living room. He ran at me yelling, I grabbed him and pushed him away, and he tripped on the rug and fell against the piano. I could tell he was dead instantly. I saw enough of that in the war to know. But it was an accident. I didn't mean to kill him. I panicked and left after that."

Mathieu hadn't said a word so far. He'd been watching Albert closely as Barnes interrogated him, never taking his eyes off him. Albert was a cool customer, but now some sweat was starting to form on his brow. Mathieu decided it was time to strike.

"When did you first see Irene Simpson with Paul Thornton?"

The question startled Albert. His jaw dropped as he turned to face Mathieu. "How do you know about that?" he asked, looking bewildered.

"Was it the night Duke Ellington played at the Dunbar?"

Without thinking, Albert nodded yes, still confused how Mathieu knew.

"Did you see Irene approach Thornton after the set?"

"Yes," he answered as he felt his heart pounding in his chest.

"You'd seen Irene before, hadn't you? Because of your boss."

"Yeah," he said, looking away. "She wasn't the kind of woman you'd forget once you'd seen her."

"And you waited in the bar while Irene and Thornton were at the party in Duke's room. Then you followed them home to Thornton's house, didn't you?"

"Yes," Albert responded, unable to lie to this detective who seemed to know everything already.

"And a couple months later, you decided to tell your boss you'd seen Irene with her Negro lover, didn't you?"

Albert made an inaudible sound.

"Didn't you?" Mathieu said, raising his voice in anger and banging his fist on the table, startling even Barnes.

"Yes."

"Why did you tell him?"

"He was acting especially arrogant one night, so I decided to put him in his place."

"He got enraged when you told him, didn't he?"

Albert looked down at the floor and said, "Yes."

"And the night of Irene's murder, you drove him to Paul Thornton's house."

"I didn't know he was going to kill her. I swear. He said he was just going to threaten Thornton. We'd been on the Ritz. He hadn't scored with any of the women and had to pay for it again. He was angry and a little drunk when we left. He told me to drive him to Thornton's. He was going to scare him off, tell him to stay away from Irene. But when Irene answered the door naked, he just snapped and shot her. You have to believe me. I didn't know he was going to kill her," Albert said, looking at Mathieu for reassurance.

"You're in deep shit, Albert," Mathieu said. "You killed Professor Patterson, and you're an accessory to the murder of Irene Simpson. You're going to hang."

"Look, can't we make a deal," Albert pleaded. "I can help you convict my boss."

"How?" Mathieu asked.

"I'll testify against him."

"A jury will never believe you," Mathieu said. "They'll think you're just trying to save your own skin. Plus, your boss will swear you killed her. Who do you think a jury is going to believe him or you?"

"But I have proof," Albert said.

"What kind of proof?"

"I have the gun he killed her with," Albert said. "With his fingerprints all over it."

Mathieu glanced at Barnes for his reaction, then turned back to Albert and asked, "Where is it?"

"In my sleeping quarters at the mansion, hidden under some floorboards. My boss gave it to me to throw overboard one night when we went to the Ritz. But I substituted another gun and kept the one he killed Irene with."

"Why did you keep it?"

"In case something like this ever happened."

"Then I guess we're going to have to see if you're telling us the truth." Turning to Barnes, Mathieu said, "Ready for another ride to Pasadena tonight, Peter?"

"I can't wait," he replied, smiling.

38

The Confrontation

Before heading to Pasadena, Mathieu called Bull at home. He didn't want to make any mistakes at this point. Bull listened quietly as Mathieu recounted the latest events and Albert's allegation that Harrison killed Irene.

"Mother of Jesus," Bull muttered after hearing the story. "We've got to do this by the book, or we'll be crucified."

"I want to retrieve the gun before Albert changes his mind, sir," Mathieu said. "Can you get me a search warrant tonight?"

"I'll have to wake up a judge," Bull said with a sigh of resignation. "That's always amusing."

"I'd appreciate it, sir."

"I'll have a warrant for you within the hour," Bull said, then added. "And by the way, excellent police work." Then he hung up before Mathieu could say anything else.

True to Bull's word, a court clerk delivered the search warrant to Mathieu just after midnight. Then, Barnes, Mathieu, and Albert got into Barnes' car and headed to Pasadena.

It was almost one o'clock when Barnes turned into the long gravel driveway of Harrison's mansion. He doused the lights and, following Albert's directions, drove around to the back of the property where Albert's sleeping quarters were located. As they got out of the car, Mathieu looked up at the mansion. It seemed quiet. Most of the lights were out, no sounds came from the main house.

Mathieu's biggest fears now were being discovered by Harrison or Albert changing his mind. Albert was still handcuffed, but not taking any chances, Barnes and Mathieu took hold of his arms and led him toward his quarters. Once inside, they left the lights off and avoided talking. Mathieu turned on his flashlight, and Albert led them to his hiding place.

Barnes removed Albert's handcuffs to allow him to retrieve the murder weapon. Mathieu shined the light on the floor as Albert knelt down and pulled up two floorboards. He reached in and retrieved what looked like a pistol wrapped in a handkerchief and tied with twine. He handed it to Mathieu, whose heart was beating rapidly in anticipation.

Mathieu laid the package on the bed and untied the string. Careful not to touch the firearm itself, he peeled back the handkerchief and stared at the pistol. A smile came over his face as he looked up at Barnes and Albert. It was the same caliber weapon that killed Irene. He carefully rewrapped the firearm and put it in his coat pocket.

In a whisper, he asked Albert, "Do you have anything else with Harrison's fingerprints on it for comparison?"

Albert thought about it for a minute and said, "Yes, he gave me a silver cigarette case for my birthday. I never used it. It's too heavy."

He led them to the dresser, opened the top drawer, and started to grab the cigarette case when Mathieu stopped him. "Use a handkerchief to pull it out."

Albert did as he was told, then handed the cigarette case to Mathieu.

Mathieu motioned to Barnes to put the cuffs back on Albert. Then he looked around the room to see if there was anything else they needed. Deciding there wasn't, he said in a soft voice, "Let's get out of here."

They left the mansion as quietly as they had arrived. Barnes didn't turn the headlights on until they were two blocks away. Twenty minutes later, they arrived back at LAPD headquarters. Barnes and Mathieu booked Albert into a holding cell for the night, on one count of manslaughter in the death of Professor Patterson. They would decide on additional charges later, depending on whether Albert upheld his end of the bargain and testified against Harrison.

After agreeing to meet back at the station in the morning, Mathieu sent Barnes home to get some sleep. Mathieu booked the gun and cigarette case into evidence. Then left a note for the lab to check them for fingerprints and for ballistics to compare the gun with the bullets found at Irene's crime scene. With nothing else to do but worry about whether the evidence would be lost, or misplaced Mathieu went home to get a few hours of sleep.

At nine the next morning, Barnes and Mathieu joined Bull in his office to go over the lab reports. The bullets from the crime scene matched the gun Albert had given them. And the fingerprints on it matched Harrison's prints from the cigarette case. Albert had been careful handling the weapon; there were no other prints on it. In addition, some blood spatter was found on the barrel that matched Irene's blood type. The report confirmed the gun was registered to Thaddeus Harrison.

Bull asked his secretary to call Harrison's office to set up an appointment for noon. She was told Harrison was working from home that day. A meeting was set up for the mansion instead.

Putting his head in his hands, Bull rubbed his eyes, then looked at Barnes and Mathieu and said, "This is great detective work, gentlemen. You two make a good team. Are you sure you don't want to work for the LAPD, Peter?"

"Thank you, sir," Barnes replied. "But I'm fine at the beach."

"Can't say I blame you," Bull said, then added. "But it's not over. How we handle the interview today will make or break the case. Any thoughts on how we should play it?"

Before Mathieu could speak, Barnes piped up and said, "With respect, sir, I think you should let Mathieu take the lead. He knows the details of the case inside and out."

"Agreed," Bull said, nodding. "But Harrison will be a tough customer. He'll deny everything. He'll accuse Albert of lying, and if things get really tough, he'll try to bribe or scare us. Most of all, he'll remind us of all his powerful friends. So, we've got to be prepared."

Turning to Mathieu, he said, "And we can't lose our cool understood?"

"Yes, sir, understood."

"Do you have a plan for how you want to handle the interview?" Bull asked.

"Yes, sir, I do," Mathieu said. "I got here early this morning and wrote up some notes. Here's what I think we should do." He spent the next fifteen minutes laying out his strategy as Bull and Barnes listened. They occasionally interrupted to offer suggestions but overall agreed with Mathieu's plan.

After the meeting ended, Mathieu went back to his desk and put the murder weapon, notes, and a few other pieces of evidence into his satchel. With two hours left before going to Pasadena, he made one last phone call to Francine at the Times. Mathieu told her about the impending arrest of Harrison and asked her to give Chandler a message. Then he waited to see if his godfather would reply.

A few minutes before noon, a caravan of three police vehicles arrived at Harrison's mansion. Bull and his assistant Leonard were in the lead car, followed by Barnes, Mathieu, and Albert in the second vehicle. Bringing up the rear was a black Ford Model AA police truck with two uniformed officers.

After parking, they walked to the entrance. Bull knocked on the front door, and the butler answered. He seemed surprised to see Albert in handcuffs but made no mention of it. He led the detectives, Albert, and the two uniformed officers through the foyer and down a long, light-filled hallway toward Harrison's study.

Everything in the twenty-thousand square foot mansion had a polished sheen, from the marble floors, wood paneling, expensive furniture, and intricately framed mirrors. The effect was overwhelming, projecting an aura of permanence and power. Its pull wasn't lost on any of them as they trailed behind the butler. They were everyday civil servants in their drab suits and uniforms, approaching a business titan's palatial quarters.

Mathieu felt it also but tried to shake it off. He imagined the mansion abandoned, its windows broken, the manicured lawn filled with weeds and trash. The mind game helped him break the aura of invincibility of the opulent surroundings. Wealth like this rarely lasts, Mathieu told himself.

Stopping outside Harrison's study, the butler knocked and waited. On hearing his master's call, he opened the door, stepped aside, and allowed the detectives to enter.

By previous arrangement, Leonard and the uniformed officers stayed behind with Albert, out of view of the open door. Only Barnes, Bull, and Mathieu entered. The butler closed the door behind them.

Like his office, Harrison's study was long and wide with floor to ceiling rosewood paneling and built-in bookcases. On the wall to their left, four arched windows let in the warm summer light. To their right, a wood-paneled sliding door led to the adjoining salon. Harrison's desk was at the far end of the room, with an unlit fireplace behind it. The detectives walked toward him over richly weaved carpeting, stopping under an ornate chandelier just in front of his desk.

Mathieu did the introductions, adopting a solicitous tone as he did. He hoped to get Harrison to believe he'd been chastised after their first meeting. For the most part, Harrison ignored Mathieu, concentrating instead on Bull, who he treated like a celebrity.

"It's a pleasure to meet you, Bull," Harrison said with enthusiasm. "I've followed your career often in the newspapers. Your reputation as a union buster for my good friend Harry Chandler proceeds you."

Harrison said all this as if he was congratulating a star employee. His tone implying that Bull was on the payroll of the elite, hired to do their bidding. Bull seemed to enjoy the praise as well as the recognition.

Mathieu wondered for a moment if Bull might let him hang out to dry. Maybe that was why he had agreed so readily to let Mathieu handle the interview. If it all went south, Mathieu would take the heat. He tried to shake the feeling off, but it lingered in the back of his mind.

After the introductions, Harrison invited the detectives to sit down in chairs arranged in front of his desk.

Mathieu began in a casual tone trying to put Harrison at ease. "Thank you for giving us your time today, Mr. Harrison. We'd just like to go over a few details with you from the previous interview. I don't think it'll take very long."

"As long as we can make it quick," Harrison said. "I have a busy schedule today."

"Of course, I'll try to keep it short," Mathieu said. "If I understand correctly from our previous conversation, Mr. Stewart drove you to Santa Monica to take the launch out to the Ritz on the evening of Miss Simpson's death. Where you stayed for several hours gambling and drinking, after which you returned by launch to shore. Is that correct?"

"Yes, as I've already told you," Harrison said. "You can easily check that with the Ritz's management."

"I did," Mathieu replied in a calm voice. "But there's a discrepancy between when you said you left and what the Ritz recorded in their ship's log. According to their logs, you left two hours earlier than you told me. I was hoping you could help straighten that out."

Harrison shrugged. "Then I must have confused it with another trip. I go out there often, and it was a long time ago."

"Yes, I understand, Mr. Harrison. However, I'm more concerned with what happened after you returned to shore. Because there are a few other discrepancies between what you told me and what we've recently learned."

"We already went over this," Harrison said, now irritated. "Albert ... Mr. Stewart drove me home. When we arrived here, I had a nightcap then went to bed. I'm sure Mr. Stewart can verify that if he hasn't already. Unfortunately, he hasn't come into work today."

"That's where the problem comes in, Mr. Harrison," Mathieu said. "Mr. Stewart recently gave us a different version of events about what happened that evening when you both returned to shore."

"What different version?" Harrison demanded. "Where is Albert?"

Mathieu ignored Harrison's questions and continued. "According to Mr. Stewart on the night in question after returning to shore, you told him to drive to Paul Thornton's house."

"That's preposterous. How would I have known where Paul Thornton lived? I don't even know him."

"Because Mr. Stewart previously told you where he lived. At the same time, he told you he had seen Miss Simpson with Thornton at the Dunbar jazz club. And that he had followed them home to Thornton's house near the beanfield."

Harrison turned to Bull and said, "I demand you get this detective under control. He's trying to harass me with this crazy made-up story."

Bull hesitated a moment, measuring his words before speaking. "Detective Mathieu is following up on a line of questioning that I've authorized."

"I demand to see Mr. Stewart," Harrison said.

"All in due time, Mr. Harrison," Mathieu said, taking control of the interview again. "Mr. Stewart also alleges that you told him to drive to Thornton's house because you intended to threaten Thornton to stay away from Miss Simpson. Upon arriving at Thornton's home, you got out of the car, walked up to the front door, and knocked. But instead of Thornton, it was Miss Simpson who answered the door. She was naked. She'd been expecting Thornton. In a jealous rage, you shot her twice, searched the house quickly, then ran back to your car and got in. At which point, Mr. Stewart turned the car around and sped off, returning you here to the mansion. In addition, we have an eyewitness who saw someone get out of a Bentley that evening and walk up to the house. Immediately afterward, they heard a scream and two shots being fired."

"That's a nice little story you've made up, Detective," Harrison said. "But you'll never be able to prove it. Albert is lying, and you don't have any evidence."

"Actually, we do," Mathieu said, pulling the murder weapon from his satchel. He approached the desk and laid it in front of Harrison.

"Recognize this, Mr. Harrison? It's registered to you. It has your fingerprints on it, and the bullets found at the crime scene match this weapon. It also has blood splatter on the barrel that matches Irene's blood type."

Harrison momentarily froze when he saw the gun as if he'd just seen a ghost. "I didn't kill Miss Simpson ... Albert did," he blurted out in panic.

Mathieu motioned to Barnes to bring Albert into the room. There was silence as Barnes went and got him and brought him to the desk.

Harrison pointed at Albert and said, "He killed her. I told him to threaten Thornton, but the fool killed Irene instead."

Albert remained impassive, not saying a thing.

Mathieu was glad Harrison had accused Albert. It almost guaranteed his testimony. "Then how do you account for your fingerprints being the only ones on the gun, including on the trigger?" Mathieu asked.

"I grabbed the gun away from him afterward," Harrison said.

Mathieu smiled. "And wiped his prints off, replacing them with your own?"

"That doesn't sound very plausible, Mr. Harrison. Albert had no reason to kill Irene. But you did. You were the one obsessed with her, not him. You were the one enraged that she was with a Negro, not him. And you were the one that killed her, not him."

"What if I did," Harrison said in a haughty manner. "What jury would convict me for killing a slut who was sleeping with a Negro?"

"Miss Simpson wasn't sleeping with Thornton. She wasn't sleeping with anyone. In fact, she probably never willingly slept with any man in her life. She was abused as a child. She was traumatized by men. As an adult, she never let any man touch her. All she did was dance naked for Thornton. As she did for you and all her other clients."

"You can't prove any of this," Harrison said.

"Oh, but I can, Mr. Harrison. I have the murder weapon with your prints on it, and I have Albert's testimony."

"I'll hire the best lawyers in Los Angeles. They'll tear your case apart and Albert's testimony to shreds. All of this is pure conjecture. And you'll never be able to prove I was obsessed with Miss Simpson or had any intimate relations with her," Harrison said with smug disdain.

"Maybe I can," Mathieu said with a smile, seeking to throw Harrison off balance. "Maybe I have intimate photos of you and Miss Simpson together."

"You tried that trick before in my office. You're bluffing."

"Am I?" Mathieu said as he retrieved the photos of Harrison watching Irene dance and laid them on the desk.

"You're pretty recognizable in these photos, Mr. Harrison. Sitting bare-chested in your underwear, watching Irene dance naked in front of you with a look of longing and desire on your face. Hopefully, the press never gets ahold of these and publishes them. Your reputation would be ruined in this town. You'd be the laughingstock of the city."

Harrison glanced at the photos then pushed them away. "The Times would never publish anything as salacious as that," he said, trying to reassure himself.

"The Times might not," Mathieu said. "But I'm sure the Herald would. William Randolph Hearst would love to stick it to you and Chandler. Then you'd really be a pariah in this town, Mr. Harrison. Chandler would dump you in a second."

"Chandler will never desert me."

"You might want to rethink that, Mr. Harrison," Mathieu said as he handed him an envelope.

"What's this?"

"There's a note inside that Chandler wrote to you this morning upon learning that you had murdered his secretary."

"I have no intention of reading it," Harrison said.

"Then I'll tell you what he wrote," Mathieu said. "'Harrison, all our future business dealings are hereby severed. May you rot in hell!' Signed Harry."

Harrison opened the envelope and looked at the note, checking to see if what Mathieu had said was true. After reading it, his face turned ashen. He sat back in his chair, trying to collect himself.

"I have nothing more to say until I consult my lawyer," he said, staring at his desk.

"As you wish," Mathieu said. "But we'll have to take you down to the station now to book you."

While Harrison sat in stunned silence, Bull called Leonard into the room. He had Harrison stand up and come around in front of the desk. Everyone else moved out of the way as Bull stood next to Harrison and handcuffed him while Leonard took several photos of them. The sound of flashbulbs popping was the only thing you could hear as Harrison endured this final indignity, posing for tomorrow's front-page headlines.

When they finished with the photos, Harrison looked at Bull and, almost pleading, asked, "May I go upstairs and get some things before we leave?"

"Of course," Bull said. "Leonard, take him upstairs and watch him, then bring him back down. And take the cuffs off so he can get his things."

"Yes, sir," Leonard said as he removed the cuffs and grabbed Harrison by the arm.

With Leonard in tow, Harrison walked toward the wood-paneled sliding door, opened it, and entered the salon. Moments later, the detectives heard the sound of their footsteps ascending the marble staircase to the second floor.

After Harrison left the room, Bull, Barnes, and Mathieu stood around discussing what had happened. They were all stunned that it had gone so well. But they knew it would be a lengthy court battle, where the outcome was far from certain. Bull called one of the officers into the room to watch over Albert as they discussed what to do next.

Bull was commending Mathieu on his restraint when they heard the sound of two gunshots come from upstairs. The detectives immediately drew their weapons, ran through the open door into the salon and up the winding staircase.

When they got upstairs, Bull called out, "Leonard … Leonard, where are you?"

39

The Aftermath

The detectives followed the sound of Leonard's muffled cries to Harrison's bedroom. Leonard was on the floor, trying to stem the flow of blood from his shoulder wound. Harrison lay face down on the bed, the silk sheets soaked in blood from a massive gunshot wound to his head.

While Harrison had packed, Leonard stood outside his bedroom door, admiring the circular skylight over the winding staircase. But after a few minutes, concerned that Harrison was taking too long, Leonard entered the bedroom and saw Harrison take a gun from his dresser.

Leonard drew his service revolver and yelled, "Stop!" But Harrison turned and fired, hitting Leonard in the shoulder. Harrison then took a step toward the bed and shot himself in the head, falling face forward onto it. When Bull and Mathieu found Leonard on the floor, they bandaged his wound with some towels from the bathroom, while Barnes fetched a deputy to get a stretcher.

The next day, instead of front-page headlines announcing his arrest, Harrison's death was buried on page seven of the LA Times. "Wealthy Real Estate Magnet Commits Suicide." At headquarters, Bull apologized to Mathieu. "I'm sorry. I should have known better. Leonard can be careless. What a cockup," he said, shaking his head in disgust. "I'll try to make it up to you somehow."

"It's okay, Chief," Mathieu said." It's a kind of justice ... maybe it's for the best. At least this way, Irene's name won't be dragged through the mud."

"You did all you could for her, Mathieu," Bull said solemnly. "You didn't let her down."

Mathieu shrugged, not convinced he had. "Do you want me to turn in my detective's shield now that the case is over and go back to motorcycle patrol?"

Bull stared at Mathieu and shook his head. "I'd be a damn fool to do that," he said. "You're not going anywhere. You're stuck with me now."

"Thank you, sir," Mathieu said, surprised.

Mathieu hadn't expected Bull's response. He assumed Bull would send him back to patrol once the investigation was complete. Maybe that was what he meant when he said he'd try to make it up to him. In any case, Mathieu was grateful. He'd gotten a taste of being a detective and liked it.

Three days later, Mathieu went to visit Sister Mary Catherine at St. Anne's. They sat in her office, both in a somber mood, after Mathieu informed her the case had been solved. He withheld most of the details, telling her instead that it was a simple case of jealousy and that the guilty party had committed suicide.

In an attempt to cheer her up, he handed her a handwritten note he had copied from Irene's diary that he wanted her to read. He watched her face brighten, then fill with tears as she did.

Sister Mary Catherine looked up at him. "I'm sorry, but it touches me to know how Irene felt about me. It's been so long since we had any contact. Thank you for bringing this to me," she said. "Sisters don't get to be mothers, but I felt like a mother to Irene. It lifts my spirits to know she felt the same."

"I have some more good news for you," Mathieu said as he handed her a copy of Irene's will that he'd obtained from her lawyer. "Irene made some shrewd real estate investments, and she left most of her estate to St. Anne's."

Sister Mary Catherine seemed astonished at the projected amount. It was the first she'd heard of the bequest. It had been held up as Irene's lawyer evaluated the total worth of her holdings.

"And this is what Irene wanted you to do with the money," Mathieu said, passing her the building plans for a new hospital wing.

Sister Mary Catherine stared wide-eyed as she paged through the architectural drawings, then sat back in her chair and tried to compose herself.

"I'm speechless, and that doesn't happen very often," she said, laughing at herself. "This is beyond anything I could have ever imagined."

"The bequest is a tribute to you, Sister. A testament to Irene's gratitude and love for you," Mathieu said. "You saved her life. It's Irene's way of repaying you. She wanted St. Anne's to be a safe haven for even more children in the future."

"And yet, in the end, I couldn't protect her," she said with sadness in her voice.

"That's not your fault, Sister," Mathieu said. "Irene made her choices freely and for good reasons. Neither she nor you could have predicted the consequences of her actions."

That sat in silence for a few minutes reflecting on Irene's life, neither feeling compelled to break the stillness. Sister Mary Catherine was the first to speak, "I sense you came here for another reason also, Theo."

In answer, Mathieu handed her a piece of paper. "It says here on my birth certificate that I was born at St. Anne's," he said. "Which doesn't any make sense. Why was I born here instead of at the French Hospital, which is closer to my parent's home? I don't think you've told me everything you know, Sister."

She turned away from Mathieu's gaze and faced the window. The harsh light accentuating the lines on her face, lines of both age and concern.

"No, I haven't," she said, turning back to face him. "Sometimes, it's hard to know who deserves one's loyalty. Did you know your boss came to see me yesterday?"

"You mean Bull?" Mathieu asked, surprised.

"Yes."

"He came here?"

"Yes," she nodded. "He's a more sensitive man than he lets on."

"What did he want?"

"He told me about all the work you had done for Irene during the investigation. He'd just finished reading your final report along with Irene's diary. He noticed a few things in her diary that he wanted to ask me about. I was reluctant at first to answer, but he persisted. I asked him if he was asking in an official capacity or a personal one. He said it was personal. He said he thought you deserved an honest answer. One that might bring you some peace."

"What things in her diary?"

"One was a passage where Irene mentions seeing you for the first time as a little boy. And another where she wonders if your father told her everything about his relationship with her mother."

The hair on the back of Mathieu's neck stood up as the nun spoke.

"You must have wondered yourself," she said.

"Wondered what?" Mathieu asked, now feeling anxious.

"If there was some connection between you and Irene."

Mathieu hesitated before answering, "I noticed some coincidences," he said. "But I didn't allow myself to think about it during the investigation. It would have been a distraction."

"And now?" Sister Mary Catherine asked.

"Now I feel adrift … a little off balance. I came here to find out who my real mother is."

Sister Mary Catherine hesitated a moment then said simply, "Your real mother is the same as Irene's."

The answer caught Mathieu off-guard. He looked at Sister Mary Catherine with an uncomprehending look; it didn't make any sense. He felt suddenly disconnected from his surroundings as if he were in a tunnel where no sound got through. Time stood still for a few moments. When he came out of his daze, he heard her say.

"Surely, you must have suspected it."

He looked at her with a blank expression and said, "No … I didn't expect this. You mean Julia … the woman my father told me about is my real mother?"

"Yes," she said, nodding her head. "Julia's your mother. Irene was your half-sister."

Mathieu was stunned. "I don't understand."

"Your father and Julia had a brief affair, and she got pregnant."

"Why did she give me up?"

"Because her husband had caught up to her again just before you were born. She needed to leave town quickly. She couldn't take care of you on the run. Your parents wanted a child, but your mother couldn't have any. So, they agreed to adopt you."

"Who knew about this?"

"Up until now, only Julia, your parents, and me," Sister Mary Catherine said. "You were supposed to be born at the French Hospital, then brought here for adoption by your father and mother. But Irene, who was eight years old at the time, was at the French Hospital having her tonsils taken out. We didn't want to risk upsetting her by seeing her mother. So, you were born here instead."

Mathieu should have been excited, but he felt numb.

"Where is Julia now?"

"I don't know," Sister Mary Catherine said, shaking her head. "Your father helped her leave town after giving birth to you. As far as I know, she went to San Francisco."

Mathieu stared at the floor, trying to make sense of it all.

"Julia did the right thing, Theo," Sister Mary Catherine said. "She was on the run from a very abusive man. She wouldn't have been able to take care of you. And your parents desperately wanted you because your mother couldn't have children. She forgave your father for his brief affair with Julia. And she has loved and cared for you ever since as her own."

"Do you have a picture of Julia?"

"Yes," Sister Mary Catherine said. "Better than that ... I have a picture of her holding you after you were born." She reached into the top drawer of her desk and passed him a small photo.

Mathieu studied her face and smiled. His father had been right all along; he did look like his mother.

"What was her maiden name?"

"Luna ... Julia Luna."

"Do you think she changed her name back to Luna?"

Sister Mary Catherine shrugged. "I don't know. It would have been safer for her to choose a new name. What are you going to do now, Theo?"

"Try and find her," he said in a distant voice.

"Do you think that's wise?"

"I don't know."

"I don't think you're being fair to your parents, Theo,

especially your mother. They wanted you, they raised you, they took care of you. Your mother may not have given birth to you, but you are who you are largely because of her."

"I know, Sister, you're right," Mathieu said. "I haven't been fair to her. I need to make amends to her. But I also need to find Julia for my own sake and hers. She deserves to know what happened to Irene. And I want her to hear it from me, not someone else."

"But how will you find her?" Sister Mary Catherine asked. "No one has had any contact with her in over twenty-one years."

"You forget, Sister," Mathieu said, now smiling. "I'm a Detective. That's what I do. I find people."

40

Epilogue

The Great Depression began two months later with the stock market crash on October 24, 1929. Its effect was felt worldwide; no country was spared from the chaos, hardship, and despair. In the United States, California was hit as hard as other states. But some cities were less affected than others.

Los Angeles was one of those, partially because of the movie business. By the early nineteen-twenties, over eighty percent of the films produced worldwide were made in Los Angeles. And fortunately for the film industry, people continued to go to movies even during the Depression.

Within Los Angeles, the effects were also unevenly felt. While the brunt of the suffering was borne by the common man, the ultra-rich didn't escape unscathed. Thaddeus Harrison's fortune had been over-leveraged before his death, heavily invested in risky stock market schemes. The crash wiped out his wealth overnight. Had he not committed suicide because of Irene's murder, he likely would have two months later anyway.

Fortunately, Mathieu and his family had managed their money conservatively. The Farmers and Merchants Bank of Los Angeles, where they kept their savings, was one of the few banks to survive. And while his father's restaurant business suffered, he found ways to keep the business going through the lean times.

Irene had also kept her money at the same bank. Her apartment leases and properties had been sold before the crash. After which, the proceeds were transferred to a savings account at the bank for St. Anne's.

A month after the stock market crash, Mathieu drove up to Harrison's mansion in Pasadena. He stopped across the street from it and parked. The mansion lay vacant, weeds growing in the lawn, windows broken by passing vandals. There were other stately homes on Orange Grove that looked equally derelict. Like rotting corpses, they sat empty, devoid of life.

As Mathieu sat there, he thought about Irene, the horrible abuse she'd endured as a child, the good she'd done as an adult, and the price she ultimately paid. Life was a mystery. You could have a pampered childhood and end up living a vacuous life. Or you could endure hardship, overcome it, and do some good. Even for the well-intentioned parent, there were no guarantees.

What would Mathieu's life have been like if Julia hadn't given him up for adoption? Would he be who he was? It was doubtful. Best not to be too angry at his own parents, he thought. They were just feeling their way in the dark like everyone else.

Mathieu took one last look at the mansion, then started his car. He pulled out, turned around, and headed back toward Los Angeles. As he drove south, he felt the warm sun on his face and smelled the fragrant scent of orange groves in the air. Bull had just assigned him a new case to work on. The search for Julia would have to wait for now.

But first, Mathieu had something personal to do. He glanced at the flowers lying on the seat next to him, then back at the road. He was on his way to the cemetery to place them on his sister's grave.

About the Author

Michael L. Nicholas lives in Los Angeles, California. This is his first in a series of novels featuring Detective Mathieu.

CPSIA information can be obtained
at www.ICGtesting.com
Printed in the USA
BVHW081216040521
606414BV00003B/206

9 781665 703420